THE GOLD STALKERS

The Gold Stalkers

COL. R.C. HARTJEN

For my wife Helen and my son Ray, without whom
this book would never have been published.

Contents

Dedication   v

                    Note   1

1   2

2   17

3   31

4   44

5   66

6   79

7   98

8   105

9   120

10   139

11   150

12   168

13   178

14   194

15   210

VIII ~

16   227

17   232

18   242

19   258

20   274

21   288

About the Author   298

Note

Man's lust for gold had been instrumental in the exploration and settlement of many areas of our world, including the western United States in the last half of the 19th century. Since dreams of fame and fortune were not limited to any one group, prospectors and farmers, gamblers and pimps, merchants and bankers; each in their own way became stalkers of the elusive yellow metal.

Chapter 1

The snow was falling harder than ever. The large, wet flakes blanketed the mountains with a white, treacherous cloak that obscured everything and transformed what was normally a dangerous trail into a nightmare for anyone foolish or desperate enough to attempt it. To make matters worse, the wind had picked up, and drifts were threatening to put an end to any travel at all. Visibility had dropped to less than twenty feet and promised to drop even further. There was no sign that the storm would let up.

Jim Horton reined his horse to a stop and dismounted. The game trail was a little wider here, and he took the opportunity to check the three mules and their loads. As he began adjusting the load on the first, the second mule groaned and collapsed. It struggled briefly to regain its feet, and then lay quietly, exhausted and panting for breath. Horton cursed softly and waded through knee-deep snow as he made his way to the animal's side. He uncinched the girth straps on the pack and dragged it from the mule, but the animal still could not regain its feet. The combination of a Ute arrow and the rapid flight to avoid both the hostile

Indians and the snow had proven to be too much for the mule.

Horton stepped back to consider his options, knowing that he really did not have much in the way of choices. He could not stop where he was and he could not leave the mule to die from the wound or from exposure. He drew his knife from his boot, reluctantly, then stepped forward and cut the animal's throat. The mule thrashed feebly for a moment, then lay still as its blood stained the snow crimson.

Horton distributed the load from the dead mule's pack evenly between the other two. The loads were not very bulky, but they were heavy. Gold always was. Horton discarded shovels, picks, and other mining gear to help compensate for the additional load he was asking the remaining mules to carry. He took his food and cooking utensils over to his own horse. By the time he finished, the animals were coated with snow and visibility had dropped to the point where Horton could no longer ride and still navigate accurately. He tied the mules behind his horse, picked up the reins and started leading the animals down toward the valley floor far below, breaking a trail for them as he went.

Within minutes Horton had to stop again. In spite of the cold, his exertions had caused him to break into a sweat. He knew that sweat was an enemy in this weather, one that drained heat from the body and froze the unsuspecting. He removed his heavy buffalo-hide coat and tied it across his saddle. The right side of his shirt was covered with dried blood. Shivering from the cold, he went back to his position in front of his caravan and followed the faint trail toward the relative safety of the tree line that he could not see but knew must be somewhere below him.

For the hundredth time that day Horton cursed the combination of greed and just plain bad luck that had caused him to stay too long in the high country, trading time for one more poke of gold, then another, and then another. The bad luck had finally forced his departure. He had known that a war party of Utes had been looking for him. He had seen their sign several times when he was hunting for camp meat. Eventually they found his camp.

Somehow, he had succeeded in driving them off, but the reprieve had been a short one. The Utes forced him into a running battle on the trail, and the dead mule and a shallow wound along his ribs were the result of that fight. The early snow had been a blessing, having both hidden his tracks and stopped the pursuing Utes. It also threatened to kill him.

Horton tripped and fell full length into the snow. He struggled back to his feet and tugged on the reins of his exhausted horse. He knew that the animals could not go much further and he was not sure that he could, either. His lungs felt as if they were on fire and he had lost the feeling in his feet long ago. He kept reminding himself that to stop on this exposed trail was to die. In the back of his mind, he thought that if he could get the animals into the tree line somewhere below, he might still have a chance. The chance was a slim one, to be sure, but it was the only one he had. With the wind howling around him, he staggered on down the mountain, dragging his horse and the mules behind him.

He lost track of time as he fought his way through the storm. Twice more he fell, and each time it took him longer to get back to his feet than it had the time before. He fell a fourth time and just lay there in the snow. Strangely, he no longer felt the cold. All that he felt was a consuming need for sleep. His eyelids blinked and then closed, and he felt himself drifting off. He lost track of how long he lay there, but suddenly a warning seemed to scream in his ears and force his eyes open again. He was certain that if he did not get up immediately, he never would. Slowly he fought his way to his knees, then to his feet. The animals were in no better shape than he was. They, too, had nearly reached the end of their endurance.

It was then that a freak break in the wind caused the air to clear for just a moment. In that instant, however, Horton saw the dim outline of the timber not quite a hundred yards below him. In the second or two that it took for the image to register on Horton's numb brain, the storm closed back around him, obscuring everything except the horse next to him.

Horton more than half-doubted that he had actually seen the tree line; nevertheless, he headed in its direction. In a matter of minutes, he could hear the wind in the branches of the pines. His horse and the mules could, too, and he found himself having to hold the animals back. A few minutes later he was among the trees, fighting his way through the snow-laden boughs to a relatively protected spot about two hundred yards from the trail above.

His horse stopped and Horton saw that the animals would go no further. He worked his way to the mules and fumbled with numbed fingers at the girths, removed the packs and turned the mules loose. He dragged the packs under a particularly large tree, then returned to his horse and removed his saddle and bridle. The gelding just stood there with its head down and its tail to the wind.

Horton dragged his gear over to the packs, then set about to make a camp where he could wait out the storm. There was little snow under the pine. Most of what had fallen or blown into the timber had come to rest on the upper branches. Horton took a small tarpaulin and, using the packs to hold down one side, dragged it over a low branch. He used a couple of thongs to secure it to the branch, then he broke off a number of low-hanging boughs from adjacent trees and wove them into a rough screen to block out the wind from the sides of the shelter. When this was done, he had a shelter large enough to contain himself, his saddle, and a small fire if he could get one started.

Horton gathered a number of dead branches and broke them into manageable lengths, then crawled into the shelter and swept the pine needles from the ground near the open end. Using his saddle as an additional wind break, he finally got a small fire started and added the larger branches as the flames caught hold. He draped his coat over his shoulders and hugged the fire until his teeth stopped chattering and the ice that had formed in his beard started to melt. He sat there listening to the tarp pop in the wind while he soaked up what little heat the fire offered. He noted that the last daylight had faded from the sky and he marveled that he was still alive.

Finally, he forced himself to remove his sodden boots and hung them to dry over sticks that he forced into the thawed ground near the fire. He broke out his bedroll and curled up in it. He was asleep almost immediately. From time to time he awoke, stuck his arm out from beneath his covers and added a few sticks to the fire. He never heard the full fury of the blizzard as it struck. The fire finally turned to embers and then to ashes. The wind continued to howl, and the snow blew into huge drifts that threatened to bury anything or anyone unlucky enough to be caught out in the open.

The storm broke about mid-morning of the second day. Once the snow stopped, the temperature began to plummet until around sunset. Horton guessed that it was at least twenty degrees below zero. The soft, wet snow deposited by the blizzard crusted over and froze solid, making any movement extremely difficult. Drifts were more than ten feet deep in some places. Even if a horse could somehow break through or avoid the larger ones, the crust would cut the animal to ribbons within minutes. Nevertheless, Horton began to get ready to leave in the morning.

The animals, of course, would not go. Only the bay gelding had survived the first night of the storm. Gaunt with hunger, the horse searched with little success for food beneath the snow. The two dead mules had provided Horton with fresh meat during the blizzard. He had stripped the hide from the dead animals before they froze solid, and now he cut the hide into strips and fashioned a crude pair of snowshoes.

That evening he prepared a small pack from what was left of his supplies. Some jerked venison, a small tin in which to melt snow, a handful of matches, a much-patched shirt, two boxes of .44-40 cartridges for his single-action Colt and Model 1873 Winchester carbine, and two leather pokes of gold made up the list of items he decided he would take with him. Horton would have to leave behind more than twenty similar pokes in a small cave that he had discovered just below his camp site. He had carefully marked its location by shooting azimuths with his compass to the two most prominent peaks in the area. He was reasonably sure that he could find the spot again, but he sketched a map of the spot just to be sure. He also decided that he would have to study his backtrail and expand the map as he traveled.

Horton rose early the following morning. Leaving his pack and Winchester behind, he went in search of his horse. He had decided reluctantly that he would have to destroy the animal rather than to leave him behind to starve. Horton finally found the gelding feeding in a small clearing where the wind had scoured about half an acre nearly clean of snow. The bay raised its head and pointed its ears at Horton as he nickered a greeting. Horton slipped the Colt from its holster as he approached the horse, then changed his mind and holstered the pistol.

"There, there, big fella," he said soothingly as he patted the horse's neck. "If you could find this grass, maybe you can find some more. You got a chance, anyway, probably a better one than me. Hope you make it, boy."

The horse nuzzled his face then went back to cropping at the frozen grass. Horton wiped the bay's slobber from his cheek and made his way back to the camp. He knew that he had been looking for an excuse not to destroy the animal, and he was glad that he had found one.

Horton folded the tarp and added it to his pack, then swung the load to his shoulders. He picked up his Winchester and made his way carefully through the trees toward the low country far below. The snowshoes made walking awkward at first, but he soon settled into a rhythm that allowed him to cover ground more quickly. His chief concern was to avoid a fall on the slippery, crusted snow. If he broke a leg or even an arm in such a fall, he doubted he would ever make it out of the mountains. Every half-hour or so he paused to study his backtrail, notch trees, and make notations on his map. By noon he had removed the heavy buffalo-hide coat and added it to his pack. Although it was still bitterly cold, there was no wind and he stayed warm enough. The hair froze in his nose, and his breath formed icicles on his moustache and beard as he walked. The glare from the sun shining on the snow hurt his eyes even though he had darkened the areas under them with soot from his campfire and keep his battered Stetson pulled low. He knew that the glare would get even worse once he left the timber.

Horton moved steadily towards the valley floor. The stiffness in his legs from breaking trail for his horse and mules days earlier soon left him, and he began to whistle softly to himself. He started to believe that he just might make it out of these mountains alive.

Jim Horton would not have called himself a miner or even a prospector. He considered himself a rancher, a full partner with his three brothers in a 100 section ranching operation in central Texas. After the War Between the States, Jim and two of his brothers had mustered out of what was left of Hood's Texas Brigade and spent a year in the Dakota and Colorado territories looking for gold. They had found traces of color on several occasions, but never more than enough to cover expenses. It had been enough, though, to light a fire in him. In the dozen years since the brothers had gone back to Texas, he had been unable to snuff out the urge to seek out the elusive golden metal. When the snows began to melt in the spring of 1878, Jim was waiting impatiently in Denver to resume the hunt. He felt a little foolish that at the age of thirty-three he was not able to control this wild urge to discover his fortune, but the ranch was doing well enough and he felt that he could afford to indulge himself in his fantasy for a year.

Luck had been with him in the beginning. He had gone into the mountains, where he took great pains to avoid boom towns, prospectors, and Indians. Several times he had found traces of gold, but in late May he found a stream that had produced more than just a trace of color. In one day, he cleaned out nearly a thousand dollars' worth of large nuggets. He worked his way upstream in search of the source and found a vein of quartz so rotten with gold that he could break it apart with his fingers. He estimated that during the five months that followed he had extracted over fifty thousand dollars' worth of the precious metal, and the vein had shown no signs of playing out.

It was the richness of the vein that had kept him too long in the high country. He had ignored the signs of approaching winter in his lust for more gold. The crust of ice on the edges of the stream, the crispness of the air, the sudden color in the groves of aspen far below—all went unnoticed. It was then that his luck turned sour,

A light snow finally convinced him that he could stay no longer, and then the Utes struck his camp. After the fight he had packed up the gold and as much of his equipment as he could take on his mules, then covered the signs of his mining activity as best he could. It was his plan to return later and clean out the rest of the vein. He had run into the Utes again less than an hour after he broke camp, and the blizzard caught him later the same afternoon. Now he was trying to walk out of the mountains with little equipment and just a fraction of the gold. If he didn't make it, he would become just one more faceless victim of gold fever.

Horton plodded on until exhaustion and darkness overtook him. He built a small fire under a large pine and counted on the branches to dissipate any smoke that the fire might give off, although he thought that it was unlikely that there would be anyone around to see or smell the smoke. After his experiences with the Utes, though, he took no chance of attracting unwanted visitors. He melted some snow in his tin, then shredded some jerky and added it to the water to make a thin stew. He ate slowly, then melted more snow and drank until he could hold no more. He knew that he could become just as dehydrated here as he could in the desert and that eating snow would suck the heat out of his body and kill him. He rolled up in his coat and the tarp and quickly fell asleep. He was unaware of the snow when it began to fall again.

In the morning, Horton found a two-inch layer of snow covering his gear and everything else in sight. He also discovered that it was much warmer. He had been told that it never snowed when it was bitterly cold, but he had not believed it until now. He judged that the temperature was well above zero. The warmth had brought the fresh snow that promised to make travel even more dangerous. From the look of the sky, more snow was on the way. Moving slowly because of the stiffness in his legs, back, and shoulders from the trek of the day before, Horton melted snow and drank all of the warm water he could hold. When he was finished, he shouldered his pack and started on his way out of the mountains again.

He came upon a high valley along about mid-morning. The floor of it was relatively open, with only an occasional tree sticking up through the snow. The snow had drifted badly, though, and Horton kept to the wood line to avoid the worst of the drifts and to make himself more difficult to see. He had no desire to run into any more Utes.

The valley was about a mile long and about two or three hundred yards wide, depending on where the measurements were taken. Always the cattleman, Horton could appreciate the value of such a place as a summer pasture. The grass would be green and plentiful, but the cattle would have to be moved to lower ground by September or risk being stranded by an early snow. Judging from the broken limbs on trees, Horton guessed that snow could reach a depth of ten or fifteen feet in some places. He filed away the information in the back of his mind and kept moving.

At noon he stopped and boiled more water for stew, then moved on. He was going slower now, and he found himself stopping more frequently to rest. He was used to hard labor at high altitudes, so the thin air did not bother him. Walking in snowshoes was a new experience, however, and he discovered muscles that he never knew he had. All of them were sore, too.

Twice during the afternoon, he had to stop in order to replace broken pieces of rawhide on his snowshoes. The sun was blocked out by heavy clouds, and snow started falling again. An additional foot of snow had fallen by the time Horton decided to stop for the night. Worse still, the wind had picked up and caused the snow to swirl and further reduce visibility. Horton dug around under the pines and built another small fire. That night, he boiled and ate the last of the jerky. After he had eaten that meager meal, he moved away from the fire and rolled up in his tarp. The heat from his small fire caused the snow on the lower branches near the fire to melt, and Horton fell asleep to the sound of dripping water.

At daybreak, Horton debated the wisdom of traveling further. It was snowing heavily and the wind made any movement difficult. He was out of food, however, and he had no way of knowing just how long the storm would last. He had seen no game since the snow had started on the first day. He could only assume that the animals were smarter than he was and were staying put until the weather cleared. With his muscles screaming in protest, Horton broke camp, hoisted his pack, and started walking. He followed the easiest route he could find as long as it kept heading out of the mountain. It was not very long before he was completely disoriented, and the falling snow made any study of his backtrail impossible. He kept the wind to his back and kept on walking, praying as he went that the wind would not shift.

Horton paused at mid-day and found that he could not get a fire started. With considerable disgust he gave up the attempt and, after a short rest, continued on his way. Twice he stumbled into clearings. Both times he followed the wood line around them, taking the longer route rather than run the risk of wandering aimlessly in an open area with only the wind to guide him.

He started to pant and his breath came in labored gasps. He began to fall more frequently, and he could no longer feel his hands or his feet. He was in serious trouble and he knew it. He needed a place where he could wait out the storm, and he needed food desperately. He was too tired to feel the hunger, but he would have to eat soon if he was to survive.

As it grew darker, Horton saw a glow in front of him. He stopped and rubbed his eyes, not sure that he had really seen it. His fatigue-numbed mind tried to determine the source of the light. It was then that he caught the faint smell of wood smoke. With the wind blowing as hard as it was, he knew that he must be very close to the fire. Slowly, hanging on to trees and using his Winchester for support, he moved toward the glow. It wasn't until he was within a dozen feet of it that he saw the shape of the cabin. It was hidden by the trees and would have been difficult to see even without the snow. Light shown through a rifle port cut in a heavy shutter.

Horton stumbled along the wall until he found a door. Gathering the last of his strength, he began pounding on the heavy planks. Moments later the door opened abruptly, and light and heat struck him like a physical force. He staggered into the room and fell to his hands and knees. The room seemed to revolve around him. He looked up and caught a glimpse of a woman. A glimpse was all that he got before darkness swept over him. He vaguely felt hands touching his coat, then he knew no more.

Chapter 2

The blizzard was not confined just to the mountains. Fifty miles to the east of the cabin in which Jim Horton had collapsed, snow was also falling on the mining town of Ruxford. Ten years before there had been only timbered hillsides where the town now stood. Ruxford owed its existence to the discovery of gold in the surrounding mountains. There was little difference between Ruxford and most other mining towns beyond the fact that Ruxford managed to endure where other towns seemed to boom and then vanish.

There was an air of permanence about this place, however. Saloons, hotels, and stores specializing in mining equipment dominated the main streets, and an active red-light district operated north of town on the far side of Crystal Creek in an area that had become known as Hogtown. Within the last few years, some of the richer members of the town had brought a veneer of civilization to the place by importing a preacher, two female schoolteachers of uncertain age, a judge, and a lawman named Sam Peabody.

Sheriff Peabody was a no-nonsense man who set about making the streets safe for anyone who wasn't dumb enough to flash a large bankroll or brag about how much gold he had dug up. The sheriff figured that nobody could protect fools like that, but he did guarantee that women, children, merchants, and people who minded their own business were free to walk the streets south of Crystal Creek without fear, day or night. He left Hogtown pretty much alone. There a man could find a card game, a drink, a woman, or a knife in the ribs any time he wanted. The citizens of Ruxford seemed to be satisfied with the arrangement, and the sheriff had no intention of changing it.

Before the war, Sam Peabody had rangered in Texas and he had cleaned up a number of towns over the past ten years. At the age of forty he was known to be a tough but fair man, not particularly fast with his Colt, but deadly accurate with a rifle, pistol, or knife. He was also known to be damned hard to kill. The story was often told about how he had come upon the Mertan gang and, in the space of less than five minutes, had killed all seven of them while collecting no fewer than six bullet wounds for his trouble. Peabody knew that the story was somewhat exaggerated, but he never indicated by how much, nor did he discourage its telling. He figured that the story had saved him considerable trouble over the years. Hardcases tended to think twice before going up against him. That was fine with him. He had nothing to prove to anyone, least of all to some young gunslick trying to build a reputation at his expense.

On the night of the blizzard, Sheriff Peabody made his rounds as usual. The town was shut down tight by ten o'clock, and even Hogtown surrendered to the weather by eleven. The sheriff made a last check of Main Street and then, as was his custom, headed to the Excelsior Hotel for a late meal before turning in for the evening. It pleased him that he would be able to call it a night several hours earlier than usual. As he mounted the steps to the hotel, he decided that the wind and snow weren't all bad. He could almost taste the steak that Charlie had waiting for him in the kitchen.

It was just after midnight when a shadowy figure emerged from the alley on the west side of the Ruxford Bank and Trust. He checked the street as far as he could see in both directions and then, seeing no one, moved silently to the front door of the bank. He reached into his coat pocket and extracted a key which he used to unlock the door, then entered the building and closed the door quickly behind him. He relocked the door to cover the unlikely chance that the sheriff would come by again, then moved to the back of the building where the banker, Morton Witherspoon, maintained his office.

The man extracted a small candle from his pocket and lit it. He walked to the calendar on the wall beside Witherspoon's deck and lifted the top sheet to reveal the sheet for December. He noted the three dates circled on the calendar and dropped the November sheet back into place. He smirked to himself as he walked over to the safe and dialed the numbers that had been circled on the calendar. The tumblers inside clicked and the man twisted the handle and swung open the door with a gentle tug. He laughed softly as he rubbed his hands together and surveyed the contents of the safe.

"Witherspoon, you're as big a fool as ever," he muttered to himself. "You are absolutely predictable. You make this almost too easy. The sad part is, you'll never know that you helped to rob your own bank." He laughed again.

The man put down the saddlebags that he had slung over his shoulder and began to fill the pouches with the packets of greenbacks from the upper shelves of the safe. None of the bills that he took were new, so there was little likelihood that they could be identified by a serial number. He was able to force a little more than ninety-seven thousand dollars into the bags and slightly less than fourteen thousand into his pockets. By then the supply of used bills had been exhausted. He longingly eyed the gold coins and pouches of gold dust stored in the bottom of the safe for a moment, then shut and locked the door of the safe before he could be tempted any further. The gold was too heavy for him to carry very far, and he needed to stick with his plan if he hoped to get away with this robbery.

The man snuffed out the candle, put it back in his pocket, and stood up. Shouldering the saddlebags, he moved back to the front door, checked the street for movement and, seeing no one, left the bank and relocked the door. He moved swiftly to the back of the building, where he threw the saddlebags over his horse's neck before he mounted and rode slowly out of town. The snow and wind quickly filled in the tracks that he and his horse had left. Within half an hour, all sign of his having been there was covered by a foot of snow.

The rider made his way to the deserted train station and turned north to follow the tracks toward Denver. The blizzard and poor visibility did not trouble him because they had been an essential part of his plan. He had waited for just these conditions. They brought risks, to be sure, but he felt that the contents of the saddlebags more than justified any extra chances he had taken with the weather.

Three miles up the track he came to an abandoned spur, which he followed until it dead-ended at the ruins of a collapsed trestle. The rider dismounted and led his horse along the rim of the gorge until he came to an old shed. He coaxed the horse to the lip of the gorge, removed the saddlebags and then shot it. The animal collapsed, its body hung on the lip for a moment and then slipped into the gorge below. The man picked up the saddlebags and walked back to the cabin. In a few minutes smoke started coming from the stovepipe that stuck out through the roof. The wind and the snow continued unabated for three more days.

Nothing stirred in Ruxford until after the snow stopped and the wind died down. It took another two days after that to dig out the town. By the time that was accomplished, the train service to Denver had resumed. Since it was a Saturday, a large part of the male population adjourned to the saloons and bawdy houses in Hogtown to celebrate the end of the storm, their personal survival, and other assorted occasions. What with one thing or another, it was the following Monday before Morton Witherspoon reopened his bank and discovered the theft. It took him another four hours before he was able to compose himself sufficiently to report the robbery to Sheriff Peabody.

When the first train after the storm passed through Ruxford, it was flagged down three miles north of town by a single man carrying a pair of saddlebags. He boarded the train and paid for a ticket to Denver with a crumpled greenback. The conductor sent the man forward to the nearly deserted passenger car and pocketed the bill. He figured that the company had plenty of money, so this fare could be added to his own private retirement fund. The train continued on its way to Denver without further interruption. The conductor went back to his caboose and his bottle. He soon forgot that the train had ever stopped at Ruxford.

Sheriff Peabody followed the agitated Morton Witherspoon back to the bank. He was puzzled about the robbery. Many times he had witnessed armed gangs robbing banks and shooting up the town. On two occasions he had arrested bank clerks who had stuffed carpet bags full of cash and then tried to leave town. Never had he encountered a situation in which the money had just seemingly vanished from a locked safe in a locked building. No one had left town as far as he knew, so the probability was that the bank robber was either still here or had come and gone in the storm. The latter possibility was highly unlikely, in his opinion, because it would mean that the outlaw would have had to make his getaway in weather that would most probably have killed him. The sheriff did not rule out that possibility, however. Stranger things than that had happened before.

When they got to the bank, the sheriff immediately examined the doors and the safe. There were no marks which would suggest forced entry. All the windows that could be opened and closed were guarded by iron bars firmly embedded in the rock walls of the building. The walls themselves were nearly three feet thick and unbroken. The roof was intact, as was the floor. The safe had not been blown up, drilled, or tampered with in any way.

The sheriff turned to Witherspoon and asked, "Who had the combination to the safe besides you, Morton?"

"No one, Sheriff," the man responded. "I change the combination on the first day of every January, just to make sure that someone has not discovered the combination by watching me open the safe. If one of my employees leaves, I change the combination again, too. There's no way anyone could have known that combination, I tell you," the banker said angrily.

"Keep your shirt on, Mort," the sheriff said soothingly. "It's pretty clear that someone did. The safe's empty an' there's no sign of forced entry anywhere, not even on the doors. This thing sizes up as an inside job to me. Any of your people likely to pull off something like this?"

"Both tellers have been with me since we opened nearly ten years ago," Witherspoon said somewhat more calmly. "The bookkeeper, old Mister Fulton, has been here for nearly two years, ever since the man before him caught gold fever and left to go prospecting. He's nearly seventy, though. He's not likely to have done it. For one thing, he's too frail to have carried off the gold."

Sheriff Peabody thought for a moment, then turned to look at the banker. "You got any ideas about how the robber or robbers got into the building? Who's got the keys to the doors besides you?"

"There are three keys," the banker answered somewhat testily. "I've got one on my key ring, and I keep a spare at home locked up in my desk. Jack Kirby, the head cashier and vice president, has one, too. All of the keys are accounted for, Sheriff. Jack Kirby's been with me for more than twenty years, even before we opened the bank here."

The sheriff thought for a few more minutes, stroking his chin with his thumb and forefinger as he made another tour around the office. "It sure is a puzzle to me, Morton. No sign of breakin' in, not a scratch on the safe, but the whole place cleaned out just as slick as you please. All your help is clean, you say. Whoever done this sure didn't leave me much to go on." As an afterthought, he asked, "Who cleans up the place?"

"Jack Kirby handles that. He hires somebody to sweep up and cart off the trash after we close every night, then locks up after them. The safe's always locked by the time they get here, and Jack always keeps an eye on them."

"Same people clean up all the time?"

"They change nearly every day. To tell you the truth, it's not much of a job. Generally, they stay around just long enough to find a better one."

"You change the safe combination each time one of 'em leaves?"

"No, I don't. In fact, the last time I changed the combination because someone left was about two years ago when that bookkeeper went off to hunt gold."

"Morton, I still think that whoever pulled this off unlocked the door an' dialed the combination to the safe. That either makes 'em out to be employees or professional safe crackers. If we was back East somewheres, I'd bet on the second choice, but since we ain't, I'm bettin' on the first one. Yep, I do believe that it's an inside job."

"That's hard for me to believe, Sheriff, but I see the logic in what you say. There are an awful lot of Easterners around here, though, and a lot of them came here not too many steps in front of the law."

"Which means we're right back where we started—nowhere. If you'll open the safe for me again, I'd appreciate it. I'd also like to talk to each of your employees in private, if you'll let me have the loan of your office."

"Certainly, Sheriff. Anything you want," Witherspoon said as he spun the dial on the safe.

The sheriff backed off as the banker worked the combination. He discovered that the banker's back blocked the view of the dial from the windows. The only way a man could see the combination as it was being dialed was by using a telescope and observing through the open door to the office. The chance of getting away with such an observation unnoticed was very slim.

"There you are, Sheriff," Witherspoon said as he stepped back from the safe. "As you can see, the only thing that the bandits left were the packages of new bills stored on the third shelf."

"Now why do you suppose they done that, Morton? There must be ten or fifteen thousand dollars there."

"Sixteen thousand to be exact. I expect that they left the new bills because we have a record of their serial numbers. We don't keep records of the numbers on used bills."

"I never would of thought of that," the sheriff mused. "Seems to me that only someone in the bankin' business would know somethin' like that."

"Or someone who makes a living cracking bank safes, Sheriff," the banker replied quickly.

Sam Peabody smiled. "You got a point there, Morton. Maybe I'm tryin' too hard to bend the evidence to fit my theory. How much did the thieves get away with all told?"

Witherspoon went over to his desk and got a piece of paper. Reading from it, he said, "There were eleven thousand, four hundred eighty dollars in gold coin; two thousand, one hundred twelve dollars and seventy cents in silver coin; and forty-one thousand dollars' worth of gold dust, measured by weight. The grand total is nearly fifty-five thousand dollars."

Sam Peabody whistled softly. "That's a lot of money, Morton. Was all of it the bank's?" he asked as he finished writing down the sums in his notebook.

"No. As it happens, we were storing the gold dust and most of the gold coins for Wells Fargo. We do that frequently when they have a lot of dust or cash on hand. The rest of it belonged to the bank and its depositors."

"Is this goin' to put you out of business?" the sheriff asked pointedly. "A lot of people had all they owned in that safe of yours."

"I'm happy to say that we were insured," the banker replied. "I've got enough money to keep things going 'til the company pays off, even if I have to have some of my own assets in Denver sold off and the money sent in."

"That'll be mighty good news to your depositors, Mort. Now tell me, how did you find the office when you came in this morning?" the sheriff asked, shifting subjects. "Was it just like this?"

"Just like this, Sheriff. The bank door was locked, my office door was closed, and the safe door was standing wide open. I closed and locked the safe when I left to get you because of the other money still in it."

Sam Peabody thought for a minute as he absent-mindedly moved a dust ball around on the floor with the toe of his boot. Finally, he looked up and addressed the banker.

"Well, thanks for your time, Morton. I won't be troublin' you no further. If you'll send your people in, one at a time, I'll ask 'em some questions an' be on my way."

The banker nodded in agreement and left the sheriff alone in the office. Soon there came a knock at the door as the first of the bank employees came to be questioned. The sheriff talked with each one and learned nothing new. When he finished talking with the last man, he left the bank and tried to walk around the building. The snow was so deep, however, that he had to settle for looking down both sides of the bank. He saw nothing suspicious. It was clear that the snow had covered any sign that the robber or robbers might have left. Reluctantly, he headed back to the office. The only thing that he could do now was to be on the lookout for some big spender throwing their money around.

Later in the afternoon, the sheriff made his way over to Hogtown. He had a contact or two there who would tell him if anyone started spending more money than usual. It wouldn't be the first time that a smart man let fast money cloud his judgment. What the sheriff needed was a break if he ever hoped to solve this case, just one little clue that he could hang his hat onto instead of a gut feeling that wasn't worth a damn in court. He was still certain that someone connected with the bank had been responsible for the robbery. He could pretty much rule out Witherspoon, since the banker had offered to make good on depositors' losses out of his own personal assets. Besides, the banker had been in business for thirty years with never a hint of impropriety. The sheriff vowed to check out each of the other employees as soon as he could. He'd check out Witherspoon, too, just for good measure. You never could be absolutely sure about a man where money's concerned. He was still thinking about the robbery when he crossed the creek into Hogtown.

Chapter 3

Jim Horton was pacing the floor as he had been for nearly a week, ever since the day he had awakened to find himself in bed under nearly a foot of duck-down quilts. It had taken him only an instant to get his bearing and to remember the events that had brought him there.

"Jim, please sit down and relax. Wearing out my rug won't bring the time of your leaving any closer."

Horton stopped his pacing abruptly and faced the girl who had just spoken. Perhaps "girl" was not quite the right word to describe Sonja Olsen. The fact was that he thought there weren't any words that were up to describing her, at least not any that he knew of. She was tall for a woman, at least matching his own six feet, and maybe she was a little taller. Her hair was the golden color of wheat, and she had a face that would do credit to an angel. The sound of Scandinavia could be heard in voice. She was just out of her teens, if he was any judge, and she had a figure that would cause most other women to cry with envy. To all this she added a sweet and gentle disposition and an almost child-like innocence. She could also cook better than anyone he'd ever known. All in all, Jim Horton was hard-pressed to understand just why he was so all-fired anxious to leave the considerable comfort of the cabin.

"Sorry, Sonja. I don't know what's gotten into me," he said. "You an' your pa have been real good to me, an' I appreciate it. But I gotta confess that I really feel penned up. I'm not much used to a roof, let alone all this," he drawled softly as he gestured at the room about him.

"Come, sit here," she said, patting a spot beside her on the bench, "and tell me more about your ranch in Texas. All that I've ever known were the mountains, first in Sweden, of course, for I was very small when we left. I should very much like to see this open country where you raise so many cattle, I think."

Horton crossed the room and sat beside her, although he positioned himself considerably farther down on the bench than she had indicated with her hand. Part of his restlessness, he knew, was caused by his desire to recover his gold and get it safely to a bank. What he was not yet willing to admit to himself was that the other cause of his increasing restlessness was his desire for Sonja. She was just about everything he had ever thought about as being desirable in a woman. She was beautiful, smart, easy to talk to, and perfectly able and willing to work alongside of a man. She would be sure to do her share of the work and maybe a little more. The calluses on her hands showed that she was no stranger to hard work, but those same hands were capable of incredible tenderness. Sonja would do to take along, he admitted. The temptation to take her into his arms was a hot, urgent thing, threatening to take control of him at any moment. The fear that she might reject him was one of the things that controlled his lustier urges. The other thing chose that moment to enter the room amidst a blast of freezing air through the doorway at the far end of the cabin.

It was a wonder to Horton that any cold air could get past Ole Olsen. He was six feet, eight inches tall in his stocking feet and claimed to weigh three hundred pounds, none of which was fat. He filled the doorway from top to bottom and from side to side. He was a man somewhere in his forties, and he had been a schoolteacher before he left Sweden a dozen or more years before. One night Horton had seen him bend a two-foot length of inch-thick steel into something that looked like a horseshoe. The bar was cold and he had used only his bare hands. He hadn't even grunted from the effort. Horton was reasonably certain that Ole could pick up and walk off with a good-sized horse if he were so inclined. He was also sure that no one, not even the horse's owner, would object. Fortunately, Ole seemed to have a disposition as gentle as his daughter's, but Jim really did not want to put that to the test. There was something in the depths of Ole's eyes that hinted that he could be a dangerous enemy if provoked. He doted on Sonja, and he certainly would look upon any unwelcome advance towards her as a terrible provocation. It was no surprise to Horton that Sonja had no callers. One look at Ole would be enough to send most strong men packing.

"So!" Ole exclaimed as he shut the door behind him and deposited a haunch of venison on a bench by the door. "I stomp around in the snow looking for food while you two soak up all the heat from the fireplace," His face split into a wide grin that revealed what seemed to be at least a hundred strong, white teeth.

"By George," I think you two got the right idea! Sonja, be a good girl and bring your poor old papa the jug so he can gather his strength."

Sonja was already halfway to the cupboard. By the time she removed the jug and made her way across the room to her father, Ole had removed his buffalo-hide coat and woolen scarf and hung them on a peg by the door. With a stern look he took the jug from Sonja's hands, raised it to his ear and shook it vigorously.

"The level seems much lower than the last time. Somebody around here drinks too much. Sonja, I tell you, drink will be the ruin of you yet. When are you going to take the pledge?"

"That whiskey will be the ruin of somebody around here, but it won't be me. The only thing I would use that stuff for is to thin paint," Sonja said as she watched her father take a long pull at the jug. After his Adam's apple bobbed five or six times, she reached up and retrieved the jug from the protesting Ole.

"You've had enough, you old soak. Jim will think badly of you."

"Well, we can't be having that. You'd better give him some, too. I hate to be in trouble all by myself," the older man said almost gleefully.

Horton steeled himself as the smiling Sonja brought the jug over to him. He had learned from previous encounters that Ole made the whiskey himself and that it was strong enough to etch glass. He raised the jug to his mouth, took a cautious swallow and broke into a fit of coughing.

"Good?" Ole inquired innocently.

"Smoother'n a snake's hips, Ole," Jim managed to gasp weakly as he handed the jug back to the laughing Sonja. "I don't know about her, but I'd be willin' to sign the pledge right now if someone was to tell me how to go about it."

Ole shook his mane in mock despair. "It's a pity that there's so few real men left in the mountains. You youngsters can't take more than a little clear creek water. Ah, well, I guess that leaves more for me," he said as he reached for the jug again.

"Oh, no you don't," Sonja said as she jerked the jug away from Ole's outstretched hands and returned it to its place in the cupboard. "That's more than enough for one day. Both of you had better get ready for supper while I put away this meat."

"I'll put it with the rest, Sonja," Ole said, picking up the haunch. "I thought you might want to use some tonight. If you got something else planned, that's fine by me. Go ahead and make the table ready."

Ole vanished through the doorway amidst another blast of cold air. It took him only a few moments to walk to a large tree near the house. In it he had built a stout plank box which he kept suspended about ten feet from the ground by a series of pulleys and ropes. The raw meat stored in it was safe there from any prowling animal. Cooked meat was stored in a ventilated meat safe inside the cabin. Ole quickly lowered the box, placed the meat inside with the rest of the deer that he had shot earlier in the day and raised the box back to its former position. In less than a minute he was back inside the cabin.

The evening meal started out well enough. Ole told of his hunt between mouths full of stew and huge chunks of bread. As the story progressed, it became clear that Ole was either a great stalker of game or a first-class storyteller. When Horton voiced that opinion, Ole just grinned and pointed to the rear of the cabin.

"Any time you want, Jim, you can go out and check the game box. The proof of the story is in there."

"I don't doubt that you brought in some poor, dead critter, Ole," Jim said with a dead-pan expression, "but it probably died of old age, or it had a heart attack when it saw you stumblin' out of the trees. Probably thought you was some big bear comin' out of its cave for a last snack before hibernatin' for the winter," he said without cracking a grin.

Ole affected a wounded expression as he said, "I give a man a place to sleep and a seat at my table, and what do I get in return? Accusation and abuse, that's what. Maybe you could give this poor old mountain man some pointers. You go with me next time, what do you say?"

"I'd really like that," Jim said as he wiped up the last of the stew from his bowl with a piece of bread. "But I'm afraid that'll have to wait 'til the next trip. The weather's broke an' I'd better make tracks before I get snowed in here for the winter."

"Would that be so terrible?" Sonja asked, pouting because Jim wanted to leave. "Besides, you can't leave yet. Your side has not fully healed."

"It wasn't much more than a scratch in the first place," Jim said as he touched his side. "I certainly find the company, if not the whiskey, to my likin', but I've still got business to take care of an' I don't want to take a chance on wearin' out my welcome 'round here."

"Leave the man alone, Sonja," Ole scolded. "He knows what he has to do. Besides, he knows that he's welcome to stay here as long as he wants."

"It's just like one man to stick up for another," Sonja said under her breath before lapsing into total silence. As she cleared the table of the remnants of the meal, she punctuated her silence with an occasional sniff, but she offered no further comment of any kind. The festive mood of the meal was quickly replaced by an awkward silence.

"I really do need to leave, Ole," Jim said apologetically. "I appreciate your hospitality an' all, but if you'll loan me some snowshoes, I'll be on my way at first light. There's a lot to do if I'm to come back in the spring." Jim had spoken to Ole, but his eyes had never left Sonja, who now pretended complete indifference.

It suddenly became important to Jim that Sonja understand the need for his leaving, but the more he discussed the details of his trip to Ruxford with Ole, the more silent Sonja became. Finally, Jim quit trying to win her over, more convinced than ever that he would never understand the working of the female mind.

Jim spent the rest of the evening preparing his pack and adjusting the snowshoes that Ole gave him. Sonja deposited a quantity of jerked meat on his pack with enough force to demonstrate that she was still angry and had not yet forgiven him, then disappeared for good behind the curtain that separated her bedroom from the rest of the cabin. Jim and Ole went over the route that he would take, then Ole, too, retired behind his curtain for the night. Jim made a final check of his weapons and equipment, then retreated behind the last of the curtains to the cubicle which contained his bunk.

As he prepared for bed, Jim once again considered his trip and decided that it was a good thing that he was going. He wanted to recover the gold, of course, but even more than that, he wanted to give Sonja a chance to get over her anger. The fact that he was so concerned about her feelings troubled him more than a little. He had always considered himself to be a man without ties, but Sonja had gotten to him as no other woman ever had before. It disturbed him to find that he didn't want to leave.

He had climbed into bed and was reaching to snuff out the candle when the curtain opened and Sonja stepped in. She had let her golden hair cascade over her shoulders, and standing there in her nightclothes she presented an image of loveliness that nearly took Horton's breath away. His jaw sagged momentarily, then he dragged the quilts up to his chin as the reality of the situation finally hit him.

"I could not let you leave with hard feelings between us," Sonja said softly. "I know that you must go, but I was afraid that you would not come back." As she spoke, she moved to the side of the bed and sat on the edge.

"I'll be back, Sonja, I promise," he said nervously as he watched her shiver slightly from the cold that had already penetrated her nightclothes. "Now you go back to bed before you catch cold or wake your father. What would he say if he found you in here?"

"Don't worry about Papa. He is a heavy sleeper. Besides, he knows that I have feelings for you. You are my man. Now, why don't you move over? It gets cold out here."

Horton started to protest, but Sonja slipped under the quilts. He was still protesting as she snuffed out the candle and turned to him.

"Hush, now," she said as she placed a finger against his lips and pressed her body against his. Horton was no fool. He hushed.

It was still dark when Horton awoke to find only an indentation in the pillow to show that the events of the past night were not just a dream. He swung his feet to the floor and then dressed quickly, anxious to escape from the cold that had deposited a light coat of frost on the clay and grass chinking between the logs of the cabin wall. Once fully dressed, he pushed aside the curtain and stepped into the main room, only to find Sonja preparing a breakfast of venison at the stove. She looked up and smiled as he approached.

"It will be a fine day to travel," she said as she turned over the steak and stirred some potatoes and onions frying in a large skillet. "The sky is clear and the wind is down. Are you sure that you must go?"

"I'd like to stay, Sonja, but I really must go." After a moment's pause, he continued, "About last night. I ...."

"Do not speak of last night. That was a special time. There will be other times," she said with confidence. "You will come back, even if you do not yet believe it.

When you do, I will be waiting here. Now sit down and eat. You will need all your strength for the trip."

Horton sat down to a table that was quickly loaded with biscuits, honey, steak, potatoes, onions, and coffee. He ate in silence, conscious of Sonja watching him as she busied herself with chores around the cabin. Strangely, there was no sign of Ole, and Jim wondered if the big man was allowing him a chance for privacy with Sonja or if he had already left for a day of running his trap line.

After he had finished off a prodigious quantity of food, Horton rose and prepared to leave. Sonja helped him to adjust his pack, then handed him his carbine as he picked up the snowshoes. Once both of his hands were occupied, Sonja pulled him close to her and kissed him soundly, then stepped back and opened the door for him

"Hurry back," she said simply as she watched him step through the doorway and stoop to put on the snowshoes that Ole had lent him. When he straightened and turned to speak, Sonja closed the door softly.

"Damn!" Horton cursed under his breath. He wanted to say something to the girl, but nothing sounded right. He was uneasy and felt a little guilty about leaving Sonja after last night. He suspected that she intended for him to feel that way. "Women! I'll never understand 'em," he grumbled in understatement as he started off toward Ruxford.

Frustration and a little anger drove Horton to cover the first mile at a brisk pace. By then the sun had risen, stiff muscles had loosened, and his common sense had returned sufficiently for him to remember the advantages of a slower, more methodical pace. He settled down to a rhythm that he reckoned would take him to Ruxford within three days. As he traveled, he identified the landmarks that Ole had described to him the night before. Horton found himself daydreaming about Sonja.

As he rounded a sharp bend in the trail, Horton saw a flash of movement from the corner of his eye only an instant before a solid blow to the left arm sent him flying into a snow drift. A little dazed and confused, he rolled to his left as he raised the muzzle of his Winchester and thumbed back the hammer.

"Ho! Ho! I got you that time," a loud voice boomed. "I think you may not be such a great hunter yourself if you let me sneak up on you. You still think that deer died of fright?" Ole asked as he extended his massive hand to help Horton back to his feet.

"Ole, I damned near shot you! You oughtn't to do things like that," Horton said as he eased the hammer on his carbine back to half-cock.

Horton shifted the carbine to his left hand, then dusted the snow from his clothes. Ole just stood there, showing all of those big teeth in a huge grin.

"Maybe you're right," Horton said somewhat sheep-ishly. "My mind was wanderin' a bit. That's not much like me. I don't understand it."

Ole laughed and slapped him on the back, nearly knocking him down again. "The only trouble with you, I think, is Sonja. You never met a girl like her before, I bet. If you pay attention to what you do, you might get the chance to come back. Now, take care of yourself and watch out for the trail just ahead. The snow drifted and makes it look wider than it really is."

"Thanks, Ole. I appreciate everything you've done for me. I don't know how I can ever repay you."

"Just come back when you can. I got a new batch of whiskey that I'd like your opinion of."

The two men laughed and shook hands warmly, each one convinced that the other was a man fit to ride the rivers and cross the mountains with. The men parted and Ole started back toward the cabin as Horton continued his descent to the flatter lands below.

Chapter 4

Jim Horton finally reached Ruxford in the afternoon of the third day after leaving the Olsens' cabin. By the time he got there he was close to exhaustion. Not being accustomed to snowshoes, he found that mode of travel far more taxing than he had expected. The journey had been uneventful, however, and for that Horton was grateful.

The first thing that Horton did when he got to town was to stop by the general store, where he picked out a complete change of clothes and a coat more suitable for town wear than the one made of buffalo hide that had served him so well in the mountains. He also selected a used double-barreled .41 caliber Derringer, a box of ammunition for it and a heavy woolen scarf. He considered buying a new hat, for the Stetson he wore showed signs of the hardships the owner had encountered over the years. Horton finally decided against it, mostly because it had taken him two years to train the one he had before it finally felt comfortable. He picked up the pile of goods and moved it over to the counter where he had left his pack.

"Anything else, sir?" the clerk asked as he moved away from the shelves of dry goods where he had been working and approached Horton.

"I don't reckon so," Horton answered as he scratched his beard. "Well, maybe you ought to toss in a razor an' some shavin' soap. I also need to know where's the best hotel in town an' the location of a bootmaker."

The clerk added a razor and some shaving soap to the pile, then tossed in a shaving brush.

"On the house," he said as he made a final tally of the purchases. "I make the total as forty-one dollars, twenty cents. We'll call it forty-one even. That suit you?"

"Sounds right to me," Horton said as he stooped to open his pack. He withdrew one of the gold pokes and passed it over to the clerk.

"Take it out of there, if you will, an' take out another forty to boot. I don't want to weigh ever' time I want to buy somethin.'"

The clerk hefted the poke and moved over to the scales, where he measured out the appropriate amount of dust, then returned the pouch and two double eagles to Horton.

"Make a good strike, did you?" the clerk asked, a little too casually for Horton's taste.

"That there represents a year's grubbin' in those hills," Horton responded evenly. "By the time I get back home, all I'll have to show for it is blisters, a couple of scars, an' an empty poke. A man can't make a livin' pannin' streams or bustin' rock."

His curiosity satisfied, the clerk nodded his head in agreement as he wrapped up Horton's purchases. Horton decided that his little deception had worked.

"Excelsior Hotel's right on down the street, next to the Nugget Saloon," the clerk volunteered. "They got a bath and a barber shop in the back. If you want a good meal and hang the cost, eat there. If you want a big feed for a lot less, try the cafe about two blocks further on down the street. There's a bootmaker and a saddle shop right across the street from the cafe. If you're looking for a little sport, try Hogtown across the creek, but I'd stash my poke first, if I was you. Them that have money have been known to disappear over there, if you catch my drift."

"I do indeed, friend, an' thanks for the advice," Horton drawled as he knelt and added his purchases to his pack. "All I want right now is a bath, a hot meal, an' about a week's sleep, not necessarily in that order." He stood up with the pack in his left hand and the carbine in his right, nodded to the clerk, and headed for the door. The clerk stood where he was for a little longer, then took off his apron and laid it on the counter. He went into the back room and emerged a few moments later wearing his hat and coat. He carefully locked the store behind him and walked briskly in the opposite direction from the hotel, toward the sheriff's office.

Jacob Melenthin, the clerk, had come west in search of gold along with an army of others, all expecting to strike it rich. Jake soon found that the only people who got rich were the saloon and brothel owners. Jake's strict New England Methodist upbringing wouldn't permit him to join that crowd, but he had found that he could make a very comfortable living by running a general store. He was the owner as well as the clerk and had done well enough to consider expanding his business if a suitable opportunity were to present itself.

Like most of the men in Ruxford, Jake had fought in the War Between the States. He did not consider himself to be a brave man, but neither did he consider himself to be a coward. He was, however, cautious. Sheriff Peabody had told every business owner in Ruxford and Hogtown to report any strangers flashing gold dust or coin, and Jack Melenthin wasn't about to disobey Sam Peabody's orders.

The snow squeaked under Jake's boots as he made his way up the street to Sam Peabody's office. He stopped and tried the door, only to find it locked. He pounded on it a few times, then gave up in disgust. He had no way of telling where the sheriff was, so he headed back down the street to his store. He generally went home every night at eight. He'd try again to talk to Peabody tonight after he'd closed up. There was a limit to Jake's devotion to duty, especially when it conflicted with his prime sales time.

Jim Horton made his way down the street to the Excelsior Hotel. It turned out to be a two-story brick building that extended the depth of the city block. It had the look of solid permanence about it that suggested that any guest could expect privacy, clean rooms, and good service. Horton entered the hotel and crossed the lobby, which was furnished with leather chairs and bright, thick rugs. He hit the bell on the desk and had to wait only for a moment before the desk clerk emerged from an office in the rear. The clerk did not seem to notice Horton's tattered clothes or his shaggy beard and hair. He turned the registration book to face Horton, dipped a pen in the inkwell, and handed it to him.

"Rooms are five dollars a night, and that includes the use of the bath downstairs at the end of the hall." The clerk eyed Horton momentarily, then continued. "Payment will be in advance."

Horton finished signing the book, then laid down the pen with enough force to make the desk clerk jump back just a fraction. The clerk looked Horton in the eye for the first time.

"Five dollars is a little steep, ain't it?" Horton asked, letting a little more of Texas than usual creep into his voice.

"There are cheaper quarters available across the creek in Hogtown, I understand, sir," sniffed the clerk. "Of course, you pay for what you get."

Much to the relief of the clerk, Horton laughed. "I guess you do," he admitted as he flipped a double eagle onto the counter. "I'll be here for a while, so just let me know when you need more." Horton watched as the clerk obviously overcame the need to bite the coin to see if it was real and deposited the money in the cash drawer.

"Room 106 down the hall, sir," the clerk said, handing him a key. "I'll have someone bring your luggage along directly."

"No need. I'll take it myself. Where can I get something to eat?"

"Right through that door," the clerk responded, pointing to a side door that apparently connected with the saloon next door.

"I was told that the hotel served food," Horton said. "Is the dining room closed?"

The desk clerk raised himself to his full height of five and half feet and said haughtily, "The hotel dining room is not open today, but the Nugget is part of this hotel, sir. You can find good food, unwatered whiskey, and a fair game in there. If you want anything else, sir, then you'll have to go to Hogtown to get it."

Horton smiled and the clerk became even more indignant. Horton's smile widened into a grin and he said, "Thanks, mister. I guess I can find my way around." With that, he turned and walked down the corridor to his room.

The room was just what Horton expected. There was a rug on the floor and the bed, dresser, and washstand all matched. The sheets were clean and the walls were thick and freshly painted. The window looked out on the alley that ran between the hotel and the saloon. He saw that the two buildings were connected by a walkway that was hidden by the false front of the saloon.

Horton put down his pack at the end of the bed and leaned his carbine against the wall by the door. He took the change of clothes that he had purchased at the store and set it aside before he put his heavy coat and the snowshoes in the wardrobe. Horton considered trying to find a place to cache the gold pokes, then decided that it would hardly be worth the effort. The floors and walls of the room were far too solid, and any place else he picked would not hide the gold for long. He stripped off his pistol belt and checked the loads in the Colt, then dropped the pistol back into the holster and hung the belt over one of the bedposts. He picked up the little Derringer, broke it open and loaded it before slipping it into his hip pocket. Grabbing the parcel of new clothes, Horton headed for the bath.

An hour later, soaked, scrubbed, shaved, and with hair trimmed and dressed in new clothes, Horton walked through the hotel lobby on his way to the Nugget and what he hoped would be a good meal. He had disposed of his old clothes at the bath, but he decided not to do anything else that day to increase his wardrobe. There would be plenty of time for that later.

What he really wanted right now was a drink, a meal, and about twelve hours of uninterrupted sleep.

Horton found the saloon to be as elegant as the hotel. The usual bar ran the length of one wall, but this one was made of polished oak to match the paneled walls set with beveled mirrors and other fancywork. Two chandeliers provided most of the light that did not come in through the etched glass windows. The floor was clean and a man was stationed at each door to collect firearms. Horton didn't mention the Derringer in his hip pocket and the man at the door didn't notice it as Horton moved into the room and selected a table next to the staircase leading to the balcony on the second floor. It was still early, but already the place was beginning to fill up. There were a dozen or more men there talking quietly among themselves. Most of them were wearing suits, and Horton decided that this must be the popular watering place for businessmen on their way home.

A waiter quickly appeared and took Horton's order for steak, potatoes, fried onions, and coffee. He also got some real honest-to-goodness Kentucky sippin' whiskey. After drinking Ole's concoction, snake venom would have seemed smooth, but this bourbon was excellent by any standard. Horton had the idea that the tab was going to be a little on the high side, too.

Horton sat sipping his drink and watching the room fill up as he waited for his meal. Before long he heard footsteps on the stairs behind him. He turned and saw a woman of about thirty, dressed in a pale blue satin gown trimmed with white lace at the throat and wrists. He watched her as she descended the stairway. Her hair was flaming red, her eyes were green, and she carried herself with an air of grace and authority unusual for one so young. She must have felt Horton's eyes on her, for she looked down at him and their eyes locked for an instant. The woman paused momentarily, then continued on her way down the stairs and over to the bar. After a brief conversation with the bartender, she made her way across the room and stopped at Horton's table.

"I saw you looking at me on the stairs," she said in a rich, throaty voice. "I know you from somewhere, but I can't quite place it. Can you help me out?"

Horton scrambled to his feet and tried hard not to be as tongue-tied as his feet were tangled. "No ma'am. I'd of remembered a woman as beautiful as you, I'm sure. You must have me confused with somebody else, an' that's somethin' I truly regret," he drawled.

"Do you mind if I join you a minute anyway?" she asked as she grasped the back of a chair.

Horton quickly moved to her side and helped her get seated, then sat down next to her. He was under no illusion that she was there just to hustle drinks. Everything about her suggested class, and he knew that her visit was purely social.

"Was that a bit of Texas I heard in your voice?" she asked, smiling warmly.

"Yes, ma'am, I suppose it is. I was born an' raised a Texican on a little ranch near the town of Benton. I guess I'd better introduce myself. The name's Horton, ma'am, Jim Horton."

"Not General Horton!" she exclaimed as color rushed to her cheeks.

"No, ma'am, I'm afraid not, though he's my older brother. I'm just plain Jim Horton, youngest of the Horton bunch."

"That explains it, then. You look very much as I remember your brother. He helped me to escape from an evil man in Benton many years ago. In fact, he staked me so that I was able to come here. My name is Myrna Meloy," she said, reaching across to shake his hand. "I'm the owner of the Nugget and the Excelsior."

"I'm honored to meet you, ma'am," Jim said as he let his eyes sweep around the room. "Brother Seth is a generous man, but he never had the money to stake you to a place like this. You must have worked plenty hard on your own," he observed.

Myrna smiled radiantly. "Your brother gave me exactly sixty dollars, a fast horse, and some sound advice. He did more than stake me, he rescued me from a life in the cribs and gave me back my self-respect. For that I could never repay him." She paused for a moment, then continued. "I've often wondered what happened to your brother after he helped me leave town. I do know that he ran Delacourte out of town. What happened to him after that?"

"Well, ma'am, ...," Horton drawled as he tried to think of a good place to start.

"Call me Myrna," she instructed,

"Thank you, ma'am—I mean Myrna," Horton stammered. "Anyway, old Seth, he married Miss Sarah an' went back to the Army at Fort Riley. That was about a dozen years ago. They've got six boys now, an' Sarah, she says that's enough. Seth, he made Brigadier General again last year. He's in Washington, doin' whatever it is that generals do there. Me an' my other two brothers have been runnin' the Circle H until I got it in my mind to try the gold fields again last spring."

"Have any luck?" Myrna asked.

"Some," Horton answered guardedly, "but not much."

Myrna laughed. "You're going to have to do better than that if you ever hope to fool anybody. The look that came over your face said that you struck it big."

Horton started to protest, but Myrna quieted him.

"You don't have to convince me. You're wise not to let on about your strike. There's people around here that would kill a man for the gold in his teeth and then steal the pennies off his eyes. But your secret is safe with me, I assure you. Did you have any trouble in the mountains?"

About that time Horton's steak arrived. Myrna ordered something for herself, then gave some instructions that he could not hear to the waiter. A moment or two later the waiter appeared with a bottle of bourbon.

"I thought you might want a refill," she said to Horton, who was attacking his steak with considerable vigor.

"Thank you kindly, Myrna, but I ain't much to drink. I never got in the practice, so I don't handle it very well. Maybe after I eat. It's been three days since I've had a hot meal."

For the next half hour, Horton alternated between eating and relating his adventures in the mountains. He downplayed the size of his strike, not really distrusting Myrna, but merely exercising some instinctive caution. He also found himself downplaying his stay with the Olsens. He didn't feel very comfortable talking about Sonja with Myrna. He couldn't help but reflect that after not having seen a woman in six months, he had suddenly met the two most beautiful creatures he had ever known, all in the space of two weeks. Somehow, he couldn't help but be a little suspicious of all his good fortune.

"You must have had quite a time out there," Myrna said as she finished the last of her meal. "Are you going back in the spring, or are you going back home to Benton?"

"I reckon I'll head back to the mountains," he answered. "I've got some stuff still out there, an' a little unfinished business, too."

"What are you going to do until then? The winters are long and cold around here," she said with a smile that warmed the room perceptibly.

"I thought I might try my hand at cards. If that don't work, I'll look into gettin' a job. I've got enough dust to keep me in comfort for a little while."

Myrna looked at him thoughtfully for a minute, then asked, "How are you fixed for cash money? I'm not being nosey," she added quickly. "There was a bank robbery here in the middle of the blizzard and whoever did it got away with a lot of dust and coin. The sheriff has put the word out to every business on both sides of the creek to report strangers, especially if they're spending dust or gold coin."

Horton looked at her questioningly, then answered, "I've got a double eagle left, before I pay for the meal. I'm paid up at the hotel for four days. After that I'll have to get into the dust again."

"How much do you have? Maybe I can change it for you so that you won't have to deal with the bank or someone who will ask too many questions, especially since you want it known that you didn't find much."

"I've got twenty, maybe twenty-five pounds of dust with me," he answered cautiously.

"Twenty-five POUNDS of the stuff!" Myrna exclaimed. "Too bad you didn't have any luck out there! Who else knows that you have that much gold?"

"The clerk at the general store two blocks down the street knows that I have it, but not how much. Nobody else knows anything."

"Jake Melenthin. He'll report you to the sheriff for sure. I'm surprised that Sam Peabody hasn't been here looking for you already. Did you tell Jake where you were going?" Myrna asked.

"He's the one who told me about this place," Horton answered. "It doesn't make any difference, Myrna. I didn't rob the bank an' I've got people who know where I was durin' an' after the blizzard. I don't have to sulk around avoidin' the law."

"Sheriff Peabody kind of makes his own law, Jim. Mostly it's good law, but if he had a choice between having an innocent stranger in town or a solved case on the books, I'm not sure which one he'd pick." With that, Myrna signaled the waiter and spoke to him in that same low voice that Horton couldn't hear very well. The waiter scurried away as soon as Myrna finished talking with him.

"If you want to, you can work here for me 'til spring," Myrna offered. "I could use someone who can help me manage things. I've got a monopoly on the saloon business on this side of Crystal Creek. The only hotel is mine, too. All the others are in Hogtown. What you see here around us is the supper crowd and some of the businessmen who stop in for a quick drink on the way home. About nine or nine-thirty, the card players show up. The games are mostly low stakes and friendly but sometimes get one that's big. Of course, any saloon in Hogtown does as much business in three or four good days as I do here in a month. The only advantage this place has is that we haven't had a fight here in ten years and wives don't complain when their husbands drop by. Hogtown measures the time between fights in minutes."

"I appreciate the offer, Myrna. Let me think about it some. If I can really be of some help to you, I'd be pleased to do it, but if it's charity that you're offerin', then I'm not needin' it right now."

The waiter came back and handed Myrna a small pouch. She thanked him and he went back to his duties with the other customers. Myrna slid the pouch over to Horton.

"Here, There's a couple of hundred dollars in there, in addition to the twenty you gave to the desk clerk." She held up her hand in a demand for silence when Horton started to argue. "Don't bother to protest. You can give me the two hundred in dust if you want to, and I can change another thousand or two for you if you can give me a little time. And we have a firm rule around here and in the hotel. No Horton ever gets a bill for anything. That's the way it is, so don't try to argue. My people have already been instructed."

Horton looked at her in bewilderment. Finally, he said, "Myrna, my brother did you the kindness, not me. For all you know, I could be some no-account drifter who could cause you a good bit of grief. I'd be a whole lot happier if you didn't do this."

Myrna laughed merrily at his discomfort. "Then you are just going to have to be unhappy. I told you, it's a rule of the house and you can't go around breaking rules."

Horton gave up arguing and thanked her for her kindness. A few minutes later he excused himself and headed back to the hotel. He had no sooner hit the lobby than the desk clerk came scooting out from behind the desk, calling his name.

"Mister Horton! Mister Horton! Excuse me, sir, but we have had to change your room. A previous reservation, you know. Your new room is 201, at the head of the stairs. Here's your key, sir," he said as he handed the new key to Horton. "We've already moved your things. If you need anything, anything at all, just ask. I am terribly sorry about the mix-up, sir."

Horton knew that the mix-up's name was Myrna, but he thanked the clerk solemnly and gave him the old key before he made his way up the stairs to the new room. When he opened the door, he found the room was really a suite, with a parlor, a bedroom, and a private bath. A fresh bottle of fine bourbon was on the parlor table. His weapons had been laid out on the bed, and his pack was on the floor by the foot board. His heavy coat and snowshoes he found in the wardrobe. Horton first checked the loads in his weapons before he got ready for bed. It was still early, but he had been walking for three days and he was bone tired.

Horton had no sooner blown out the lamp when someone began to pound on the door. Horton relit the lamp, then put on his pants, took his Colt from the gun belt hanging at the head of the bed, and positioned himself against the wall next to the door. The pounding started up again.

"Take it easy. I hear you. Who is it?" Horton asked irritability.

"Sam Peabody," the answer came. "I'm the sheriff here. Open up."

Horton thumbed back the hammer of his Colt, then unlocked the door, turned the knob, and allowed it to swing open. For a moment or two nothing happened.

"Alright, Horton, you're no greenhorn, I'll give you that. I ain't neither, so just move out into the room where I can see you," the sheriff instructed.

"What we got here, Sheriff, is a Mexican standoff," Jim answered. "Anyone can call himself a sheriff. Prove who you are an' we'll dance to your tune."

A badge sailed through the doorway and landed about four feet inside the room. Horton waited to see if the sheriff would follow it through the door. When he did not, Horton edged away from the wall and eased down the hammer of his Colt. The sheriff heard the distinctive sound made by the pistol and peered around the corner of the doorway,

"Just set that hog leg down an' we'll talk a might," Peabody directed as he walked into the room, pistol in hand.

Horton deposited the Colt on the parlor table, then turned to face the sheriff.

"Now that you've woke up the whole hotel an' ruined my sleep, what can I do for you, Sheriff?" Horton asked.

"Heard we had a stranger in town flashin' gold. Thought I'd see where you got it," the sheriff answered, never letting the muzzle of his pistol waver from Horton's middle. "Thought maybe you might want to tell me so's we don't have any misunderstandin'. How about it?"

"Since you're askin' so polite, seems a shame to ignore such a simple question," Horton said with more than a little sarcasm in his voice. "I dug the gold, an' it's a little enough to show for six or eight months of damn hard work. If you want the exact location, I hope you brought along your lunch, 'cause you're likely to be here for quite a spell. I ain't about to share that with anyone, least of all some rude, over-the-hill lawman."

"You can save the tough talk, Horton. I've heard it all before. Hold out your hands, palms up."

Horton did as he was told, but he couldn't help but wonder what Peabody was up to.

"You've got enough callouses, split nails, an' dirt worked into those paws to be what you say, I guess," the sheriff said grudgingly. "Where did you get that?"

the sheriff asked, pointing to the scab along Horton's side.

"Same place as I got the gold. Some Utes thought my hair'd look good on a lance."

"Yeah, an' maybe some partners had a fallin' out over splittin' up the loot. Where's the gold now?"

"In my pack in the bedroom. What me to get it?"

The sheriff smiled coldly. "Maybe I just better go with you so's you don't manage to get lost," he said as he gestured towards the doorway with the muzzle of his pistol. "Take the lamp with you an' hold it in both hands."

Once in the bedroom, the sheriff positioned Horton where the light shown on the pack, then he dumped out the contents, revealing the pokes.

"Leather pokes, just like what was stolen," the sheriff said as he hefted one of the bags. "Ten, maybe twelve pounds apiece. Mister, you got a lot of explainin' to do."

"Sheriff, you know as well as I do that every prospector in the mountains makes his own pokes, an' he makes 'em out of what's at hand, namely hide," Horton explained. "What makes you think I'd steal the bank's gold, then keep it in the original pokes? I may not be real bright, but I ain't completely dumb, either."

Sam Peabody looked at Horton and smirked. "Far as I know, boy, nobody said nothin' about no bank. How'd you know it was what got robbed if you ain't the one who did it?" he said, congratulating himself on his logic.

"That's practically the only topic of conversation around here these days. I heard it in the barbershop, the bath downstairs, an' in the Nugget, all durin' the last three hours. It ain't hardly a secret no more."

The sheriff grunted, reluctant to lose his advantage, then continued. "Just where was you for the last two weeks? You got any witnesses that you can line up who can swear to your whereabouts?"

"I got caught comin' out of the mountains when the blizzard struck. You'll remember what day that was. A couple of days later I made it to the cabin of some folks named Olsen. I stayed there until three days ago, when I walked down to here."

"This Olsen fellow. He that little fellow, kinda bald, with a wife runnin' to fat?" the sheriff asked.

"Must be some other Olsen, Sheriff. This one's bigger than a horse an' hairy as a bear. He has a daughter about my size, too."

"Oh, that Olsen," the sheriff said, unable to keep the disappointment completely out of his voice. He paused a minute to think, then seemed to make up his mind about something. He looked Horton directly in the eye and said, "Boy, I don't know if you're lyin' or not. Like you say, you ain't stupid. But there's enough question left in my mind so's to cause me to take you in 'til I get the answers I need. You're gonna be the guest of the city for a while," the sheriff said as he looked around the suite. "You probably ought to thank me. This will save you a bundle for the room, too. The city don't charge no rent at all."

Horton set down the lamp and started to protest, then saw the expression on the sheriff's face and gave up. He dressed quickly, conscious of the fact that the sheriff wanted very badly to pin this robbery on him. For that reason, any attempt to escape would be dealt with harshly and probably permanently.

Once he was fully dressed, Horton walked over to the wardrobe and selected his buffalo-hide coat instead of his new town coat, knowing that heat rarely made it all the way to the cells in the back of a jail. He started to pick up the gold, but the sheriff stopped him.

"Don't worry none about that. I'll send my deputy back to get all this stuff. You just walk on outta here kinda slow an' I'll tag along behind. Don't trip or do anythin' real sudden. I'm an old man an' I scare easy. I might even panic an' squeeze this here trigger. Be a real shame if I was to ruin that nice coat you got there."

"Wouldn't want to put you out any, Sheriff," Jim said, smiling thinly. "I'll be real careful. Shall we walk together or should I carry you? Bein' so old, you might need help on the stairs."

"Boy, you got a smart mouth. I'm gonna enjoy your company. Maybe I'll enjoy it so much I'll make you a permanent guest. Now move along an' keep your big talk to yourself."

Horton shrugged, then carefully made his way to the staircase and down to the lobby. The clerk looked at him questioningly, but Horton silenced him with an icy stare and a quick shake of his head. He didn't know what was going around here, but he didn't want Myrna brought into it, at least not yet.

The trip to the jail was a short one, and when the cell door clanged shut, Horton found ample confirmation of his wisdom in coat selection. It was cold in the cell and the two thin blankets covering the straw pallet looked none too warm. As he looked around the cell, he said to himself, "Well, it ain't the best I've had, but I've been in worse. Guess I'll just wait an' see what tomorrow brings." And with that, Jim Horton rolled up in the blankets and went to sleep.

Chapter 5

Horton woke the next morning to the sounds of keys rattling in the lock of his cell door.

"Hey, you!" a voice hollered unpleasantly. "Hey! Get your sorry ass up and get over here!"

Horton rolled over and looked at his would-be tormentor, a gangling kid of about twenty who sported a tied-down gun belt and wore a star. He carried a tray of food in his left hand.

"Hey, dung head, get over here and get this tray, I ain't your damned personal waiter!" the kid yelled.

Horton swung his boots to the floor and walked over to the deputy, who had opened the door and entered the cell. As Horton reached for the tray, the deputy dropped it, spreading the food all over the floor.

"Now ain't that too bad," the kid smirked. "You're pretty clumsy, mister. Maybe you better clean that up before I get back." With that advice, the deputy turned and walked out of the cell.

As the deputy was locking the cell door, he heard a "click" and looked up. What he saw was Horton's right eye looking directly into his left. Between those two eyes was a cocked Derringer held very firmly in Horton's right fist.

"Don't run off, Deputy. I hate to eat alone. Come back in here an' join me," Horton said, a cold smile forming at the corners of his mouth.

The deputy turned very pale and his Adam's apple bobbed several times as he tried very hard to swallow. Something had gone badly wrong, he knew, and now he was at a loss to know how to correct it. Near-panic seized him.

Horton saw the fear grow in the younger man's eyes. "Don't do somethin' stupid, kid," he said softly, "I could kill you where you stand. Now, ease that door open an' come back in here, real slow."

The deputy got ahold of himself and moved carefully into the cell. His hands were shaking badly.

"D ... don't shoot me. I ... I didn't mean nothin'," the youth stammered.

"Of course you didn't, son. You were just bein' friendly. Just lay face down on the floor an' put your hands behind your back," Horton instructed the youth.

The deputy quickly complied with Horton's instructions. Once he was on the floor, Horton removed the deputy's Colt and returned the Derringer to his own pocket.

"Take off your belt an' then wiggle over to that pile of food there," Horton directed. The deputy squirmed around and did as he was told. "Now stick your feet through the bars." Again, the deputy complied.

Horton stepped through the doorway to the cell, knelt and tied the deputy's ankles together with the belt, one leg on each side of a bar. He walked back into the cell, tore a strip from a blanket and tied the man's hands firmly. He stepped back from the prostate youth and said, "Feel free to help yourself," as he used his foot to grind the deputy's face into the mess on the floor. The deputy moaned in misery and Horton, more disgusted with himself than with the deputy, walked out of the cell and went out to the front office.

There he found the deputy's breakfast tray. Horton smiled, then sat down and ate a few bites. The foot was good, but there was little warmth left in it, so he pushed it away. He would just have to eat later, he decided.

Horton got up and walked slowly over to the gun rack, unlocked it with keys he had found on the sheriff's desk, and selected a shotgun. He relocked the rack, checked the Greener to see that it was loaded, then cocked both barrels and found a seat along the front wall from which he could keep an eye on the street and the door. He settled down to wait.

About an hour later the sheriff opened the door and walked into the office.

"Curly, I've ... what the hell!" he exclaimed.

"It's just me, Sheriff," Horton said as he pointed the shotgun at the lawman's chest. "Suppose you close that door an' have a seat. We need to talk."

The sheriff closed the door and walked over to a chair without saying a word, but if looks were bullets, Horton would have been a dead man.

"Before you sit down, Sheriff, take off your coat real slow." The lawman did as he was told. "That's good," Horton observed. "Now take off the gun belt with your left hand." Horton watched as the sheriff removed the belt. "Now take off the shirt," he said.

The sheriff looked up sharply. "What is this? You want me to do a striptease?"

"Nothin' like that, Peabody. Now turn around."

Horton found what he had suspected, a long, thin-bladed knife tied so that the hilt was at shoulder level and the blade extended down the sheriff's spine.

"Toss that toad stabber into the corner an' then sit down in that chair with the arms on it."

Sam Peabody did what he was told, then asked, "Why this chair?"

Horton smiled at him and said, "Why, you told me yourself that you were an old man who scared easy. I don't want you to faint an' fall out of your chair. You might hurt yourself. Besides," he said as his smile faded, "those chair arms'll make it harder for you to pick anything out of your boot real sudden."

"Where's Curly? If you've killed him, you'll hang for it," the sheriff promised.

"If you mean your deputy, that maggot-mouth is eatin' the breakfast he brought in for me this mornin'. Seems that he didn't think there was enough room on the tray, so he spread the grub around on the floor. Must be some kind of cute little trick of his that he uses to impress visitors. I thought that it was a poor way to treat a guest, so I convinced him to trade breakfasts. He seemed anxious enough to do it. He'll live, but he may have to change his pants. He was smellin' a little ripe when I left him."

"If you've done anything to Curly, I'll ...," the sheriff started to say before Horton cut him off.

"You're startin' to repeat yourself. Curly is a mean, nasty kid, Sheriff. He likes to bully folks who he thinks can't fight back. He deserves whatever he gets. The only thing that got hurt this time was his pride. I can't answer for the next time. My advice to you is to find someone a little older for your next deputy. I don't think that this one will last much longer if he don't change his ways."

The sheriff stared hard at Horton, then relaxed a little. "You're probably right about that. Curly's a little on the touchy side, always tryin' to prove just how tough he is. Maybe this'll teach him some manners. Now you tell me somethin'. How come you're still here? You could have been long gone by now."

"I just wanted to find out what's goin' on. Seems to me that I remember you sayin' that you wanted some more answers. I thought that I might be able to help you out. Besides, the only fast way out of this town right now is by train, an' it would have taken you about two minutes to figure that out. You'd have met me on the platform."

Horton paused a minute for that to sink in, then continued. "I didn't hold up the bank, so there's no need for me to run off anywhere. I just ain't goin' to stay in your jail no longer. I've seen your brand of hospitality, an' I don't think that it'll be necessary for me to impose on you or your deputy anymore. You can find me at the Excelsior or at the Nugget if you need me. Oh, an' I'll take my dust with me. I'd be surprised if some of it hasn't found its way into Curly's pockets already."

"Are you accusin' a lawman of theft?" the sheriff asked angrily as he started out of the chair.

"Hold on, now. You're not in much of a position to take exception to anythin' I have to say, Peabody," Horton said as he waved the muzzle of the shotgun at him. "Suppose you settle back in that chair an' tell me what you had in mind for today."

The sheriff didn't like it, but he sat back down and struggled to get control of himself. He could not remember ever having been as angry as he was right now. Somehow, he managed to say calmly, "I was headed up to the Olsen's place to check on your story. I was also goin' to try to find out where you came from."

"Sounds like a good plan to me, Sheriff. Ole can sure tell you I was there. You had better take the deputy with you. He might try somethin' stupid if he was to stay. Me an' my guns an' my gold'll be at the hotel when you get back."

"How do I know that you'll still be here when I get back? You could be long gone on the train."

"Because I'm here right now an' you're still alive," Horton explained. "If it'll make you feel any better, you can post a guard. I won't leave the buildin'. Call it 'house arrest' if you like."

The sheriff thought for a minute, then said, "Well, I don't like it, but you can go to the hotel. Maybe I'll post a guard, an' then again, maybe I won't. But the gold is goin' to stay right here until such time as I know for sure that it's really yours an' not the bank's."

"That's just fine with me," Horton said, "just as long as Curly doesn't have the combination to the safe. If he does, change it before you go."

The sheriff nodded in grudging agreement. "Since you're being so all-fired agreeable, how about tellin' me where you come from so's I can check up on you?"

"Sure thing," Horton said. "I'm from Benton, Texas. Aside from the war, I've lived in Texas all my life. My first name's James, an' I've got three brothers still alive. We own a little ranch called the Circle H. In another year or so, when you get too old to be useful, come on down an' maybe we can find a job for you muckin' stalls or somethin'."

Sam Peabody's neck started getting red again and the veins in his forehead bulged. "I've said it before an' I'll say it again. You got a smart mouth on you, Horton.

Someday I'm gonna take you down to size an' teach you some manners. You can count on that!"

"Like I said, Sheriff, I'll be at the hotel. Just remember. You started pushin', not me. You come lookin' for me to come back here, you better have a gun in your hand. I've been pushed around all I'm goin' to be. Now stand up an' take off the rest of your clothes."

Peabody looked at him incredulously. "What?" he said, unable to believe what he had heard.

"You heard what I said. Get up an' take the rest of your clothes off. All of 'em. Then throw 'em in the cell with Curly. I've got the keys to the gunrack an' the cell. By the time you fish your clothes out an' get dressed again, I'll be far enough down the street not to have to worry about gettin' shot in the back. Now, move!"

Muttering oaths and threats under his breath, Sam Peabody took off his clothes and threw them into Curly's cell. Horton checked the lock on the cell and the knots restraining Curly, then started for the door.

"Before I go, Sheriff, how about tellin' me where you put my guns? I'll take them off your hands, too, while I'm at it." The sheriff pointed sullenly at the desk.

"I have a bit of shoppin' to do," Horton said as he retrieved his pistol from a drawer. He found his Winchester leaning in a corner. "I'll leave your pistol an' the keys at the front desk at the hotel. You can just keep the scattergun." He snapped the gun shut, then smashed the barrels down on the edge of the desk, bending the tubes badly. "Have a good trip, Peabody," he said over his shoulder as he went through the doorway. "Don't catch cold."

Sam Peabody swore as the door closed behind Horton, then he headed for the cell. "Curly, if I ever get you out of there, you're fired. When I get you untied, you hand me my clothes."

Curly nodded his head in embarrassment. As soon as the sheriff freed him, he passed the older man's clothes out to him. The youth was smart enough to keep his mouth shut. He could see quite plainly the sheriff was mad as hell. As he dressed, Peabody amused himself by thinking of ways to strip the hide from Horton an inch at a time.

Horton walked briskly down the street to the hotel. It was not much past seven o'clock, but already businesses were open and there was a fair amount of traffic in the street. The air was crisp and cold, and the snow squeaked and crunched under foot. He took the steps to the hotel two at a time and paused briefly to check the street before he entered the lobby. There was no sign of pursuit from the jail. Horton grinned to himself as he remembered the sheriff trying with only limited success to cover himself with his hat, and he knew that Peabody would try to find a way of making him pay for the indignities that he had suffered.

A new desk clerk was on duty, so Horton asked if his things had been cleared out of his suite. The clerk checked and found that only the gold and his guns had been removed. Horton thanked him for his trouble, then put the keys from the jail and the lawman's pistols on the desk.

"Sheriff Peabody will be in sometime soon. I borrowed these from him a while ago. See that he gets them when he comes in, will you please?" he asked.

"Certainly, sir. Is there anything else I can do for you?" the clerk asked politely.

"I'd like to know when Miss Meloy comes in," Horton said. I need to talk with her."

"Miss Meloy generally comes down around nine, sir. I'm sure that you can see her then if you want. I can wake her up now if it's an emergency, or you could leave a message if you wish."

"I'll check back later, thanks," Horton said. "If anyone comes lookin' for me, tell 'em that I'll be at the cafe down the street or at the bootmakers."

The clerk nodded in understanding and Horton went back outside, checked the street for signs of the sheriff and, finding none, walked another two blocks to the cafe. He spied the bootmaker's shop across the street and was pleased to see a tailor shop next to it. Since he planned to try his hand as a gambler, he decided that a suit or two might be more appropriate garb than the rough work clothes that he was wearing.

The cafe was just what the clerk at the general store said it would be. The place was crowded and it took him a while to finally find a spot at the counter. A minute or two later a plump, middle-aged woman with a maverick strand of hair that kept falling into her eyes asked him what he wanted. The deputy's breakfast hadn't been much, so Horton ordered some flapjacks, side meat, and coffee. The coffee arrived quickly, strong enough to dissolve a spoon. The flapjacks and side meat followed close behind.

Horton lingered over the meal. Aside from getting a pair of boots to replace those that were falling off his feet and looking into the possibility of buying a suit or two, he had nothing to do with his time. The cafe had nearly emptied by the time he had finished his third cup of coffee, so he paid his bill and followed the others out the door.

The bootmaker was a gnarled old man who happened to have a pair of boots in his size already on hand. They were of the cavalry style, with lower heels than those found on boots in cow country. Horton stomped them on and left his old ones in the trash. It was only after he paid for them that Horton discovered that the boots had been ordered by a previous sheriff who had been knifed before he could pick them up.

The tailor was an obliging man who turned out to be the brother of the bootmaker next door. Horton stood still long enough to get measured for two suits, then made his way back to the hotel. He decided that the

Excelsior would be his headquarters until the sheriff got back from the Olsen's place. Horton figured that he had pushed the sheriff far enough, at least for a while.

As soon as Sam Peabody finished dressing, he headed directly for the hotel. He retrieved the keys as well as his and Curly's pistols at the desk, then paused for a minute to decide whether to have it out with Horton or wait until later, when he wasn't quite so mad.

"Horton still upstairs in his room?" he asked the clerk.

"No sir. He said to tell anyone who asked that he'd be at the cafe if he was wanted."

The sheriff pondered the answer and thought a little more about the situation. By now the edge of his anger had been blunted a little and in spite of himself he began to see the rough humor of the situation he had just experienced. The start of a smile played at the corners of his mouth, then vanished when he remembered Curly, still locked up at the jail.

"When he comes in, tell him that I'll see him in a few days," he said to the clerk, then he turned on his heel and left.

Before going back to the office, the sheriff stopped by the livery and had the hostler get his horse ready. His second stop was at the general store, where he picked up some food, and then he went back to the jail. He let Curly out of the cell and sent him home to change his clothes. Before Curly left, the sheriff gave him some specific instructions.

"Curly, I want you to stay clear of that fella Horton. You were a damn fool for tryin' somethin' with him in the first place. If you mess with him or even look like you're thinkin' about it, he's just likely to kill you, an' I can't say that I'd blame him none. I want you to stay here or your ma's 'til I get back in four or five days. You understand me, boy?"

"Yeah, I hear you," Curly answered sullenly. It graveled him to know that the sheriff didn't think that he could handle Horton, but he was more than a little relieved to have an honest excuse for avoiding the man. To tell the truth, Curly didn't think that he could handle Horton, either.

On his way out of town, the sheriff stopped at the train depot and sent wires to the sheriff in Benton, Texas and to the Texas Rangers in Waco asking for information on Jim Horton. As he rode out of town, the sheriff watched the train from Denver pull into the station. The steam from the engine created a huge cloud in the cold air. He didn't see the five men who got off and headed for Hogtown.

Chapter 6

A smile of triumph spread across Willard Simpson's face when he stepped down from the train. He had not seen the sun shine on Ruxford for more than two years, when he quit his bookkeeper's job at the bank and headed for the gold fields. He hadn't had two dimes to rub together when he left, but now he had a suitcase full of money and a burning desire to be a major power in Ruxford, starting with Hogtown. He had learned long ago that money brought power, and he fully intended to become the most powerful man in the territory. He stood on the station platform for a few minutes, savoring the feeling of triumph that he felt at his return. He was sure that Caesar had felt this way when he had returned from conquering Gaul.

The cold finally brought an end to his revelry, and he turned to the men who stood in a group behind him. He pointed to the obvious leader, a stocky man of average height with streaks of gray in his beard and hair.

"Jackson," he said with authority, "pick one of the men to come with us and have the other two round up the baggage and wait in the station. We'll know where we're staying in the next hour or two,"

Del Jackson nodded in understanding and relayed the instructions as he had been told, even though the men were fully aware of the plan that had been worked out on the train during the night. Jackson was more than a little peeved with the way that Simpson ordered him around, as though he needed to let everyone know that he was in charge. As he thought about it, a surge of anger bordering on madness swept over Jackson, but he quickly controlled it. Things had not gone well for him over the past few years and he needed the job. Besides, he was the number two man and Simpson's plan was good. If something were to happen to Simpson later on, no one would be surprised if he took over. One never knew when an opportunity would present itself ....

With Simpson in the lead, the three men left the station and made their way across the creek into Hogtown. Little had changed since Simpson had seen the place two years before. Unlike Ruxford, the proprietors of the sporting establishments in Hogtown displayed little civic pride and seemed unwilling to divert profits into such activities as building maintenance or the construction of sanitation facilities. Hogtown was well named. It was one of the worst pigsties in Colorado. Even the freezing weather could not mask the smell. Simpson vowed that the first thing he'd do when he took over was to get the place cleaned up.

The men made their way through the deserted streets, walking around garbage and piles of debris as they went. Nothing much moved in Hogtown before noon because the place usually ran wild until an hour or two before dawn and then spent the morning hours recuperating. The men went directly to the dominant building on the main street, a brick and clapboard structure with a weathered sign that declared the place to be the Golden Palace.

Ephram King was a short, rotund, and balding man of about sixty who looked more like a choirmaster than the man who controlled virtually all the gambling, drinking, and whoring that went on in Hogtown. He kept a dozen or more toughs on the payroll for the sole purpose of enforcing his dictates. The sporting crowd had learned long ago that it paid to do business with Eff King. To ignore his wishes was to go out of business in a hurry, usually with several broken bones as a reminder of such folly. For the privilege of staying in business, proprietors of the various establishments paid King a percentage of their gross, the percentage determined by King based on the nature and volume of the business. In spite of King's appearance, the system worked. No one could remember the last time that his authority had been seriously challenged.

The three men mounted the steps of the porch and entered the building. In contrast to the weathered exterior, the interior was relatively plush, with a number of gaming tables scattered around the main room and a bar backed by several mirrors and paintings of nude females extending the length of the room. That the mirrors were still intact was a tribute to the efficiency of the bouncers. Along the back wall was a stairway that led to the second story rooms visible directly behind a balcony rail. Access to the storeroom was gained through a doorway located on the back wall near the bar. A huge man with masses of scar tissue over his eyes and a nose that had been flattened over a large portion of his face stopped sweeping the floor and looked at the men as they entered.

"We ain't open yet, gents. Come back after noon," he said in a high-pitched, hoarse voice that suggested he had caught more than one punch in the throat.

We don't want anything to drink, my friend," Simpson said as the men walked up to the swamper. "We're here to see Eff King."

"In that case, come back after four. Mister King, he don't see folks much before then." The swamper eyed the trio suspiciously, then continued. "The boss send for you?"

"No, but he'll want to see us now. He still got the same room upstairs?"

"Yeah, but you can't go up there now. The boss, he didn't tell me he was expectin' nobody. Come back later when he ...."

The swamper never got a chance to finish what he was going to say. As he was talking to Simpson, Jackson had eased around beside him and struck him a wicked blow with a sap loaded with sand and lead shot. The big man crashed to the floor without uttering another sound.

"Is he dead?" Simpson asked in a tone that suggested only mild curiosity.

The third man in the group, a large, stocky man with bulging eyes who went by the name of Frog Mayeaux, bent down and checked the swamper. "He ain't dead, but if he's ever been hit harder, it ain't been anytime lately. You want me to finish him now?" he asked expectantly.

"No, but tie him up real good," Simpson replied. "Maybe we can use him later. If not, you can finish him then. Jackson, go lock the front door so we won't be disturbed."

Jackson did as he was told, then followed the others up the stairs as soon as the swamper was securely tied. The men stopped in front of the last door at the far end of the balcony. Simpson nodded to Jackson. All three men drew their pistols, then Mayeaux kicked in the door.

Jackson and Mayeaux quickly moved into the room and crouched on either side of the doorway, covering the room against any possible resistance. Simpson walked between them and moved up to the form in the bed who was struggling to untangle himself from the quilts. As King's head emerged, Simpson gently pressed the muzzle of his Colt against King's left eye.

"See here! Who are you men? What do you want? What is the meaning of all this?" King blustered as he eased his head back and away from the muzzle of Simpson's Colt.

"You remember me, Eff. Will Simpson, the man who used to be the bookkeeper at the bank a few years ago. I came back to buy you out."

"You must be crazy!" King said with emotion. "You haven't got enough money or muscle to do that. If you're smart, you'll leave right now while you've got a chance to get away, and I mean leave the territory. I don't know how you got past Cleary downstairs, but I've got a dozen more just like him who would sure like to get their hands on you three."

"Eff, old man, I have all the money and muscle I need right here," Simpson said with confidence. "Your goons won't be able to help you now. Jackson, you and Mayeaux get Mister King here into that chair by the table. He's going to fix me up a bill of sale for this place."

King started to protest, but a glimpse of the madness in Jackson's eyes shocked him into silence. He allowed himself to be dragged from his bed and enthroned none too gently in a chair near the table in the center of the room. Simpson toed another chair over to the table and sat down across from King. He laid his pistol down gently and removed from an inside pocket of his coat a paper which he placed in front of King.

"Jackson, get a pen and some ink from the desk in the corner so that Mister King here can sell me his place," Simpson said as he picked up his pistol.

King unfolded the paper and quickly scanned the print. His pale face reddened as he brought his gaze back to Simpson. "It says here that I agree to sell out to you for one dollar and 'other consideration!' Just what is this supposed to mean?"

"I could say that it means that you get to keep your life, Eff, but I'm going to be a generous man and pay you a thousand dollars besides," Simpson replied, a smile playing across the corners of his mouth.

"A thousand dollars!" King exploded. "Why, I clear that much on a bad day around here. A million's more like it."

"Now that you've priced the operation here to me, all we're really doing is haggling over the details. I'm not interested in what you used to clear on a bad day, old man. Trust me when I tell you that this could very well be the worst day of your life. If you want that life to extend beyond today, I'd advise you to sign the paper."

"Look, Simpson, why don't you save yourself a lot of grief and get out of here?" King suggested. "I'll even give you a break and forget you were ever here."

"I've made you an offer, King, and I'm going to do my best to see that it's taken. Boys, let's see if we can help Mister King see the generosity of my offer."

Mayeaux moved up behind King and pinned his arms while Jackson grabbed hold of King's left wrist. "Boss, look at the size of the ring on this guy's little finger," the gunman said. "I bet it cost a bundle."

"I think you're right, Jackson," Simpson replied, "but I'd like a better look at it. Have you still got those clippers with you?"

"Sure do, boss," he said. With that, Jackson took a pair of wire cutters from his pocket and placed the open jaws around King's little finger, just behind the ring.

"No!" King screamed in disbelief. "You can't do that to me!"

His protest was cut off by a clipping sound as Jackson separated the little finger from King's hand. King looked stupidly at the blood as it began to pour from the stump of his severed finger. He began moaning. Mayeaux let go of his arms and King grabbed some of his nightshirt to bind up his injured hand. He was very pale and started to shake badly.

"You bastard!" he spat as he looked at Simpson and cradled his wounded hand in his lap.

"Now, Eff, name-calling isn't going to solve anything. As I see it, you've got four more tries to sign that paper before we have to start on your toes. We'd have more, but I'd hate to have you leak blood from your right hand all over that pretty document of mine. Why don't you be a reasonable man and sign the paper before we have to do any more trimming?"

King looked at Simpson with hard, cold eyes, then reached for the pen and signed his name hurriedly at the bottom of the page. When he finished, he pushed the paper over to Simpson and said, "I'll take the thousand in cash."

Simpson laughed and passed a roll of bills. "Thanks, Eff. I knew that you'd see the light. You can get dressed now. One of my boys will stay with you until you can get on the train tonight. We wouldn't want anyone to steal your fortune, now would we?"

King grimaced as a stab of pain shot through his hand and arm. "You're laughing now, Simpson, but remember this: someday, some slimy bastard will show up and take it all away from you, just like you did from me."

"Is that how you got your start?" Simpson asked sarcastically.

"I forced someone out, yes, but he walked away a whole man. I hope you rot in hell for what you did to me."

Simpson laughed. "If I do, Eff, you'll be there to see it happen. Now shut up and get dressed. I've got other stops to make today."

Simpson gave instructions to Mayeaux while King dressed, then Jackson followed him downstairs. They checked on the swamper before they left. Cleary was still out cold and showed no signs of waking soon. Jackson kicked him hard enough to make a rib pop just to see if he was faking, then shrugged when Cleary made no response. The two men left the Palace and walked on down the street.

The business with King had taken far less than an hour. The streets had not yet come alive, and the two men saw no one as they made their way to the far end of the street. They stopped in front of the last house, where two red lamps still burned dimly on the porch. The men tried the front door, found it open, and walked in. A little bell jingled as they closed the door, and a moment later the curtains on the far side of the room parted to admit a short, plump, middle-aged woman who still retained much of what once must have been considerable beauty. Simpson judged her to be barely five feet tall, and that was including the high heels that she wore concealed beneath her long, elegant dressing gown.

"You boys are a little early," she said as she patted her hair into place. "The girls are still sleeping. It would be better if you could come back in a few hours, but if you're in a hurry and have someone special in mind, I'll go wake her up."

"It's me, Miss Ellie, Will Simpson. Do you remember me?" he asked, smiling gently.

"Why, sure it is. You've been gone a long time, Will. How long has it been, anyway?"

"It's been far too long to be away from you, Miss Ellie. I see that you're prettier than ever."

"Go on with you, and save that line for one of the girls," she said, but Simpson noted that she patted her hair again and had broken out with a smile that fairly lit the room.

"As I remember," Miss Ellie said, "you used to be real partial to that redheaded girl, Lilly. She's not here anymore, though."

"Oh?" Simpson responded. "Where did she go?"

"Somebody killed her not too long after you left town. Strangled her with a length of wire and left the body in the woods, they did. A lot of people were really broken up about it, including your old boss, Morton Witherspoon. Yes, Lilly was one of our most popular girls. Sometimes people still come in and ask for her."

"They ever catch the man who did it?"

"As far as I know, no one ever tried very hard. There wasn't much law in Ruxford then, and there never has been any on this side of the creek. You know as well as I do that nobody cares much about one whore more or less. We buried her and business went on as usual. I probably wouldn't have even remembered it except that we all thought it was a pretty good joke that you and your boss were both bedding the same girl. Did Old Man Witherspoon ever catch on?"

"As far as I know, it was our little secret," Simpson said, still smiling. "The fact is, Miss Ellie, I didn't come here to see Lilly. Is there someplace where we can talk without being disturbed?"

Miss Ellie looked at the pair for a moment, then made her decision and nodded towards the curtains through which she had recently emerged. "We can talk in the office, although nobody would bother us here at this hour," she said as she led the men into her ornate office. She seated herself in a chair in front of a large oak roll top desk and gestured for the men to be seated in a pair of chairs nearby. She said, "Now, what's on your mind?"

"Miss Ellie, I know that you control the girls here in Hogtown. Lilly told me how you bring in new talent to work this house and rotate others through the saloons and other sporting houses. I also know that you're in partnership with Eff King at the Golden Palace." Simpson paused as though to catch his breath.

"Lilly talked too damned much," Miss Ellie said as a frown creased her features. "She must have been pretty sweet on you to tell you all that."

"I'm sure that she was, but that has nothing to do with my proposition," Simpson said curtly. "Now when I left here, I hit the gold fields and made a good strike, but you and I both know that the biggest strikes in any gold town are in the saloons and sporting houses. What I propose to do is to buy you out, Miss Ellie. How much money do you want for your operation?"

"Sorry to disappoint you, Will," she said sweetly, "but my business is not for sale. Like you say, the real gold mine is in the houses. Besides, Eff King wouldn't approve of a change in partners."

Simpson toyed with his hat for a moment, then fixed his gaze on Miss Ellie. The cold look from his pale eyes sent a shiver of fear through her and she found that she was hugging herself as if to restore warmth to her body.

"Actually, Miss Ellie, I've already bought out Eff King. In fact, he sent along a message for you in case you proved to be reluctant to sell," Simpson said as he extracted a small, slender box from his pocket and handed it over to her.

Miss Ellie hesitated for an instant, then took the box from Simpson and opened it. The color drained from her face as she gasped and dropped the box to the floor. King's severed finger, with the ring still in place, rolled out onto the luxurious oriental rug. Miss Ellie looked at Simpson with terror-filled eyes and finally managed to whisper, "What kind of man are you?"

Simpson reached into an inside pocket of his coat and withdrew a bill of sale. His movement caused the woman to shrink back into her chair, suddenly looking a decade older. Del Jackson produced his pair of wire cutters and grinned wickedly, revealing ill-fitting false teeth.

"A man who is rich and intends to get richer, and I don't much care who gets hurt in the process," Simpson answered her. "I trust that you will be quicker to sign than Eff was. It would be a shame if something were to happen to hands as pretty as yours." He handed her the paper. "Just sign there on the bottom, by the 'X.'"

Miss Ellie took the pen from her desk, dipped it in the inkwell, and signed her name with a shaking hand. Simpson picked up the bill of sale, blew on it several times until the ink was dry, then refolded it and returned it to his pocket. By that time Miss Ellie had re-gained some of her composure.

"Are you going to kill me?" she asked, her voice once again steady.

"I wouldn't do anything like that as long as you co-operate," Simpson answered. "In fact, I'm going to let you keep your clothes, the money in the safe, and whatever cash that you have in the bank"

"You're very generous," she answered skeptically. "Just what else do you want?"

"Very little, actually. I want you to buy some tickets for you and Eff on the evening train to Denver, then I want you to spread the word around town that I bought you and Eff out and that the pair of you are off to start up a new business in the Dakotas. It goes without say-ing that you will give the impression that you are very happy with the arrangement."

"And if I don't?" she asked as a note of defiance crept into her voice.

"Then I fear that you will always need help eating," he responded as he gestured toward Jackson, who grinned even more madly and operated the jaws of the cutters a few more times for effect. "If you live, that is. And don't even think of a double-cross. There's a lit-tle matter of a dead miner that you and Lilly buried in the stable out back. The law might want to know how he got there and how come his head got all bashed in. They might also wonder what happened to his poke."

Miss Ellie got very pale. "He attacked one of my girls. He'd have killed her if we hadn't brained him first. There's no law against self-defense."

"The law might not look at it as self-defense, especially since you went to so much trouble to cover it up. They might just want to hang you by that pretty neck of yours 'til your eyes pop out. That missing poke wouldn't help your case, either."

"You have such a graphic way of expressing things, Will. I see your point," she said as she sank back into her chair, utterly defeated. "What do I tell the girls?"

"The same story, of course. If one of them can think, put her in charge until I can send someone up later to take over. Just don't try to cross me," he added almost as an afterthought. "King's survival as well as yours depends on how you act from now on. My friend Mister Jackson here will stick with you until my other man shows up just to make sure that you don't have a change of heart. I'd hate for you to disappoint me."

"You don't have to worry," she said with a quivering voice. "You haven't left me with much choice. And I thought you were such a nice young man." Tears were rolling down her cheeks.

Simpson smiled coldly at her, then gave a few specific instructions to Del Jackson. When he was sure that Jackson understood what he wanted, Simpson buttoned his coat and made his way back to the Golden Palace. As he went, he marveled that, although he had been in Hogtown for less than two hours, he was now the major power there, with a part of every dollar spent in any of the establishments going directly to his pockets. His smile changed into a grin, and he allowed himself to swagger a little. He knew that the key to his success had been surprise, timing, the isolation of his intended victims, and the shock that controlled violence nearly always produced. If there had been any recent attempt to wrestle power from King, he would have been better guarded, and the plan would have failed. If the attack had not been made in the early morning, King's goons would have made short work of Simpson and his crew. The severed finger had taken all the fight out of both King and Miss Ellie. That violent brutality had paralyzed the pair and robbed them of all capability for resistance.

As elation surged through him, Simpson felt certain that the events of the remainder of the day would determine whether he would keep the power he had just grabbed or lose it to a counterattack that would very likely cost him his life. Suddenly he felt very alone and vulnerable. He quickened his step and vowed never again to go anywhere without an escort.

Back at the Palace, Simpson sent Frog Mayeaux after Adams and Jones, the two men he had left at the station. He locked King in a storehouse behind the saloon and then went through King's books as he waited for the men to get back from the station.

When Mayeaux, Adams, and Jones entered the Palace, Will Simpson briefed them on the events that had taken place, then sent Adams to relieve Jackson as Miss Ellie's guard. Adams was a ferret-faced man of average size who Simpson had discovered running a bordello in Denver. An able manager, he was also deadly with a knife or a pistol, and he had a reputation for being brutal with his fists and boots. He had been the one who had suggested the use of wire cutters to demoralize King. Simpson had no doubt that he could handle the bordello operation.

Jones, on the other hand, was a large man, well over six feet tall, who had been a bare-knuckle prize fighter until he lost an eye in Saint Louis to a river boatman who had never heard of the Marquis of Queensbury or his rules. He was now an expert in saloon management, and his job was to supervise the saloons in Hogtown. Jackson and Mayeaux were experts in violence, men without conscience who would kill or maim on order. They were to control the goons needed to maintain Simpson's hold over Hogtown and its residents.

When Jackson returned from Miss Ellie's, Simpson sent him along with Jones to convert or eliminate Cleary, who had begun to show signs of consciousness. The conversation proved to be easier than Simpson thought possible. Cleary, too, had been demoralized by the swiftness of the attack that had left him senseless and trussed up like a hog for slaughter. It had not taken long to convince him that he should join Simpson and the others.

As soon as he had been cut loose and had applied a cool rag to his aching head, Cleary suggested that he contact the rest of King's old group and inform them of the change in management. Simpson readily agreed with the plan when Jackson presented it to him, and shortly thereafter Cleary and Jones made the rounds of Hogtown, notifying King's old crew. By nightfall Simpson's crew had been expanded by more than a dozen men, none of whom appeared to care that King had been replaced by Simpson. Their only concern seemed to be that their pay would keep coming. As a group, the men looked tough and able to deal with any situation. None appeared to be overburdened with a conscience, either.

After the evening train pulled out with Miss Ellie waving goodbye to a town that largely ignored her departure, Simpson sent Jackson and Jones to dispose of King. "Nothing fancy," he told them. "When they find his body in the spring, I want it to look like he got killed for the money he got for selling out,"

"Boss, why did you give King the money if you was plannin' on snuffin' him all along?" Jackson asked.

"Quite simple. To keep him quiet until it got dark enough to get rid of the body without being seen. As long as he thought that we were going to let him go, he'd have been a fool to try anything. Miss Ellie left here a rich woman, and the body is still buried in the stable if we need it. She won't make any trouble for us, so we could afford to let her go. King would come back after us with an army. Now go take care of him before he starts to get wise. You boys can keep the money he's got on him as a bonus."

Jackson flipped him a half-salute and left Simpson alone in the office. He leaned back in the desk chair and lit a cigar. As the smoke curled above his head, he put his feet up on the corner of the desk and smiled as he thought of his new empire.

Chapter 7

In her shack at the edge of Hogtown, Cyclops Mary eased out from under the outflung arm of a drunken, snoring prospector who had purchased her company for the night. He came in from the mountains to get a drink, a meal, and a woman, he had announced in a loud voice earlier that day. He had gotten all caught up with a woman in less than a minute. He never did get a meal. Now he lay on the soiled sheets in his dirty underwear with the flap buttons missing, snoring loud enough to make the windows rattle.

Cyclops Mary swung her feet to the cold floor and searched with her toes until she found her slippers. She stood up and slipped into a robe that she took from a nail near the head of the bed, then shuffled over to the wash basin near the window to clean herself up. She hoped with all her heart that the prospector would sleep until morning. Then she could pat him on the cheek, tell him what a great lover he had been, and send him on his way. She certainly wanted no more to do with him tonight. It had been a rough week and she needed some rest.

Looking back, Mary decided that all of the weeks for the past fifteen years had been rough, ever since her father had discovered her pleasuring Charlie Pruitt, the parson's son, in the woodshed behind her house. Her father had gone looking for his shotgun while Charlie had acquired a sudden burst of patriotism and had run off to join a local Boston regiment on its way to put down the rebellion in the South. He had never even stopped to put on his boots or his trousers. When her father returned and found that Charlie had made good his escape, he worked out his rage by lathering Mary's naked buttocks with his razor strap, then he threw her out of his house. At sixteen, Mary found herself out on the street, alone and without a means of support other than her well-endowed body. She was busy practicing the world's oldest profession well before the marks left by the razor strap had faded.

Mary had drifted from bordello to bordello, patron to patron. The profession had been a hard one, one which aged her beyond her years. She no longer commanded the attention of the big spenders. Drunken prospectors were all who were left to her now. Three years before she had been caught in a knife fight in the town of Leavenworth, Kansas, where she had acquired a cut that ran from her hairline to the right corner of her mouth. Fortunately for her, the blade had not touched her eye. While she was wearing a bandage to cover the wound, one of her better-read customers gave her the nickname "Cyclops." Mary had liked it well enough to wear an eye patch even after the wound healed and, strangely enough, her business had picked up. Now she considered the patch and the name her personal good luck charm.

As she was busy washing herself by the flickering light of the stove, Cyclops Mary looked out the window and saw three men emerge from the curtain of falling snow and walk towards the cliff just beyond her shack. The two men on either side of the third were strangers, but the center man looked a lot like Eff King. She wondered why he would be out there in that weather, then saw that the two other men were half pushing, half carrying Eff down the path. Mary stepped well back from the window. She knew instinctively that this was no time to call attention to herself. She continued to watch as the three men faded back into the falling snow.

Jones and Jackson cursed as they pushed King along the path. "Hurry up, King, or you'll miss your train," Jackson said mockingly.

"Yeah, you'll miss your train," Jones echoed, then cackled to himself.

King clutched his throbbing hand. "Where are we going? This isn't the way to the station. There's nothing out here past the town," he said just before the realization finally hit him that Simpson had never intended for him to catch the train. Suddenly his legs refused to work, and a groan escaped his lips.

"You're right, King. The only thing out here is your destiny," Jackson said as he saw the edge of the cliff just ahead.

"Don't do this," King pleaded. "I'll go away and you will never see me again. I give you my word."

"Sure you will," Jackson said as he slipped his pistol from its holster and slashed viciously at King's head with the barrel. King folded into the snow without uttering a sound. Jackson stooped and felt for a pulse at the man's throat and finding none, straightened up and turned to Jones.

"He's done for," Jackson said. "Grab his feet and we'll throw him over the edge." Jones picked up the feet as Jackson grasped the dead man's arms and together, they threw King's body over the edge. They did not hear it as it hit the ground more than a hundred feet below. The men turned silently and walked back toward the town.

Cyclops Mary watched as the two men approached her shack from the cliff. King, she saw, was no longer with them. As they drew even with her window, she saw one of the men stop abruptly and grab the other by the arm.

"Jones, we forgot the money!" she heard the shorter of the two exclaim.

The man called Jones swore bitterly and at length. Finally, he seemed to run out of swear words and said, "We'll break our necks goin' after that money tonight. What'll we do?"

The shorter man thought for a minute, then said, "We'll come back after the sun comes up. We can pick up the money and then hide the body again. How does that sound to you?"

"Suppose the snow covers the body tonight or we can't find it in the morning?" the tall man whined.

"Then we'll be out a thousand dollars, stupid! Now let's get out of here. I'm getting cold."

Cyclops Mary watched as the two men walked back toward the town. She waited until the pair had disappeared from sight, then walked over to the stove and selected a short length of stove wood, which she promptly used to bash in the head of the snoring prospector. The snoring stopped immediately. Mary did not stop to see if he was alive or dead. She dressed hurriedly in the prospector's filthy clothes, then left the shack and made her way to the edge of the cliff. The marks in the snow were rapidly disappearing under the fresh snow. Mary did some rapid calculating and made her way past the shack and down the hill, then turned and approached the face of the cliff from the bottom. It took her a few minutes before she was able to locate the strange lump under the snow and investigate it further. She found Eff King's body under about an inch of snow. The former gambler, pimp, and chief whoremaster was no longer a symbol of power. He was just another broken piece of trash that had been discarded over the cliff.

Cyclops Mary quickly went through his pockets and found a roll of bills, which she slipped into her pocket. Then she pushed, pulled, and rolled the body until she had moved it from the base of the cliff to a break in the ice of Crystal Creek. The water at that point ran swiftly enough to keep ice from forming, and Mary pushed King's body along the ice until it slipped over the edge and into the torrent, where it finally disappeared.

Cyclops Mary hurried back to her shack, where she discarded the prospector's clothes. She washed herself again carefully, then let down her hair and dressed in her one respectable dress. She picked up her eye patch, walked to the stove, opened the door and tossed it in. She watched as it was consumed by the flames. Cyclops Mary existed no more. She was a whole new person. She didn't know just who she was yet, but she was confident that her identity would come to her in time.

Mary went over to the table and counted the money that she had removed from the prospector's pockets. With the cash she already had and what she had taken from King's body, the total came to nearly sixteen hundred dollars. Her hands shook as she put the money in her handbag, then she sat down in her rocking chair near the stove. She covered herself with a blanket and settled down to wait for the morning.

When the sun came up the next day, Mary stepped onto the southbound train just as Jones and Jackson made their way past her old cabin on their way to the cliff. The two men spent more than two hours searching for King's body, then, stiff from the cold, they made their way back to the Golden Palace. By that time the fire in Mary's stove was long out, and the old prospector came to in an ice-cold room. He thought that he had the granddaddy of all hangovers until he touched his matted hair and felt all the dried blood. The next thing he looked for was his bankroll, knowing as he looked that it was gone. He wasn't surprised; it had happened before and he was reasonably sure that it would happen to him again. He dressed slowly, then left the cabin. It was going to be a long winter and he needed a drink.

Mary sat in the passenger coach and planned the rest of her trip to San Francisco, where her new life awaited her. She thought that she would become a widow of some means, at least until her money ran out. By then she meant to have a husband. She was done with whoring forever, she decided.

While Mary was making her plans, the snow stopped and the sun shone brightly on Ruxford.

Chapter 8

Sheriff Sam Peabody was cold, stiff, and more than a little disappointed that Jim Horton's story had checked out. He had been looking forward to repaying Horton for the humiliation that he and Curly had suffered at his hand nearly a week earlier. It had taken the sheriff two days to ride out to the Olsen's, a day to talk and rest up, and two days to return to Ruxford. All that he had to show for his trouble was an empty belly and a light case of frostbite on his nose and one cheek. By the time he made it back to his office he was cussing Colorado, the winter weather, the bank robber, Jim Horton, and a legal system that assumed the innocence of the accused. He was not a happy man.

The sheriff dismounted in front of his office, flipped the reins of his horse's bridle over the hitching rack, and stomped on numbed feet up the steps and into his office. He found Curly with his feet propped up on the sheriff's desk and his hat pulled down over his eyes, sound asleep. Peabody delivered a mighty kick to the chair, which resulted in Curly being deposited in a heap on the floor.

"I told you a hundred times to stay the hell out of my chair. You're gettin' paid to protect the town, not sleep the afternoon away at the city's expense." The sheriff paused for breath, then continued with un-abated anger. "Take my horse down to the livery an' take care of him. Make damn sure you rub him down good. He's worked a hell of a lot harder this week than you have."

Curly, showing a flash of wisdom, was smart enough to keep his mouth shut and do what he was told. He headed for the door on the run, snatching his coat and scarf from the wall rack as he went.

Still growling under his breath, Sam Peabody hung up his hat and coat, then righted the chair behind his desk. He spied a pair of telegrams lying on top of a pile of wanted posters and other mail that had arrived in his absence. The sheriff was still too cold to sit, so he grabbed the telegrams and walked over to the stove, where he could read them and get warm at the same time.

The telegrams did nothing to improve his humor. The reply from the Waco Ranger Company stated that not only was Jim Horton not wanted for any criminal activity in the state of Texas, but that Horton had been a member of that company of Rangers for more than three years prior to his departure for the gold fields in Colorado.

"A regular damned pillar of the community," Peabody growled to himself as he wadded up the telegram and fed it to the hungry flames in the stove. The second telegram said the same thing, then asked just why Peabody was snooping into the affairs of an honest Texan. This telegram was signed by the Benton, Texas sheriff, Matthew Horton.

"That's all I need," Peabody mumbled. "A suspect with kin in high places."

The second telegram followed the first into the flames. The sheriff went back to his desk and sorted through some of the other papers stacked there. Before long he came across yet another telegram. This one was from some functionary in the office of the Governor of Colorado, who said that he had received an inquiry from Washington, D.C. wanting to know what was going on in Ruxford and offering to impose martial law there if the governor asked for it. The inquiry was signed by Brigadier General Seth Horton. The governor's assistant demanded to know what the sheriff was doing down there.

"That's the last straw," the sheriff said as he tore up the telegram and flung the pieces into the wastepaper basket. "The sooner that hombre leaves town, the better I'll like it," he said as he drew his Colt, thumbed the hammer to half-cock, and opened the loading gate. He spun the cylinder to check the loads, then eased the hammer back into place as he holstered the pistol. Within moments he had donned his overcoat and was making his way toward the Excelsior Hotel to find Jim Horton.

Jim Horton traversed the nearly deserted lobby of the Excelsior Hotel and made his way into the Golden Nugget. It was late afternoon and already the room was becoming crowded with townsmen who were looking for a little bracer before going home for the night. Horton worked his way across the room to the bar, where he found a beer waiting for him. Horton nodded in thanks to the bartender, then turned his back to the bar and surveyed the room.

In the last four days Horton had established a routine. He rose at noon, ate, took care of whatever business he had, then presented himself at the bar just before the main rush hit the floor. He nursed the beer until he found a card game to his liking, then spent the rest of the night playing games of chance. He was a good player and he won consistently, if not heavily. He figured that he was nearly two hundred dollars ahead so far. The men with whom he played were businessmen and merchants in town who were just looking for a friendly game. The high rollers who wanted to play for big stakes generally went to Hogtown, where the action was faster and the risks were greater.

Horton was enjoying himself. The life was easy, the food was good, and the companionship was pleasant. He was the closest thing to a professional gambler that Myrna Meloy allowed in her place, and so far, his presence there had caused no problems. He had managed to acquire a decent wardrobe, but clothing alone could not hide the fact that he had been earning his living by breaking rock. His work-thickened hands were covered with callouses which caused him to be a little clumsy with the cards, and his complexion was brown and well-weathered in contrast to the indoor pallor of the townsmen with whom he played.

His relationship with Myrna troubled him. She continued to refuse payment for his room, food, and drink, but she had allowed him to repay from his winnings the money she had advanced to him just before the sheriff had impounded his gold. Horton did not like to be obligated to anyone, but he could see no way in which he could gracefully extract himself from the present situation without insulting her. That he was determined not to do.

Horton had just about decided on which game to join when he saw Sheriff Peabody enter the room. The sheriff spied him at once and gestured for Horton to join him by the doorway. Jim set his nearly empty glass on the bar and walked over to Peabody. The noise in the bar suddenly diminished as the patrons shifted their attention from whatever they had been doing to watch the pair.

"How was the trip, Sheriff?" Horton asked as he stopped in front of Sam Peabody.

"Damned cold, thank you. Olsen backs up your story, just like you said he would. It looks like I can't hold you for the robbery, but I want you out of town by this time tomorrow."

"What for?" Horton asked. "Just because you made a damn fool of yourself an' don't want to be reminded of it? Seems pretty unreasonable to me."

"Don't give me any of your lip, Horton. Trouble follows you like a shadow, an' you're too damn smart by half. Now you got your kin breathin' down my neck, an' even the governor is askin' questions. I don't allow gun slicks or card sharps in this town. If you ain't long gone by tomorrow, I'm comin' after you."

Horton looked the angry sheriff right in the eye and in a low, cold voice answered the lawman. "If you do, Peabody, you had better have a gun in your fist. I'm not wanted for anythin' an' I got money in my pocket, not countin' what you're holdin' of mine in your safe, so you can't get me for vagrancy. I've read Blackstone a time or two, an' I know you've got no legal right to run a man out of town unless he's broken the law or a town ordinance. I haven't done either, so if you come for me, you're the one who'll be outside the law an' I'll just be defendin' myself."

"You callin' me out?" the sheriff asked angrily.

"No, Peabody, I'm not!" Horton said in a cold voice. "I'm just tellin' you that I don't push worth a damn an' I've never run from a fight in my life. Maybe that makes me out to be not very smart, but that's just the way I am. If you want to push this, then you'd better be ready to shoot!"

The sheriff cut off his reply as he became aware of the eyes of the crowd watching him expectantly. His anger had clouded his good judgment, and he'd let his mouth talk him into doing something that his brain knew was wrong. Still, he had committed himself and he could see no way to back down and still be able to control the town later.

"I'll be ready, Horton, you can be sure of that," Peabody said. "If you're still here by this time tomorrow, I'll shoot you down where you stand."

"You can try, Peabody. Others have before you." Horton paused, then lowered his voice and continued in a more conciliatory tone. "You've let your temper get you into a tight spot, Sheriff. If you don't show, you've got to leave town. If we shoot it out, you'll probably get yourself killed an' for no good reason. Even if you were to win, you'd be operation' outside the law an' would surely be branded as an outlaw an' maybe even hung. Why don't you just cool off an' we'll meet somewheres an' talk this thing out calmly in the mornin'? I've got to collect my dust from you anyway."

The sheriff thought for a moment. Deep inside he knew that he was pushing so hard because Horton had humiliated him at the jail. Sam Peabody was a brave man, one who had faced death many times in his life during the war and while bringing law and order to towns across the West. Always before he had fought for what he believed to be right. This was the first time that he had ever had any doubts about the rightness of his actions, and it caused him to hesitate for a minute.

"Have it your way, Horton," the lawman said finally. "I won't have it said that I ain't a reasonable man. I'll meet you at the cafe at seven tomorrow mornin'. I'll decide what I'm goin' to do with you then. Just don't you count on me changin' my mind." He fixed Horton with a look that would raise a blood blister on a rock. "Make real sure that I don't have to come lookin' for you."

"Fair enough. Bring my money with you. Now, if you'll excuse me, I think I'll play some cards." Horton turned his back on the sheriff and walked over to a group of men at a table and sat down.

The sheriff stood there a little longer, then left quietly after conversation in the room had resumed. He still wasn't quite sure who had won that exchange. As he walked back to his office, he decided that if neither of them had won, at least neither of them had lost, either.

Willard Simpson had been sitting at the back of the room while the exchange between Horton and Peabody was taking place. He waited for more than an hour after the sheriff left before a player got up from the game at Horton's table. Simpson made his way over to the table and joined the game. The men played poker for about two hours before the game broke up.

As Horton got up to leave, Simpson laid a hand on his arm and asked him to wait for a minute. Horton looked questioningly, then resumed his seat and waited until the other three men left.

"I heard you put the sheriff in his place tonight," Simpson said as he tilted back in his chair. "It's about time someone knocked that old man down a peg or two,"

"That 'old man' is about the toughest man in the valley," Horton responded testily. "Don't get the wrong idea. I won nothing from him tonight but some time. He'll still be here in the mornin', tougher than ever."

Simpson smiled easily. "Whatever it was that you did, you showed everybody here that you could hold your own against anybody, including the sheriff. I need a man like you to manage the floor at my place."

"You'll have to pardon me, but I'm new around here. Which place is yours?" Horton asked politely.

Simpson laughed and introduced himself. "I own the Golden Palace over in Hogtown. There's no reason why you should know me. I just got here this week, and the first thing I did was to buy the place from the previous owner. I understand he had a health problem. What I need now is a man with guts enough to control the floor and who's honest enough not to try to rob me blind. I think that man could be you. You can keep your winnings, and I'll cut you in for ten percent of the take. What do you say?"

"Your offer sounds right interestin' Mister Simpson, but I'd be wantin' twenty percent of the gross," Horton said finally.

"Fifteen and we've got a deal," Simpson replied.

"Fifteen it is, boss," Horton said as he extended his hand. "I'll start tomorrow, if that suits you."

"Good enough," Simpson said as they shook on the deal. "There's a room that you can have upstairs at the Palace if you want it, or there's a couple of places that pass for hotels just down the street. I wouldn't recommend them to you, though. I doubt that either one of them has ever been cleaned, and some of the tenants would kill a man just to steal his busted two-dollar watch."

"The room at the Palace sounds fine to me," Horton drawled. "I'll move my things over in the mornin' right after my talk with the sheriff."

After a little more conversation, Simpson left and Jim Horton went to search for Myrna. He was not looking forward to breaking the news to her. As he looked for her, he carefully framed in his mind exactly what he wanted to say. The last thing in the world that he wanted was to offend a woman, especially one as generous and beautiful as Myrna Meloy.

Will Simpson had a lot on his mind when he picked up his two bodyguards and left the Golden Nugget that night. First of all, he was glad to have found a man as tough as Jim Horton to manage the gambling operations in his saloon. If things worked out as he planned, Simpson could see Horton running all of the gambling in Hogtown. Simpson chuckled to himself when he remembered the look on the sheriff's face when Horton refused to let himself be posted out of town. There was no doubt in his mind that Horton would be able to control the other gamblers in Hogtown.

Mixed with the satisfaction of having found the right man for a key job was Simpson's new concern, one which also involved Horton. During the last few minutes of their conversation, Jim Horton had indicated that he intended to leave in the spring. "Some unfinished business in the mountains," was how he expressed it. Simpson knew that Horton had made a strike of some sort and that the Utes and the weather had driven him into town, but all indications pointed toward that strike having been a small one, barely large enough to pay his expenses. For a man to give up a job with the potential of the one he had offered Horton, Simpson thought there was a good chance that the strike had been one of major proportions, a situation which raised some interesting options.

He wondered if he should try to convince Horton to stay in Hogtown and forget about the strike. He would undoubtedly have to increase the percentage of the take that he was offering to Horton, and there was always the chance that the strike had indeed been minor and that Horton was only maneuvering and manipulating in order to cut himself in for a bigger share of Simpson's profits. The other option was to let Horton leave in the spring, then follow him into the hills and take over his strike. More than one man had gone into the mountains, never to be seen again, and it was already widely known that Simpson had made a large gold strike himself. No one would be surprised if a proven winner were to discover yet another seam of gold.

The more he thought about it, the more Simpson leaned toward the second option, and the prospect of acquiring large quantities of gold played a surprisingly minor role in the decision. In the back of his mind, Will Simpson was beginning to think that Jim Horton just might become difficult to control. If the sheriff couldn't keep him in line, there was no guarantee that he could either, even with Del Jackson and the rest of his men there for backup. Yes, perhaps the best solution was to use Horton to consolidate his holdings, then turn him loose to locate the gold. He could have Horton killed then, thereby eliminating any challenge to his authority and nobody would be the wiser.

Simpson made straight for the Palace and his office, gesturing for Del Jackson to join him there immediately. He had barely enough time to shed his hat and coat before he heard a knock on his door. Before he could answer, Jackson let himself in and eased his stock form into a chair.

"I'm glad that you were here, Jackson," the younger man said, "I've made some changes tonight and I want you to know about them so there won't be any trouble,"

"You know me, boss. Whatever you want is just fine with me," Jackson said cunningly.

"I hired a man tonight to run the gambling downstairs. Jones does well enough with the bar and the girls, but he's over his head when it comes to the tables. I don't mind when the dealers fleece the fools who come in here, but I draw the line at skimming from the house." Simpson paused long enough to pick up the ledgers on his desk. "After looking at King's books, I've discovered that the house profits have dropped more than twenty percent since we took over."

"An' you think this new man can turn it around?" Jackson asked skeptically.

"If he can't, nobody can. He's a tough, hard man who knows his business. Maybe you've heard of him. His name is Jim Horton, and he's ...."

Del Jackson heard little beyond Horton's name. He felt blood rush to his face as if he were blushing, and his ears began to ring. Simpson's face blurred in his vision, and he felt himself slipping toward the edge of madness. Memories of his humiliation and near death at the hands of another Horton years ago in Texas came flooding back, threatening to drown him. From somewhere deep inside himself he recognized what was happening and he fought desperately against it. Gradually the room came back into focus, and he was conscious of Simpson looking at him strangely.

"Well, do you?" Simpson asked forcefully

"Um, do I what?" Jackson somehow managed to say.

"Do you know this man Horton?" Simpson repeated.

"No, I never heard of the man, boss," Jackson lied. "Why?"

"No reason. You just acted funny when I mentioned his name, and I thought you might have run across him somewhere before. It doesn't matter. He'll be here tomorrow night. See that the room at the far end of the hall gets cleaned up for him. He'll be living here, at least until he can find something more to his liking."

"I'll take care of it," Jackson promised. "You want me to show him around?"

"No, have Jones do it. And while we're on the subject, don't get too close to him. He's kind of touchy, and I don't know how long he'll be staying."

"I got you, boss," Jackson said, trying hard to suppress a malignant smile. "I'll take care of him without gettin' too close. You got anything else for me?"

"No, you can get back to the floor. While you're at it, tell the boys I'll be staying in for the rest of the night."

Jackson nodded as he eased himself from the chair and left the office. He told Cleary to get the room ready for Horton, then went in search of Charlie Houseman, one of the gunmen that Simpson had inherited from Eff King. Jackson had settled on a proper reception for Mister Horton. All that he needed was a little time in which to get it ready. He could hardly wait to see Horton's reaction to it.

Chapter 9

Jim Horton gathered his gear together and checked out of the hotel by six o'clock the following morning. He made arrangements with the desk clerk to have his bags delivered to the Golden Palace that afternoon, then walked down the still dark street to the cafe. Ruxford was already awake and people were moving about in preparation for another day's work. In contrast, the saloons, gambling dens, and bawdy houses across the creek in Hogtown were just closing up after a typical night of debauchery. Horton still had a few reservations about working in a place like that.

Last night Myrna had tried her best to talk Jim out of working in Hogtown. When she finally realized that he was going to take the job in spite of anything she said, she accepted the inevitable and filled him in as best she could on the situation he could expect to find on the northside of Crystal Creek. About Willard Simpson, she could tell him little, except that when he worked at the bank he seemed to be a nice enough young man who had never been in trouble. The word around town was that he had made a big strike in the goldfields and had come back here to turn a small fortune into a larger one. Horton could find little fault with that, as long as Simpson ran a place where the games were honest and the whiskey unwatered. When Myrna told him that Simpson had also bought out Miss Ellie's bordello, a furrow had appeared on Horton's brow. Running a saloon was one thing; running a whorehouse was quite another. Horton had not quite made up his mind about Mister Willard Simpson.

Horton stepped up onto the boardwalk in front of the cafe and let himself in. The heat from the stove hit him even before he stepped through the doorway. It was close to zero outside; inside the temperature was at least sixty degrees warmer. Horton quickly shed his coat, scarf, and hat before selecting a seat at a table where he could command a view of both the front door and the entrance to the kitchen. As always, he instinctively kept his back to the wall. Habits picked up during three years of ranger duty were slow to leave a man, and a smart man did what he could to improve his chances of survival on the frontier.

The cafe started to fill up shortly after Horton sat down. The waitress came with a cup of scalding coffee and took his order before she left. Horton had eaten his meal and was working on his third cup of coffee when Sheriff Peabody came through the front door. It took him only a moment to spot Jim at his table. The older man made his way through the crowd and pulled up a chair next to Horton.

"I guess you really was a ranger after all. I always favor the wall seats myself," Peabody said conversationally.

"I'll move over a bit an' we can share the wall if it'll make you feel more comfortable," Horton offered as he slid his chair part-way around the table.

"'Preciate that," the sheriff said somewhat grudgingly. "I don't ever feel comfortable with my back to the room. You eat yet?"

"Some time ago, Sheriff," Horton said as he signaled to the waitress. "Have you decided how's the best way to get out of the predicament you talked us into last night?"

The sheriff took the coffee from the waitress and ordered some breakfast, then looked over the rim of his cup at Horton. "It's just possible that I was a might premature last night, but that's water under the bridge, as they say. I don't like you, Horton, an' you're the kind of man who draws trouble to 'em like a magnet. If you're goin' to play gambler, then I want you out of my town. It's only a matter of time before you have gun trouble."

"Why do you say that?" Horton asked.

"Because you got no back-up in you. Somebody nudges you, then you just naturally got to push back. Seems to me that you always got to give back more than you get, too. That means that sooner or later you'll end up killin' some damn fool. The folks who go to the Nugget are good, solid citizens that I don't want to see layin' dead on some saloon floor."

Jim Horton thought for a minute, then started to speak. Just then the waitress arrived with the sheriff's breakfast. Horton waited until she left, then said, "I came into the town to find a place to hole up for the winter. I made no trouble an' paid cash for anything I wanted. The first time we met, you came after me like you had a thorn in your paw, accused me of bein' a thief an' threw me into jail. If that wasn't enough, then that snot-nosed kid you like to call a deputy shoots off his vile mouth an' throws my food on the floor, just to prove what a tough hombre he is. Now you got the gall to call me a troublemaker when I can prove that I ain't a thief. Seems to me, Peabody, that you got your back arched up so high because you made a bunch of mistakes an' got called on 'em. As I look on it, there ain't one hell of a lot of difference between you an' Curly."

By the time Jim Horton quit talking, Sam Peabody's complexion had turned a dark shade of red, and his mouth was working like he had a lot to say and didn't know which words to let out first. Just as it looked like he was about to speak, Horton said, "Don't have a stroke, Sheriff. I think the reason you're so damn mad is that you know I'm right. I came here as an honest citizen who deserved your protection, not your abuse, an' you know it."

Sheriff Peabody waited until he got better control of himself, then said menacingly, "Maybe you're right, Horton, an' maybe you ain't, but I got to tell you that

if your carcass was to show up dead in an alley somewheres, I'd be hard-pressed to shed any tears."

"As long as you don't try to put the carcass there,"
Jim said evenly, "I'll have no complaints. Now, I got
what may be a solution to our predicament. You want
to hear it or are we goin' to keep on threatenin' each
other?"

"Yeah, go ahead," the sheriff said as he pushed away
his breakfast, still untouched. "I lost my appetite on
any account."

"A fellow named Simpson offered me a job runnin'
the tables at the Golden Palace over in Hogtown. Since
that place is sorta wide open an' you don't patrol it,
you might count that as leavin' town an' I could count
it as stayin'. That way nobody had to back down. What
do you think?"

The sheriff thought for a while, then said, "I'd like
it a lot better if you hadn't of thought of it, but I suppose that it'll work. I never heard of this Simpson fellow, though. Eff King owns the Palace."

"Miss Meloy told me that Simpson bought him out
while you was up to the Olsen's," Jim informed the lawman. "She's also heard that he bought out Miss Ellie's
place, too. Simpson seems like a pleasant enough fellow, but you never know. As long as he runs an honest
game, we won't have no trouble."

"Hope you're right, Horton, but I wouldn't count
on it. Eff King had his hand in everything dirty that
took place over there. Between him an' MIss Ellie, they

controlled all the bawdy houses, whores, saloons, gamblin' an' anything else you could think of that had the smell of money about it. He had a dozen or more men who'd cut your throat to get at the loose change in your pocket. If Simpson was able to take over that operation so quick, I would not be willin' to wager more than a pile of old horse apples that he's honest."

"Well, I guess that I'll find out soon enough," Jim said. "I start workin' there tonight. If you brought along my pokes, I'll be leavin' now. Maybe the food'll taste better when I'm gone."

"Maybe, but I won't count on it. You ain't goin' anywhere near far enough," the sheriff said as he slid the two pokes of gold across the table to Horton. "There's a chance that I've been wrong about you, boy. I doubt it, but there's always a chance. Just stay out of trouble an' we'll get along. Now get out of here so I can at least try to eat."

Horton slid the pokes into his coat pockets, then gathered his gear together and left without saying another word. As he walked back to the hotel, he was surprised that he felt considerable relief that he had come to some sort of truce with Sam Peabody. There were still a few things that Jim wanted to do before he crossed the creek into Hogtown. The first item on his agenda was to retrieve his Colt from his bags. Hogtown was wild enough to make the Derringer he carried seem inadequate. The second thing that he intended to do was to take his gold to the bank. It would be far safer there than in his new room in Hogtown. Besides the matter of safety, Horton really wanted to look over the place where the robbery had occurred. Since he once had been accused of the crime, he now felt that he had a vested interest in discovering what really happened.

Jack Kirby peered through the bars of the cashier's cage at the tall, well-dressed Texan who wanted to open an account at the bank. As he prepared to weigh out the gold in the pokes that the man had presented for conversion and deposit, Kirby tugged gently on a thin cord beneath the counter that activated a small bell in the office of the bank president, Morton Witherspoon. It wasn't that Kirby thought that he was being robbed or that anything was amiss. He had been instructed to summon the president if anyone attempted to deposit a large sum of raw gold, and Jack Kirby considered twenty or more pounds of gold to be a large sum.

Jim Horton watched as the door to an inner office was opened and a heavy-set, middle-aged man of average height emerged and walked over to the head cashier.

"Hello, Jack. Is everything going alright?" he asked.

"Just fine, Mister Witherspoon," Kirby responded, then introduced Horton to him as a new depositor.

"Pleased to meet you, Mister Horton," the banker said as he stepped around the cage and shook Horton's hand. "Call me Morton. Everybody does."

"Pleased to meet you, Morton. Fact is, I wanted to talk with you. I heard that the bank was robbed a while back an' I wanted to be sure that my money'd be safe. Would you mind showin' me your safe?"

"Not at all, sir, not at all," Witherspoon said, smiling. "While Jack finishes up here, why don't you come back into my office and take a look?" Horton noticed that the banker's smile did not extend to his eyes. It was clear that he really did mind showing the safe to Horton.

The two men walked into the office and over to the safe. "As you can see, it's the finest safe that money can buy," the banker said boastfully.

"Yet somebody cleaned it out without leavin' a clue," Jim responded.

"How come you know so much about the robbery?" the banker asked as his smile deserted his face entirely.

"Fact is that the sheriff accused me of doin' it; that is, before he checked out my alibi," Horton admitted. "That robbery got a bit personal along about then. You got any ideas about who might have done it?"

"No, I don't," the banker replied in a cold voice. "The only theory I have is that a professional bank robber did it. The sheriff thinks that it might have been an inside job, but all of my people checked out clean."

"If you don't mind me askin'," Horton said, "what have you done to make sure that this hombre doesn't come back an' do it again?"

"We've hired two night guards who stand watch with pistols and sawed-off shotguns. If he comes back, he'll get a reception that he'll never forget, I assure you," Witherspoon said with some feeling.

Horton nodded his head as if in agreement, then took one last look around before following the banker back out of the office. After a minute or two of polite conversation with Witherspoon and Kirby, Horton picked up his bank book and started to leave the bank.

"Oh, by the way, Morton, do you happen to know anything about a man named Will Simpson?" he asked.

"Sure," Witherspoon answered. "He was an employee of mine for several years. He resigned a couple of years ago to do some prospecting. As I remember, he was most conscientious. Why do you ask?"

"Oh, no particular reason," Horton said evasively. "He's back in town, you know."

The banker looked surprised but not alarmed. "No, I did not know that," he said as he turned to Jack Kirby. "Do you suppose that he'll be wanting his old job back?"

The cashier shrugged his shoulders as Jim said, "I doubt it. He's bought a place across the creek, I hear."

"That doesn't sound much like the Will Simpson that I knew, but if it's true, then I wish him the best of luck. He'll need it over there."

Horton nodded in agreement, then shook hands with both men and left the bank with not much more information than he'd had when he entered.

Jim Horton spent the remainder of the day talking with Myrna Meloy. Much of the conversation dealt with Morton Witherspoon and the bank. He learned little about the robbery that he had not already known. He did learn that the banker had a wife and several children whom he kept in a big brick house at the edge of town. He was also a regular patron at Miss Ellie's, generally choosing to stay with a specific girl rather than sampling the variety of pleasures available at that particular town landmark. Myrna also told him that before the robbery there had been rumors that the bank was in some sort of financial difficulty. Horton knew that there wasn't a bank in the west that wasn't the subject of rumors now and then, but he wondered if there might not be some connection between the rumors and the robbery.

Jim checked with the hotel clerk before he left and learned that his bags had been delivered to his new room at the Palace. He slipped the clerk a twenty-dollar gold piece over the man's strenuous protests and thanked him for all the help that he'd been. The clerk looked about nervously before pocketing the money, then thanked Horton profusely for his generosity. Horton felt just a little guilty, for it had been his intent to buy a little good will with the tip when apparently none needed to be bought.

It was full dark by the time that Horton reached the Palace. He dropped his hat off in his room and went downstairs to survey his new job. It was early yet, and few customers were present. Horton managed to say a few words to each of the dealers and bartenders, then selected a table in the rear of the room across from the bar. Cleary brought over a bottle and a reasonably clean glass, then took the chair Horton offered. There followed a few minutes of pleasant conversation, after which Cleary left with a promise to send Horton over some hot food. Horton poured himself a drink and sipped it while he waited for the food to arrive.

More customers came in and the noise level in the bar increased. One of the assistant bartenders whose name escaped Horton brought over a platter laden with steak, potatoes, and some bread. Horton was a little surprised to find that the food was still hot. He thanked the bartender and had just started to eat when a shadow fell over his table.

"Mister, you're sittin' in my chair," said a large, dirty man who wore his much-broken nose like some sort of badge of honor.

Horton pushed back his chair a little and looked up at the man. "I'd be pleased to have you join me, mister. Pull up a chair," he said calmly.

"Maybe you didn't hear me, Horton. You're in my chair. This here's my table. I ain't sharin' either with the likes of you. Now git!" the big man spat.

Horton sat there for a moment, sizing up the visitor. The man had him by at least three inches in height and by fifty pounds in weight. The nose suggested that the loudmouth had fought often, if not well. Jim decided that for the sake of business he'd move to another table. He also wanted to prove that the sheriff had been wrong when he had accused him of never walking away from trouble.

As Horton started to rise, the loudmouth pointed to the empty table next to him and said, "An' that one there belongs to my two friends here."

"Yeah, that there table's our'n," a small, toothy man whose face was badly pox-marked nodded in agreement.

Horton sat back down and addressed the first man. "Where do you suggest that I look for a table?" he asked evenly.

"Ya might try El Paso. Yeah, I hear there's an empty table in El Paso," the large man said, obviously pleased with his attempt at humor.

"Well, boys, if I ever get down that way, I'll be sure to drop in an' see. Right now, you're disturbin' my supper. Suppose you either sit down an' join me or hit the road. Makes no difference to me," Horton said as he reached for his fork.

The large man stepped around the table and grabbed Horton by the lapel of his coat and started to pull him to his feet. "Maybe you still didn't hear me, pilgrim. I said ...."

At that point the big man lost his train of thought because Jim brought his fist up from the floor in a powerful uppercut that caught the loudmouth flush in the crotch. The big man's stale breath rushed from his mouth, and he folded at the waist, clutching at his damaged parts.

Horton stood up, placed his hand behind the man's head and drove his face into the table with all of the force that he could muster. From the gore that he left on the table, it was evident that the loudmouth would have another notch in his nose and several fewer teeth as souvenirs of this ill-advised encounter.

Horton turned to the other two men, who stood there in astonishment as they looked down on their boss lying unconscious on the floor. The fight might have ended there, but the man with the smallpox scars chose that moment to come out of his trance and go for his gun. Horton palmed his Colt and fired twice, the shots so close together that they sounded like one. The two .44 caliber slugs caught the man just above and below his belt buckle and propelled him backwards across the room. He hit the floor just short of the bar, a confused look crossing his face. He rolled onto his side and began to vomit blood. A few moments later he was dead.

Even before the pox-marked man hit the floor, his companion went for his gun. Horton fired once more, the slug catching the man in the throat, breaking his neck and killing him even before he began to fall. He crumpled into a heap several feet short of his companion in death. Neither of the men had been able to get off a shot.

Horton surveyed the crowd coldly and said, "Anyone else want to buy into this pot?" No one answered and most of the men in the room hurriedly found something else to occupy their attention. Jim thumbed the hammer of his Colt to half-cock, flipped open the loading gate and punched out the empty cases. He reloaded the cylinder with the spare cartridges from his belt, eased the hammer all the way down and holstered the pistol. He turned to look at the first man just in time to see him try to draw his pistol. Horton kicked the Colt from his fist, then ground the heel of his boot into the loudmouth's outstretched hand. Horton was rewarded with a scream and the sound of breaking bones. The man on the floor passed out.

"He won't try to back-shoot anyone else very soon," Horton said to himself as he walked back to the table. He picked up his glass and poured himself a fresh drink. He had lost all interest in eating. He set down his empty glass and walked over to the two dead men. Although he had never seen either of them before, he knew the type. They were little men who felt much bigger with Colts in their fists. In death they looked very small and pathetic. The had lost control of their bowels and the smell was beginning to permeate the room. Horton saw Cleary approach with a couple of men in tow. They grabbed the bodies by the feet and dragged them out of the room, leaving only a thin trail of blood on the floor to mark their passage. Two other men took charge of the unconscious leader and followed the men with the corpses out of the saloon. Cleary dumped some sawdust on the larger pools of blood and then went back about his business as if nothing had ever happened. Horton was impressed with how little life meant in Hogtown.

Del Jackson was in Simpson's office when he heard the shots. He ran to the door and let himself out onto the balcony overlooking the saloon floor. When he saw Horton kick the pistol from Charlie Houseman's hand, he knew that his plan had failed. He drew his pistol and took aim at Horton as the Texan walked over to look at the dead men. Just as Jackson was preparing to fire, Will Simpson grabbed his arm.

"Don't shoot, you fool!" he exclaimed. "Horton's on our side."

"Maybe," Jackson said. "Maybe not. Those men he shot worked for you, too. You goin' to let him get away with it?"

"You're well-told I am," Simpson replied. "At least for now, I am. Right now, I'm going to find out just what happened. Knowing Houseman, Horton had ample cause for what he did. Ferret and Lacer never had enough intelligence between them to do anything except back up Houseman and you know it. We're well-rid of the bunch of them. Horton's worth far more to us than they ever were," he said as he released Jackson's arm.

Jackson holstered his pistol and stalked off, his anger still unabated. Simpson waited until Jackson had closed the door to the office behind him, then went downstairs to talk with Horton.

Horton waited patiently while one of the swampers mopped up the gore and remains of his dinner from the table, then sat down in a chair from which he could observe the action taking place in the saloon. No more than three minutes had passed since the shooting, but except for the thinning gun smoke and the thin blood trails on the floor no one would have known that there had even been a fight. Jim was more than a little concerned that fights of this type were so commonplace that no one paid much attention to them anymore.

Will Simpson came up to the table, pulled out a chair and sat down. Jim acknowledged his presence with a nod, then went back to scanning the crowd. The men sat in silence for a minute or two until Simpson could contain himself no longer.

"What started it, Jim?" he asked.

"I'm not quite sure. I take it you saw what happened."

"I saw the end of it from the balcony. The shooting was over by the time I got out of my office." Simpson made no mention of his run-in with Jackson.

"Well," Jim explained, "the big fellow came up an' started to harangue me. He acted like he wanted me out of town, but I think he was dead set on gunplay. I didn't play his game an' he got confused an' made a stupid move. He won't do it again. The shootin' part of it was unnecessary. The real fight was over when the runty pair decided to buy into it. They were too far away for me to get at 'em with my hands. You got any idea who they were?"

"The big man's name is Charlie Houseman. The other two used to hang around with him. They all worked for the previous owner of this place and they've been working for me since I took over."

Jim thought for a moment before he spoke. "Funny thing about all this, Simpson. This Houseman fella called me by name, an' I'd never laid eyes on him before. If I were a suspicious man, I'd think that someone set them on me. You got any idea who might want to do that?"

"You can be sure it wasn't me," Simpson said defensively. "I didn't go through the trouble of hiring you just to run you off or kill you before you even got started on the job."

"I believe that," Jim said evenly, "but what I can't understand is why you need people like those on your payroll. They'd sell out their mothers if the price was right. It's plain enough that somebody hired them to come after me."

"Now, Jim, we run a big operation around here. Besides this place, we have a piece of the action in every other establishment in Hogtown. A business of this size requires a certain amount of muscle to keep it operating smoothly. I know that Charlie Houseman had his faults, but every big business needs a few people like him if it hopes to survive."

"So, you're sayin' that you took over King's action, lock, stock, an' barrel," Horton stated flatly.

"Yes, I did. And a profitable business it is, too. It's going to make both of us rich men."

"It may make you a rich man, Simpson, but it's goin' to make me unemployed. I heard that King had his hand in every piece of dirt on this side of the creek, but I'd hoped that you were above that sort of thing. I was wrong. I want no part of that kind of operation. As soon as I can get my bags, I'll be leavin'."

"Just who in hell are you to be making moral judgments?" Simpson said angrily. "You're just another gambler who killed two men and maimed a third not ten minutes ago, and you did it without batting an eye.

I may do a lot of things, Horton, but I've not killed any-one."

"That may be true, Simpson," Jim said softly. "You're more the type to hire your killin' done. Now, if you'll excuse me, I'll be goin'." And with that, Jim Horton walked away from the speechless Simpson, collected his bags, and left Hogtown.

Chapter 10

Jim Horton sat his bags down in front of the counter in the lobby of the Excelsior Hotel and tapped gently on the bell. The desk clerk emerged from the doorway behind the counter.

"Back so soon, sir?" he asked respectfully. "How can I help you?"

"I need a room, Amos. You got any openings? It seems I just can't hold a job," Horton said, smiling broadly.

"I'm sure that Miss Meloy would want you to have your old rooms back, sir, and we almost always have that suite available. Shall I have your bags taken up?"

"I'd 'preciate it. Would you also tell Miss Meloy that I'll be imposin' on her hospitality for a little while? I'd tell her myself, only I suspect that I'd better have a chat with Sam Peabody before I do anythin' else."

The desk clerk assured him that he would, and Horton went back out into the night to look for the sheriff. As he walked towards the jail, he noted that the temperature was falling rapidly again, diminishing the chance of more snow. Horton had never been fond of cold weather, and this was more than he had ever experienced before in his entire life. Texas was looking better and better to him with every passing day. Sure, it got cold there and snow wasn't all that unusual, especially in the upper half of the state, but no self-respecting Texan could ever get used to the bone-numbing cold of the Colorado Rockies.

Horton saw a light burning in the jail as he approached. Inside he found the sheriff at his desk, laboring intently on some paperwork. Horton was surprised and not just a little amused to see that the sheriff was wearing a pair of eyeglasses as he worked. Sam Peabody looked up as Horton closed the door. Jim noted that he immediately slipped off the glasses and shoved them into a drawer.

"You get lost, or what?" the sheriff asked quickly. The beginnings of a smile at the corners of his mouth saved the comment from being sarcastic.

"As a matter of fact, Sheriff, I came to report a shootin'," Jim answered almost apologetically. "Better make that a pair of 'em. Like you said, sooner or later I was goin' to have gun trouble, an' tonight was the time. I believe it was a put-up job. Some hombre wanted me out of the way, permanently. Has anybody else reported it?"

"Hadn't heard a word," the sheriff responded. "But if it took place in Hogtown, I don't suppose I would. Most folks think that it's out of my jurisdiction."

"Isn't it?" Horton asked.

"Not hardly. I'm responsible for the whole town, that part of it included, but the truth of the matter is that I can't police it all, an' nobody expects me to. Every time I get a decent deputy, he either runs off prospectin' or else he gets himself shot. Besides, minin' towns all got to have somewheres for miners an' prospectors to blow off steam, an' that means whiskey, gamblin', an' whores. By puttin' them all over in Hogtown, the decent folks can walk the streets of Ruxford with some kind of safety. If I could find a couple of good men, I'd like to clean up Hogtown a little, too. There's still too much killin' an' thievein' goin' on over there to suit me."

"I couldn't agree with you more," the younger man answered. "For the record, let me tell you what happened tonight," Horton said as he pulled up a chair and sat down next to the sheriff's desk. For the next ten minutes he related the story without once being interrupted by the lawman, who grunted occasionally as if to indicate grudging approval. When Jim finally finished, the sheriff leaned back in his swivel chair and put his feet up on the desk.

"Seems to me that you didn't get left too much choice. Too bad you didn't shoot Houseman, too. Him an' that pair Ferrett an' Lancer was all overdue for killin'. The sorry part of it is, they ain't the worst of King's old bunch. There are some others who was on King's payroll an' who probably are on Simpson's that make them three look downright tame. I can't help wonderin' who put them up to killin' you. Did you get a chance to pry it out of Houseman?"

"No, I didn't," Horton said disgustedly. "By the time I thought of it, they'd dragged him out of the Palace. I doubt that there's any chance of findin' him alive now. He's either holed up, left town, or whoever put him up to it has finished him off to keep his mouth shut. If I'd been a little smarter, I'd of thought of that before it was too late to do anythin' about it."

The sheriff thought for a minute, then looked Horton in the eye. "No matter," he said finally. "If someone brings the shootin' to my attention, then I guess I'll have to look into it. I suspect that I'll never hear about it, though, an' the two dead ones'll just turn up missin'. That happens a fair amount across the creek. If I was you, I wouldn't lose no sleep over it," he advised as he swung his feet off the desk and stood up. Jim Horton stood up with him.

"Now that you've gone an' shot your way out of a job, just what are you plannin' on doin' for the rest of the winter?" the sheriff asked.

"I hadn't thought about it much, to tell you the truth. I'll probably go back to playin' cards at Miss Meloy's if you aren't goin' to lock me up for what happened tonight," Jim drawled.

"I can't lock you up for somethin' I don't know about, son. I got an idea that you ain't goin' to be any too happy sittin' around all winter dealin' cards an' ruinin' your liver on bar whiskey. Why don't you get rid of them fancy duds you're wearin' an' be my deputy? I pay fifty a month an' furnish all the ammunition you can use. In your case, that might break the city's ammo budget. You can even sleep in one of the cells if it ain't in use. What do you say? Have we got a deal?"

"What about Curly?" Horton asked. "He's goin' to be real upset if he loses his job, especially to me/"

"Well, it would serve him right if he did, but maybe between the two of us we can teach him a little about how to be a peace officer. I got to warn you, though. If you take the job, we're goin' to make a stab at cleanin' up Hogtown a little. I've needed a man with some ca-jones to back my play, an' I figure that you're him."

"In that case, Sheriff, you got yourself a new deputy," Jim said quickly. "I got to say, though, that I was beginnin' to think that I was goin' to have to fight you, not work for you. Why the sudden change of heart?"

The sheriff barked out a laugh. "Hell, son, we're both cut out of the same bolt of cloth. Things'll be much better around here if we're on the same side. An' while we're at it, you can start callin' me 'Sam.' Now raise your right hand an' take the oath."

Jim Horton did as he was told and became Deputy Sheriff Jim Horton, with a monthly pay roughly equal to what he had earned on a bad night at Myrna Meloy's.

Jim rose early the next morning, ate at the cafe, and walked through the front door of the jail shortly after six-thirty. He found Curly dozing in a chair in the corner of the office closest to the stove. He woke up as Jim closed the door firmly behind him.

"Oh, it's you," Curly said sullenly.

"Yeah, an' a good thing it was, too. The sheriff would have had your hide if he'd caught you sleepin' on duty. Is that coffee fresh?" he asked as he pointed to the pot on the stove.

"I made it about an hour ago, if it's any of your business," Curly answered, his mood plainly not improved by Horton's rebuke. "Before he turned in for the night, the sheriff told me that he done hired you. I don't think too highly of the idea, myself."

Jim grabbed a cup from the shelf and walked over to the stove. He poured himself a cup of the steaming coffee, then pulled up a chair across from the other deputy and sat down.

"Whether you like it or not, Curly, I'm going' to be workin' here at least 'til spring. Now, I can kick your butt every day when I come in here or we can work together an' help Sam clean up Hogtown. It's your choice; it makes absolutely no difference to me. Right now, I see you as more of a problem than a help in any kind of serious law work. If you can learn to shut your mouth an' pay attention, I think you can become a real good deputy." Jim paused for a while before he continued. "I came in early today to have a little talk with you, an' now I've had my say. You want to get anythin' off your chest?"

Curly looked at him angrily for a moment, started to speak, then thought better of it. Horton was a little amused to watch the youth struggle with his emotions, but he kept his expression hard. Finally, Curly found the words that he wanted.

"I admit that I was out of line when you was locked up back there, an' I guess we might as well get along if'n we're goin' to work together. Just don't get the idea that I'm afraid of you, 'cause I ain't," the younger man bristled.

"Fair enough, Curly. I'll believe you aren't afraid of anything as long as you don't try to prove how tough you are. When a man tries to look too tough, he usually gets to prove it. It's goin' to take all three of us to clean up Hogtown, an' you can bet that somebody is goin' to call our hand before we're through." Jim extended his hand to Curly. "What say we start all over, Deputy?"

Curly looked at Horton's hand for a moment, then shook it as a smile spread across his face. "Nice to meet ya, Deputy. Just tell me one thing," he said as he released Horton's hand. "Who slipped you that damned Derringer?"

Jim laughed. "Nobody. The sheriff made a mistake an' never searched me. He'd picked up my Colt an' Winchester already an' didn't figure me for somebody who'd have a holdout hidden somewhere. If I hadn't of gotten mad, you never would have known, either. I was perfectly willin' to let the sheriff verify my story. If you ever are in a position to arrest somebody an' don't want to get embarrassed, make real sure that you search him good before you take him in."

"Thanks. I'll remember that," Curly promised. "Is that why you stripped the sheriff down to the buff?"

"Partly. The sheriff's an old curly wolf, an' I figured him for havin' a knife or two hidden somewheres. I also wanted to slow him down enough so I could leave without tradin' lead with him. It's kinda like wrestlin' with a grizzly bear. The trick of the whole thing is in figurin' out how to let go without gettin' yourself killed. I figured that the sheriff wouldn't be too anxious to run out into the middle of the street with his appendages danglin' in the breeze."

Curly started to laugh at the thought of the sheriff standing naked in the middle of the street and Jim joined in. The sheriff picked that moment to walk into the office.

"What's all this?" he asked grumpily. "I figured I'd have to pull you two apart, an' now I find you both laughin' your fool heads off. What's so dadblamed funny, anyway?"

"Nothin', Sheriff, nothin' at all," Curly said as he tried unsuccessfully to choke back his laughter. "An' you don't have to worry none about me an' Mister Horton buttin' heads. We've come to an understandin'."

"Is that so?" the sheriff said crossly. "Then suppose you understand your way right on home. I want you back here at noon. We're all goin' to pay us a call on Mister Simpson an' I want you bright-eyed an' bushy-tailed when we go."

"You got it, Sheriff," Curly said as he ducked by Horton, grabbed his hat and coat, and headed out the door. "You can count on me!" he added enthusiastically as he closed the door behind him.

"I ain't never seen him move that fast before. I wonder what come over him?" the sheriff mused.

"I think that the boy is just growin' up," Jim observed. "If he lives through it, he might just do to ride the river with."

The sheriff nodded as he thought that over for a bit, then settled down behind his desk and started going through some papers. Jim brought him some coffee, and the two men spent the rest of the morning discussing the town and the plan that the sheriff had outlined for making the presence of the law felt in Hogtown.

The train pulled into Benton, Texas, belching smoke and vast quantities of steam as the engineer slowed the huffing iron monster. The brakes screeched and the cars shuddered and banged against each other as they came to a halt. A small group of people stood together on the station platform, waiting for the conductor to open the door to the passenger car. One of the men wore a badge on his coat.

"You sure that you want to go, Marcus?" the lawman asked the tall, powerfully built man with streaks of gray in his hair and handlebar mustache. "If Jim needed any help, he'd have sent a wire."

"He would if he could," answered the man called Marcus, "but I got this feelin' that somethin's wrong up there. I won't rest easy 'til I check it out. Joe here," he said, pointing to the oldest of the three men standing on the platform, "he an' Marta can keep things goin' at the ranch. It's slow this time of the year."

"You're damn well told I can," Joe said, bristling. "I was doin' it while you pups was wearin' three-cornered pants an' playin' with cow chips in the front yard. An' things wasn't always so slow, neither!" he added indignantly.

"Now take it easy, dear," the handsome gray-haired woman said as she took her husband's arm. "I'm sure that Marcus didn't mean that you couldn't handle things," she said soothingly.

"I'm sure that you can take care of anything," Marcus said in a conciliatory tone. "As far as I'm concerned, you're still the best segundo in Texas, in spite of your age."

"An' don't you never forget it, neither!" Joe snorted, his anger largely pretended. If Joe had ever said a kind word to either of the younger men, they would have been sure to keel over from the shock of it. Joe Penbrook took great comfort in being irascible, but he thought of the Horton boys as his own and couldn't have been prouder of them if they really had been his. The brothers knew this and returned the feeling.

"I'll send a wire when I find out what's goin' on in Ruxford, Matt," Marcus said to the lawman. "If I need more help, I'll let you know."

The men on the platform shook hands and Marta hugged the older Horton, then stepped back and took Joe's arm again. Marcus boarded the train and waved from the doorway of the car as the conductor hollered, "Board!" The train groaned, bumped, and screeched as the puffing rhythm of the engine accelerated, and the train pulled away from the station. Soon only a smudge of smoke on the horizon marked the passage of the train, then it, too, was gone.

Chapter 11

Curly showed up at the jail on the stroke of noon. He, Sam Peabody, and Jim went directly from there to the cafe, where they consumed a prodigious quantity of beef stew, cornbread, and hot apple pie topped with thick wedges of cheese. The owner of the establishment, Dooly Doolittle, hobbled out of the kitchen as the men were finishing the last of their coffee and sat down with them. Dooly was an old cowboy who had gotten busted up once too often and had turned to cooking to provide his livelihood. Although he was an excellent chuckwagon cook, he had no head for business, so his wife ran the cafe while he toiled in the back. His two attractive and sturdy daughters waited on tables and dodged propositions as well as proposals, both of which were tendered only after Dooly was safely out of sight in the kitchen. Dooly was known to take exception to anyone messing around with his womenfolk, and it was rumored that he was deadly with either a meat cleaver or the ten-gauge Parker he kept loaded with nails and broken glass in the kitchen. It was clear that Dooly and the sheriff were old friends. The sheriff introduced Horton to Dooly and informed him that Jim was from Texas.

"Texas, eh?" the old man said, more as a statement than as a question. "I worked down thata way right after the war. There was big money to be made in Big Thicket country pullin' wild cows outta that there brush. You from that part of the state?"

Horton shook his head. "'Fraid not. I'm from the middle part, about seventy or eighty miles north of Austin. It's a whole lot dryer there an' the graze is more open."

"Know the area. Went through there once on the way to El Paso. Now there's a place for you. The cows got no fat meat on 'em 'cause they gotta run so hard to get from one tuft of grass to the next before they starve to death. An' hot? I hope to spit! Had a partner once who came from down there. One day he ups an' dies on me an' goes direct to hell. Anyway, he ain't there more'n a couple of days afore he has to send back for some blankets." The old man slapped his knee and broke out into a fit of laughter. Curly and the sheriff joined in while Horton smiled politely. The cook's joke was too close to the truth to be really funny, he thought.

After a while the old man excused himself and went back to the kitchen. The three men paid their tabs and made their way back through the busy street to the office. The morning's bright sunshine had been replaced by heavy clouds that promised more snow before the day was out. The men were glad that the afternoon was gloomy. The sun glaring off the snow would have made their jobs just that much more difficult.

The sheriff got out his keys and unlocked the rifle rack. Each of the deputies selected a ten-gauge shotgun and stuffed a handful of extra shells into his pockets. The tubes of the shotguns had been cut off at twenty inches, a modification which made them deadly when used against a crowd or in a small room. The sheriff picked up a Model 1876 Winchester carbine that fired a .45 caliber slug which was pushed along by seventy-five grains of black powder. The weapon itself looked like a larger version of the Model 1873, but with a walnut forearm that continued nearly to the muzzle. The sheriff dropped a box of extra shells into his pocket, although experience told him that he wouldn't need them. All three men loaded their weapons and left the office, headed for Hogtown. As they walked, the sheriff gave instructions to Curly, who nodded his head in acknowledgment and swallowed nervously.

The three lawmen went directly to the Golden Palace. The streets were largely deserted, and there were only a handful of hungover customers in the saloon. Horton covered the bar area to the sheriff's left almost casually while Curly nervously kept watch over the tables to his right. The sheriff kept his eyes on the balcony.

Horton spoke softly to Cleary. "Go get Simpson for us, will you? And tell your man behind the bar to keep his hands where I can see them."

Cleary nodded and did as he was told. He ascended the stairs two at a time as he hurried towards Will Simpson's office. A minute or two later Simpson came out of his office and put on his coat as he came down the stairs. Horton shifted his position so that he could cover both the bar and the balcony.

Simpson stopped about two paces from the sheriff and smiled broadly. "Welcome to the Golden Palace, Sheriff. To what do we owe the honor of this visit?" he asked cheerfully.

The sheriff moved a foot or two closer to Simpson and unbuttoned his coat. "Thought I'd tell you about the new rules for operation' around here," he said. "Startin' now, the law's patrollin' this side of the creek, too. All saloons an' bawdy houses'll close by two in the mornin'. Get rid of the brakes and magnets on the roulette wheels. If we find any after tonight, we'll close up the saloon. If the patrons start any trouble, you call me or one of my deputies an' we'll put an end to it. If one of your men starts anything, you'll answer to me, personal. I'd advise you not to put me to the test. I guarantee you that you'd live to regret it."

"Harsh words, Sheriff," Simpson said, still smiling. "I'm sure that we can come to some sort of an arrangement that will keep both, or perhaps I should say, all of us happy. I believe that in cases like this, the usual arrangement is five percent. Is that satisfactory with you?"

Peabody looked at Simpson coldly. "Listen closely, Simpson, 'cause I'm only goin' to tell you once. The only arrangement we're ever goin' to have is for you to live by the rules I just gave you. An' that goes for everyone else in Hogtown. The law ain't for sale, at least not here."

The smile faded from Simpson's face. "Why tell me all this? I'm only one owner. There must be more than a dozen others on this side of the creek."

"There's thirty-one, to be exact, an' you got a hand in all of 'em," the sheriff responded. "You also control the muscle over here. I know it as well as you, so you can cut the innocent act an' save us both some time. I'm puttin' the lid on Hogtown. If things stay quiet, people don't get cheated an' nobody dies, you get to stay in business. If not, you an' your bunch get to leave, by train or in a box. Makes no difference to me. You understand what I'm tellin' you, boy?"

"I understand perfectly, Sheriff," Simpson said coldly. "I can vouch for the Palace, but I can't make guarantees beyond these doors, regardless of what you think. I'll pass the word to the other owners for you, but don't try to shut me down. If you do, there'll be trouble, and more of it than two men and a boy can handle."

"Just what do you mean by that?" snapped Curly, his face suddenly turning red.

"Take it easy, son," the sheriff said. "Just do what I told you to do." To Simpson he said, "Do what I said an' no one gets shut down. Try somethin' fancy an' I'll come for you. Not for one of your boys. For you. If a fight starts, one of us would live long enough to take you with us. You can count on it. An' that's all I'm goin' to say on the subject." With that, the sheriff turned and walked out of the saloon while Jim and Curly covered the room.

"I hate a turncoat, Horton," Simpson said, still angry from his exchange with the sheriff. "You'd do well to remember that and stay clear of me and my boys."

"Like the sheriff said, Simpson, we'll be around," Jim answered. "Clean up your operation an' we'll have no problem. From what I've seen so far, you an' your boys ain't much to worry about, so you can spare me your threats."

Jim signaled to Curly and the two men backed out of the saloon and joined the sheriff in the street. The lawmen started walking back towards the creek, watching windows, doorways, and alleys as they went. By the time they reached the creek the snow had started to fall again, large wet flakes that immediately reduced visibility to a matter of yards. The men walked faster then, no longer worried about the chance of ambush.

Back in the office, the sheriff gave instructions for the two deputies to meet after supper to make the rounds. All three men knew that the issue of law and order in Hogtown wasn't settled yet. For the edict to work, the lawmen must enforce it, and the prime time for a challenge to come would be that night. The men settled down to clean their weapons and wait. Horton moved over to a chair next to Curly's and talked softly to him for a few minutes. Curly nodded several times in agreement, then went back to cleaning his Colt. Horton moved back to his original position near the stove. No one spoke after that. Before long, Horton went back to the hotel and Curly went home. The sheriff dozed quietly at his desk.

When the three lawmen left the Golden Palace, Will Simpson stood immobile, struggling to contain his anger. It took him a minute or so, but he finally cooled off enough to go back upstairs to his office. Del Jackson was there, waiting.

"What's the sheriff want?" he asked Simpson.

"The sheriff thinks that he's going to call the tune in Hogtown," he said angrily. "He's slapped a 2 a.m. curfew on us and he's going to make sure that our games are honest. What's more, he's holding me personally responsible for everyone's compliance with his rules."

Jackson laughed, "An' where's he goin' to get the army he needs to enforce those rules?"

"All he's got is that kid deputy and Jim Horton, but I have a feeling that we couldn't get them all at once from ambush. If we try to get rid of them and fail, it'll mean the end of everything we've done here. What we need to do is to arrange for something to happen to them that can't be traced back here to us."

"You ain't askin' for much, are you, boss?" Jackson said with considerable sarcasm.

"If you can't say something useful, keep your damned mouth shut!" Simpson snapped.

Jackson started to get up, then caught himself and sat back down. This, he knew, wasn't the time to challenge Simpson. But the time would come, Jackson vowed.

Simpson started to pace back and forth across the room. "Peabody, Horton, and the kid have to go, and we can't use our own men to do it. Does that suggest anything to you, Jackson?"

"Yeah. I need to go to Denver an' hire some fresh talent. How many do you suppose we'll need?"

Simpson stopped pacing and walked over to the safe. "Four good men ought to do it," he said as he knelt and spun the dial. Once the safe was open, he extracted a stack of bills, counted it, and tossed it over to Jackson. "There is enough for you to hire the men we need and to pay for the train fare. You can catch the train tonight. How long do you think it will take you to get back here?"

Jackson thought for a moment, then replied. "Four days, maybe a little more or a little less, dependin' on who's available an' whether the trains stay on schedule. What're you goin' to do about the sheriff 'til then?"

"Absolutely nothing. We're going to do everything just the way the man wants until he gets careless. When you get back with the men, keep them out of sight somewhere until we need them. Remember, I don't want anyone to be able to tie us in with them."

"I'll remember," Jackson promised as he got out of his chair and walked out of the office. The idea crossed his mind that this might be a good time to pocket the money and keep on going. Then he remembered Horton and decided to delay his permanent departure until he had a chance to see Horton dead. That was something worth waiting for.

Simpson sat down at his desk and lit a cigar. A smile creased his face. With the sheriff gone, he and his men could take over the whole town, and maybe even more. He might just end up in the governor's chair. He allowed himself to gaze out the window and daydream about that possibility as the snow began to pile up against the window ledge.

Jim ate supper that night with Myrna Meloy in the Excelsior's dining room. Myrna was dressed in a green velvet gown with a high lace collar that hugged her neck like a second skin. White lace also adorned the cuffs of her sleeves. The dress accented her full figure and complimented her red hair and flawless complexion. He had heard that some men had ridden a hundred miles or more just to see Myrna Meloy. Tonight, Jim believed those stories. There was no doubt that he was the most envied man in the Excelsior Hotel. Myrna was a vision of loveliness, and very much the perfect lady.

Horton had discussed the impending cleanup of Hogtown with Myrna the previous evening. While she had expressed enthusiastic support for the venture, secretly she was deeply concerned for the safety of the lawmen who would be called upon to maintain order in an area that had heretofore been a law unto itself. Mostly she was concerned for the welfare of this tall, quiet Texan who sat next to her at the table. She had grown to like the man—really like him as she had never liked a man before. He was her friend and confidant, and given the slightest encouragement, she would gladly become his lover. The thought of such a prospect brought a flush to her cheeks, and she realized with a start that she could actually be in love with this man. This bit of knowledge brought with it a stab of fear, for although her past was somewhat checkered, she was inexperienced in affairs of the heart.

For his part, Jim was firmly impaled on the horns of a dilemma. He had feelings for Sonja, but he wasn't sure if those were feelings of love, lust, or obligation. He was also very attracted to Myrna, whom he both liked and respected. When he looked at her, he got a tightness in his throat and his mouth turned to cotton. Several times he had been tempted to invite her to his bed, but he was equally afraid of the possibility that she would accept him or that she would reject him. Finally, he decided to do nothing and just wait to see where the relationship led. The decision did not, however, stop his palms from sweating whenever he was close to her.

Jim finished his meal and wiped his mouth carefully with a glistening linen napkin, then snapped open the case of his watch. There was no doubt about it; he could delay his departure no longer. He made his excuses to Myrna, then left the hotel and walked to the jail. The snow was still falling heavily, although the temperatures continued to drop. More than a foot of the white stuff had fallen since noon, he noted as he made his way along the nearly deserted street. By the time he reached the jail, dampness had crept into his boots and his feet were cold. He stomped the snow from his boots on the boardwalk, then entered the jail.

Curly and the sheriff were waiting for him. Jim brushed the snow from his hat and coat, then hung both on a peg near the door. When he turned back towards the center of the room, Sam Peabody tossed him the shotgun that Jim had used earlier in the day.

"Better keep this with you from now on," the sheriff advised. "I figure that Simpson's got to make his move soon or put up with a hell of a cut in his profits, which don't seem likely to me. We'd be foolish to think that the only place he'd try somethin' would be in Hogtown."

"Makes sense," Jim said. "If it were me, I'd either try somethin' tonight or pretend to go along with the new rules an' wait 'til we get careless. Then I'd try to take us all out. My guess is that it'll depend on whether they think they can get us all at once or if they'll have to try to get us one at a time. That's assumin' that they're not goin' to accept the new rules, of course."

"I think we can assume that, sure enough," the sheriff said. "If you're right, and I think you've hit the nail square on the head, then we'd better not put all our eggs in one basket. Maybe Curly'd better hold things down here an' me an' you'll pay a visit to Hogtown."

"Now wait a minute!" Curly objected. "You ain't goin' to leave me outta this!" he exclaimed as he stomped across the room to join Jim in front of the sheriff.

"Curly's got a point, Sam," Jim said. "He's young, but he's a good man. If he doesn't go, those yahoos across the creek'll think we don't trust him. Then they'll never take him seriously. It might be better if me'n Curly make the rounds tonight an' you keep an eye on the rest of the town."

The sheriff thought about it for a minute or two, then looked at the deputies and said to Jim, "I don't like sendin' the pair of you out to do my job. Seems to me that we ought to send the most experienced men an' that means me an' you."

Before Curly could argue, Jim said, "Curly can back me up just fine, Sam. We talked this afternoon an' he knows better to let them bait him into doin' somethin' besides what he's supposed to do. Besides, he's got to learn sometime, an' it might as well be right now."

"Yeah," Curly added in agreement. "I know they was tryin' to get me mad so's I'd mess things up today, but I ain't goin' to let 'em get to me no more."

The sheriff thought for a minute about what Jim and Curly said before he spoke. "When I hired you, Horton, I didn't think that you two would team up against me. 'Pears to me that I'm outvoted on this one." The sheriff leaned back in his chair and pointed his finger at the pair. "Now, I don't want you both to think we're goin' to do everythin' by vote from here on in, but just this once I'm goin' to let you give it a try. Make the rounds in Hogtown tonight, then we'll rotate the duty after that."

"Thanks, Sheriff!" Curly exclaimed as he pumped Sam Peabody's hand. "I won't let you down, I promise!"

"Take it easy, Curly. I may need that hand later," the sheriff responded. "Besides, you may not take it as such a favor if you get your butt shot off tonight."

Curly disengaged himself from the sheriff and managed to look like a little boy who had been caught with his hand in the cookie jar. Although somewhat abashed, Curly could not completely contain his excitement or his gratitude to Horton for the role with which he was expected to be entrusted.

"When're you goin' to make your rounds?" the sheriff asked Jim.

"Thought maybe we'd hit the Golden Palace around eight, then check out the other places at random, maybe half tonight and' the rest later on in the week. When we're done, we'll come back here, then check again later after they're supposed to shut down for the night. Does that suit you?"

"It's fine with me. I'll plan on bein' on this side of the creek bed nearby if you need some help. If I hear gunfire, I'll come arunnin'."

"It'd be better if you stayed put, Sheriff," Jim said. "Then we won't be likely to shoot you by mistake. Besides, if there's trouble, you couldn't cross the creek an' get to us in time to help. If you hear shots, I'd be obliged if you'd come back here an' wait. If we don't show up soon after, you can fetch the undertaker in the mornin'."

The sheriff thought about that for a minute, then reluctantly agreed to the plan. The two deputies put on their hats and coats, picked up their shotguns and made their way out of the jail and into the snow-filled night.

After all the planning and anticipation, the first night under law and order in Hogtown was a real letdown. Simpson was polite but cool to the deputies, and Horton could find nothing wrong with the roulette wheels. The crowd was noisy but not sullen; in fact, they hardly noticed the lawmen as they made their way from table to table. The other twelve establishments that the deputies checked were equally docile.

Only two things Horton found noteworthy during his rounds. The first was the absence of Del Jackson. Jim was a little uneasy because he could not account for the man and he was sure that if there was going to be any trouble Jackson would be right in the middle of it. The second instance was bumping into Morton Witherspoon on the street in front of Miss Ellie's former establishment. The banker mumbled a vague apology and hurried off in the direction to town, clearly embarrassed at having been found in such a place. Horton wondered idly if Witherspoon would tell his wife that he'd been working late at the bank. He also wondered if she'd believe him.

By two a.m. Hogtown looked deserted, and Horton felt both relieved and troubled. He was relieved because there had been no need to force compliance with the new rules, and he was troubled that the confrontation he knew would surely take place was still to come. He pondered the possibilities as he made his way back to the hotel.

As he was about to enter his room, he noticed a light coming from under Myrna Meloy's door. On impulse he walked softly down the hall and rapped gently on her door.

Myrna flung open the door and, when she saw who was standing there, flung herself into Jim's arms. He could feel the heat of her through the thin nightgown that she wore, and the pressure of her body against his excited him.

"Jim! I was so worried about you!" she exclaimed as she pulled down his head and kissed him soundly.

Horton found himself returning her kiss with ardor. After what seemed like forever and yet at the same time only an instant, they broke apart, both a little breathless from their passion. Myrna was the first to recover and, taking Jim by the hand, led him into the room. He closed the door behind them.

Jim tried to speak but words seemed to clog in his throat. He moved as if he were in a trance, and in moments he found himself in Myrna's bed. Myrna leaned over the bed and kissed him gently, then stood back and pulled the nightgown over her head. Myrna blew out the lamp and slid into Jim's waiting arms. Neither of them knew or cared that the snow had stopped falling.

Light flooding through the windows finally succeeded in waking Jim. He was a little disoriented at first until he felt Myrna stir beside him. He felt a twinge of excitement as he looked at her sleeping there, her long red hair spilling across the white pillow like a fiery stream. There had been little time for talk the night before and indeed there had been little reason to talk. The events of last night had complicated his life and he felt a need to talk now, but he was reluctant to wake Myrna.

Jim slipped quietly out of bed and retrieved his clothes which were scattered across the floor from the bed to the room that served as a parlor. He dressed quickly and silently let himself out into the hall, taking his shotgun with him as he went.

Back in his own suite of rooms, Jim kicked himself mentally for being ten different kinds of a fool. He had not yet resolved his feelings about Sonja and here he was getting involved with Myrna. And involved with her he truly was. He knew that there was no way that he could see her, touch her, talk with her, or even smell her perfume without wanting to take her to his bed, and from her ardor last night he knew that it would be no different for her. He could either leave for Denver now or spend the winter sharing a bed with Myrna, and he knew as he thought it that there really was no choice at all. He found himself hoping that there would be a late spring.

Jim managed to get cleaned up and shaved without cutting his throat, which he considered to be a major achievement given his mental state at the time. He put on his coat and hat, and with some difficulty, forced thoughts of Myrna from his mind as he made his way down the stairs and into the street. It was mid-morning and the town was busy. Jim dodged a couple of freight wagons and walked around several knots of men as he traveled the two blocks to the cafe for a late breakfast. Several people looked at him curiously as he passed, for they were not used to seeing lawmen with sawed-off shotguns walking down Main Street. Horton suspected that before spring came, they would become very used to it.

Chapter 12

The next two days passed without incident. The establishments in Hogtown were complying with the rules laid down by Sheriff Peabody and there had not been a shooting or a knifing in three days. Everybody agreed that this was some sort of a record. It was also noted that the crowds were thinning in Hogtown and that ticket sales at the train station were up. Prospectors and miners holing up for the winter were beginning to look for more wide-open towns in which to blow their money. Few people in Ruxford were sorry to see them go, primarily because little of the money was spent anywhere else but in the saloons and brothels of Hogtown. There was one very unhappy man there, however. Will Simpson spent an inordinate amount of time watching the train station platform through a spyglass whenever a train came in from Denver.

On the morning of the third day, Jim arrived late again at the cafe for breakfast. It was nearly ten o'clock and the town was teeming with people as usual. As he made his way through the crowd, the men smiled and tipped their hats to him. A few came over and shook his hand or patted him on the back. The ladies looked at him coyly and batted their eyelashes. Word of his affair with Myrna had taken less time to spread around town than it took to tell it. Jim found that he was a celebrity, and it rankled him considerably.

Oddly enough, Myrna was being treated with more respect than ever. It was almost as if the town decided that she deserved a reward for having been lusted after unsuccessfully by every male in town for all these years, and Horton was that reward. The married ladies of the town breathed considerably easier knowing that Myrna Meloy was finally spoken for. Myrna just ignored the whole situation and almost everyone admired her all the more for it.

Jim entered the cafe, removed his coat, and took his usual seat against the wall where he could keep an eye on the doors. He laid the shotgun across the arms of the chair to his right, where it would be handy if he needed it and slipped his hat and coat onto the seat beneath it. By the time he had settled in good, the younger of Dooly's daughters had brought him a steaming cup of coffee and had disappeared again into the kitchen. A few minutes later Dooly hobbled out carrying a platter of steak, eggs, fried potatoes, and biscuits with butter leaking out from their centers.

"Steak's a little rarer than usual," the old man advised, trying with little success to keep a smile from his face. The result of his effort was something between a grin and a grimace. "Never know when a man's gonna need his strength," he added as he winked meaning-fully.

Jim looked at him sharply, then decided to say the hell with it. If Myrna could ignore it, he could too. "You're right, old man. I never know when I'm goin' to have to slap around some smart-assed old cook," he said smiling.

"Yeah, but you better be careful. Them old cooks can be a whole lot tougher than they look," the old man responded.

"Kind of like this here steak?" Horton asked innocently as he poked the piece of meat with his fork.

The cafe owner barked out one of his frequent laughs and slapped the table. "Yer absolutely right, young feller. Did I tell you that one before?"

"You an' half the folks in Texas. That one was old when dinosaurs was roamin' the earth an' you were a young fella yourself."

"Sassy! Everybody's gettin' sassy these days," the old man grumbled good-naturedly as he threaded his way through the maze of tables and chairs on his way back to the kitchen.

Jim attacked his food hungrily. As always, it was excellent. He was just mopping up the last of the grease with his biscuit when Dooly's daughter showed up at his elbow with a wedge of hot apple pie that had to be at least four inches wide. Sugar and cinnamon covered the golden crust.

"Papa said you'd be wantin' this, sir." she said as she set the pie down beside the now-empty platter. "Watch that you don't burn yourself. It's hot from the oven." For some unexplained reason she found it necessary to stand so close to him while she was delivering the pie that he could feel the pressure of her hip against his arm and, as she bent over the table, view the cleavage of her bosom through a gap in her dress made possible by two or three buttons that had somehow managed to come undone. Jim wondered idly if every woman in town had managed to come into heat at exactly the same time.

Horton managed to eat the pie without exploding, then paid his bill and walked down to the office, feeling bloated every step of the way. He vowed that in the future he would show a little more restraint where food was concerned.

When he entered the jail, a loud voice assaulted his ears. "Well, the deputy finally made it to work, an' about time, too, what with all the lawlessness in the streets an' all."

Jim's eyes were still adjusting from the glare of the sun on the snow outside to the relative gloom of the jail's interior, but he could recognize that voice anywhere.

"Marcus, you old curly wolf! What are you doin' here?" he exclaimed as he moved quickly across the room and put a bearhug on his older brother.

"If you'll quit tryin' to break my ribs, I'll tell you," the older man managed to gasp. "Damned if you ain't gettin' strong in your old age."

Jim released his brother, tossed his hat and coat in a chair and pulled up another next to the stove. Marcus pulled up a third one and sat down next to Jim.

"It's like this," Marcus said as he settled back into his chair. "When Matthew got that there telegram inquirin' into your character, or lack of it, I went an' figured that you'd gone an' got yourself cross-threaded with the law again. After talkin' with Sam here," he said, gesturing towards the sheriff, "damned if I didn't find out that I was right. Seems like I can't let you out of my sight for a minute without you gettin' involved in somethin' you can't handle."

"Now that ain't exactly the whole truth," the sheriff interjected from behind his battered oak desk. "He managed to get himself outta jail right quick. Off hand, I'd say that the man can take care of himself pretty good. If he couldn't, he wouldn't be wearin' one of my badges."

"Sam, he's worn 'em before an' it aint never kept him outta trouble yet," Marcus advised. "I suppose I'd better hang around for a while just in case you an' him need some help."

Jim looked at his brother. "If you're serious about stayin', we could sure use your help. Has Sam told you what we're up against?"

"Heaven knows he had enough time. I've never known you to be so slow gettin' outta bed. You been feelin' poorly lately?" Marcus asked with a twinkle in his eye.

"I'm given' you fair warnin', big brother, an' I mean every word. Don't you start on me, too. I don't need any more grief from you. How about givin' me a straight answer just one time in your life?" Jim demanded testily.

"Sorry, brother. I didn't know you was so damned touchy. Yeah, Sam told me what's goin' on. Fact is, I was fixin' to ask him for a job when you come stompin' in."

"Sure like to have you, Marcus," the sheriff said, "but the city fathers won't allow me to pay three deputies."

"You don't need to pay him, Sam," Jim said. "Marcus doesn't really need the money anyway. He probably brought enough to keep himself from starvin' to death for a week or two."

"Say, Marcus, just how big is that little spread that Jim keeps talkin' about, anyway?" Curly asked from the corner of the room closest to the cells.

"Oh, I'd say around a hundred, give or take a few," Marcus answered modestly.

"A hundred ain't very much to make a livin' for two growed men off of," Curly stated. "Why, out here ten- or fifteen-thousand-acre ranches ain't all that unusual."

"In Texas we measure the size of a ranch in sections," Jim instructed Curly. "There's six hundred an' forty acres to a section, or one square mile, whichever way you want to figure. Even so, there's a bunch of spreads bigger than ours."

"A hundred square miles?" Curly asked incredulously. "An' you want a job as a deputy sheriff? Man, you've got to be plumb crazy!"

"Runs in the family, Curly," Marcus said. "If there's goin' to be trouble involvin' my brother, I'd just as soon be alongside him than standin' on the sidelines. Fact is that he don't shoot none too straight an' I might get hurt by accident if I ain't standin' real close."

Anything further that Marcus might have said was cut off by Jim, who shoved out his foot and upset the chair in which Marcus was balancing preciously. Marcus and the chair crashed to the floor.

"If you get shot by me, brother, you can count on it not bein' no accident. Why don't you get up off the floor? You look pretty damn silly down there."

Marcus got up and dusted himself off, then righted the chair and sat down again. "One of these days, brother, one of these days ...," he warned, not exactly joking as he spoke.

"One of these days you're going to shut that big mouth of yours an' quit pickin' on your kin," Jim advised him. "You ain't nearly as funny as you think you are."

Marcus sat quietly for a moment, then suddenly smiled broadly and stuck out his hand. "Maybe you're right, brother. I'm sorry if I rubbed your hair the wrong way. Let's forget it an' start over."

Jim took the offered hand. "That's fine with me. It's just possible that I've been a little thin-skinned myself. I'm really glad you're here. I don't know about these two, but I can sure use your help."

"Now that you done kissed an' made up, suppose I swear your brother in, Jim, an' then you can take him down to the hotel an' get him a room. Think you can handle that?" the sheriff asked.

Jim nodded and the sheriff swore in Marcus. After a few more minutes of conversation, Jim and Marcus left the jail and headed for the Excelsior Hotel.

"Marcus, there's somethin' goin' on here that you don't know about," Jim said as they walked along the street.

"I know that you've met a lady, if that's what you mean," Marcus said, grinning broadly. "Fact is, I wouldn't be surprised if word hadn't gotten all the way to Texas by this time."

"It's a little more than that. She owns the hotel. If she knows who you are, you won't be allowed to pay for anything. Now, don't get any ideas," Jim added quickly. "It's none of my doin'. Seth did her a favor back in Benton, an' she won't take a dime from any Horton. At least, that's what she says. Besides, I got a feelin' that we'd be better off if folks around here don't know who you really are. I can't put my finger on the reason yet, but maybe it'll come to me. I'd be pleased if you'd just go along with me on this."

"You want me to use another name, is that it?"

"That's it. Like I said, I couldn't tell you why if my life depended on it. All I got is a feelin', an' it's a strong one. Will you humor me about this one?"

"You've had these feelin's before, Jim, an' I can't remember a time when you was wrong. I'm your old boyhood pal Marcus Smith, 'Smitty' to you. That suit you?"

"I appreciated it, Marcus. I'll tell the sheriff an' Curly when I get back to the office. Anybody else know who you are?"

"Not that I know of. I went straight from the station to the jail. Thought that I'd find you in it, not workin' for it."

"Sorry to disappoint you. Did you bring any bags along?"

"At the station, Jim. I'll collect them later. Tell me, am I likely to run across any more Smiths around here?"

"There's one or two on this side of the creek an' a couple of hundred on the other side," Jim guessed. "I doubt that anyone'll question you about the name."

The two men remained silent for the rest of the walk to the hotel. Inside, Jim got Marcus registered and was starting for the stairs when Myrna came out of the dining room.

"Jim! What a pleasant surprise! What are you doing here at this time of day?" she asked as she walked over and took his arm.

As he always did whenever he was near her, Jim felt his heart beat faster. "An old friend of mine's come to town. He's goin' to be a new deputy here." Jim introduced the two, then cut the conversation off and took his brother upstairs to his room. Myrna watched them until they disappeared around the corner at the top landing, then went about her business.

"She's a real beauty!" Marcus exclaimed when they had closed the door, "How'd you ever find a woman like that in a town like Ruxford?"

"Pure luck, but as beautiful as she is, she's still part of a big problem for me. Maybe I'll tell you about it later. Right now, I've got to get back to the jail an' relieve Curly. Why don't you get settled in an' meet me back there a little before eight tonight? I'll take you over an' introduce you to some of the other Smiths in Hogtown."

When Marcus agreed, the two brothers parted company and Jim walked back to the jail. He took special care to avoid Myrna on his way out of the hotel. He was all too aware that if he saw her again, there was a very good chance that he would be late showing up for work. Jim thought that he had enough problems without taking any more ribbing from Sam and Curly.

Chapter 13

Five days after leaving Ruxford, Del Jackson returned on the early morning train from Denver with four men he had been sent to hire. They were tough men who had long made their way with their guns. Frog Mayeaux met the men at the station and led them through the nearly deserted streets to the edge of Hogtown, where Mayeaux had discovered an empty shack near the cliffs. Mayeaux had stocked the place with provisions and Jackson repeated Simpson's instructions that the men must stay out of sight until they were needed. The men had no objections; they were being paid whether they worked or not.

Jackson and Mayeaux went from the shack directly to the Golden Palace to report the men's arrival to Simpson. The saloon owner dismissed Mayeaux and gestured for Jackson to take a seat. Simpson sat on the edge of his desk as the gunman related the significant parts of the trip. When he finished, Simpson brought him up to date on the events in Hogtown, including the mass exodus of patrons and the hiring of a third deputy.

"Do you think that the four men you hired are good enough to take these lawmen?" Simpson asked.

"I know Kelly an' Schmidt pretty well," Jackson answered. "They're good, dependable men you can count on to follow orders. They won't back away from a fight, either. Dawson an' the other guy, Fowler, I never heard of. They seem reliable enough, an' Kelly vouches for 'em, so I guess they'll do. What bothers me is that these four law dogs are never together all at once. That means that we've got to stage two ambushes at once or keep ambushin' 'til we get them all. The surest way would be two ambushes at the same time, an' for that we need more men to be absolutely sure. I could go back to Denver an' ...."

"No, we can't wait that long," Simpson interrupted. "Every day we wait people leave Hogtown for places where the law isn't interested in cramping a man's style. Business this week has been less than half of what it was, and pretty soon we'll be doing good just to make expenses."

"Then Mayeaux an' I'll have to go along, too. We could get Fowler an' Mayeaux to stage a fight an' have somebody go after the law to stop it. The other boys an' I could be waitin' for 'em an' gun 'em down when they cross the bridge into Hogtown. That's when the lawmen will be easiest to get at. We get the others when they come after the first ones. The only thing is, we better have the fight in somebody else's place. They might get suspicious if something like that started here."

Simpson thought about the plan for a minute and could find little wrong with it. He did veto Jackson's involvement in it, however.

"You set it up but get one of the other boys to go along. If anything goes wrong, I don't want you or Mayeaux involved with the shooting. Send Fowler along with the other three, but wait until just before eight, when two of the lawmen will start to make their rounds. That way, there will be no need to start a fight or send for the law. There will be no warning at all," Simpson said as he rubbed his hands together in anticipation. "If we're careful, no one will know who started what. I think that you and Mayeaux ought to be on the main floor of the Palace where any number of people can swear you never left the place. I want you to do it tonight, too."

"It'd be better if we did it tomorrow. We'd have more time to set it up an' give us a better chance to get 'em all," Jackson advised.

"Do it tonight!" Simpson exclaimed. "Every day we wait costs us money. Scout the place and brief the men. They'll do the job that they were hired to do. You do yours!"

Jackson came out of his chair like he had been propelled by a catapult. He grabbed Simpson by the lapels, pulled him off the desk and slammed him against the wall with enough force to knock a picture to the floor.

"Don't you dare tell me how to do my job. If you don't like the way I do it, you could always try doin' it yourself," he spat. "Of course, that would take some guts."

Suddenly Jackson felt something cold under his chin and heard the click of a hammer being cocked.

"Let go, Jackson," Simpson said coldly.

Jackson did as he was told, and Simpson moved the Derringer in his hand so that Jackson could peer directly into its twin muzzles.

"You've underestimated me, Jackson," Simpson said menacingly. "I've done my own dirty work before. Now I hire trash like you to do it for me. You'll do what I tell you when I tell you or you'll be just a vulgar, unpleasant memory. Now get out of my office and take care of those lawmen tonight, like I told you."

Jackson's hands trembled a little, more from anger than from fear, but he managed to mutter, "Yes, sir," before he turned and left the office. He knew Simpson was right. He had underestimated the man badly, and it had nearly cost him his life. He promised himself that he would never make that mistake again.

Jackson spent the rest of the day setting up the events for that night. He briefed Kelly and the rest of the men, then left them to prepare themselves for the killings.

The plan was quite simple and therefore had a good chance for success. One man would cover the bridge over Crystal Creek while the other three waited in ambush about four hundred yards away, on the near edge of Hogtown. The deputies would cross the bridge, Jackson reasoned, and go directly to the main street. When the lawmen were within fifty to severity-five yards of the town, the ambush would be sprung. If, for some reason, one of the lawmen escaped the ambush and tried to get away, the man covering the bridge would get him as he headed back to the jail. If everything went according to plan, the three men in the ambush would move forward to a second position two hundred yards from the bridge. When reinforcements came from town, they would be caught between the one man at the bridge and the second ambush. After that, there should be no law left in Ruxford. As Jackson headed back to the Golden Palace, he could swear that Hogtown was holding its breath.

Jim and Marcus ate dinner with Myrna in the Excelsior's dining room, then made their way to the jail. It was a fine, cold night, with the temperature hovering just above zero. The moon was about three-quarters full, and visibility was not much reduced from daylight. Stores were mostly closed along the main street, and the stillness of the night was broken occasionally by the yapping of a dog who thought that his privacy had been invaded. The two brothers kicked snow from their boots on the doorsill and entered the jail, shedding coats and hats as they closed the door. Curly and the sheriff were already there.

"Glad you boys could make it," the sheriff called from behind his desk. "Seems like you get later every night."

"Just about didn't come at all," Marcus said. "I can tell you that our dinner companion was a whole lot nicer to be around than you two. Smells better, too. What she sees in Jim, here, is beyond me. If he said ten words at dinner, I'd be surprised."

"Couldn't get a word in, Sam," Jim explained. "Marcus never stopped flappin' his mouth the whole time. We'll all know when he dies. The silence will deafen us."

Marcus was about to reply when they heard a knock on the door a moment before it opened and Cleary slipped into the room.

"What do you want?" the sheriff asked crossly.

"I know that you don't think much of me, Sheriff," the big man said, "what with me workin' for King an' now Simpson, but a man's gotta eat. Whether you believe it or not, I ain't never done nothin' foul or low-down to anybody in this town, an' you ought to treat a man with a might more respect."

"You here to give me a lecture or have you got some business to conduct?" the sheriff responded, clearly not impressed with Cleary's words. "Make up your mind. I ain't got all day."

"You ain't got any manners, neither," Cleary observed, "but I'm gonna say what I come to say, irregardless. Somethin's wrong in Hogtown. Jackson's back from Denver, an' him an' Simpson's nervouser'n a long-tailed cat in a room full of rockin' chairs. Mayeaux is actin' queerer'n usual, too. Everybody's tight-lipped an' not talkin' to nobody. It may not be nothin', but I thought you ought to know. I gotta be gettin' back before I'm missed," the big man said as he turned and reached for the door latch.

"Cleary, I'm sorry I shot off my face," the sheriff said. "I 'preciate what you've told me. Thanks."

Cleary looked over his shoulder at the sheriff, a grin spreading across his ugly features. "You welcome, Sheriff. I hope it ain't nothin' to worry about, but if it is, then good luck." A moment later he was gone.

"Now what do you make of that, boys?" the sheriff asked the other three men. "You think he's settin' us up for somethin' or what?"

"Cleary's a simple man, Sam," Jim said. "I don't think he's got what it takes to be a good liar, an' I don't think he was lyin' to us tonight. I think we're goin' to have to act like Simpson an' his crowd have somethin' planned for us tonight." The other two deputies nodded in agreement.

"Is there any other way into Hogtown except for the bridge?" Marcus asked.

"The bridge is it in this weather," the sheriff said with a questioning look on his face. "Why?"

"I think that tonight would be a real good time to make a change in our routine, is all. Maybe go early or an hour or two later, so anyone who's waitin'' will be damned stiff an' cold," Marcus offered.

The sheriff thought about what Marcus had said, then asked the others for their thoughts. Each spoke his mind. The sheriff looked at his watch, then issued very careful instructions to each of the men. There was some discussion among themselves after that, then they settled back to wait.

Shortly after nine o'clock that night, four figures emerged from the shadows at the back of the jail and made their way stealthily towards the bridge. All four wore white, poncho-like covers made of sheets and belted at the waist, making them more difficult to see against the snow. Each man was also carrying a carbine instead of his usual shotgun. They moved in two separate teams, each covering the other while it moved in short bounds. Progress was slow, but the men were in no hurry that night.

At the bridge, one team covered the other as it crossed, then the second team turned and followed the creek bed, heading for the back of the buildings fronting on the only street in Hogtown. The first team made directly for the main street, the men keeping about ten yards between them as they went. Nobody rushed and the men walked without talking or making any discernible noise.

Jake Fowler sat in the snow in his position overlooking the bridge. His teeth were chattering so badly that he was afraid that they would break. He cursed Jackson for sending him out there and leaving him without relief for more than an hour, and he cursed the weather that had long-since robbed him of any feeling in his feet and ears. He had his hands stuck inside his coat, up under his armpits, trying to keep them warm enough to squeeze a trigger when the time came. He wanted a smoke so badly that he could shout, and he had about decided to take a chance and roll one when he saw a dark shape loom over him.

Fowler jumped in alarm and tried to jerk his hands out from inside his coat. His rifle slipped from his knees into the snow, and he had just enough time to lose control of his bladder before Marcus slid his Bowie knife into his neck. Steam rose from his body as Marcus eased him into the snow. He wiped the blade on the dead man's coat and returned it to its sheath, then moved on towards the rear of the buildings looming before him in the distance.

"You have any trouble with him?" the sheriff whispered.

"No, he was so cold that he wasn't payin' any attention. I swear I heard his teeth clickin' down by the bridge," Marcus whispered back. The two men moved on into the night.

Jim and Curly were about a hundred yards from the edge of Hogtown when flame lanced out of the darkness directly in front of them. Jim felt a giant hand grab his coat and spin him to the left, sending him sprawling into the snow. He heard Curly give a grunt of pain and watched him fall backwards into the snow a few yards to his left.

Jim swung to face the direction from which the shots had come, slapped his Winchester to his shoulder, and fired three shots at the next blossom of flame he saw. He was rewarded with a scream of pain. More shots filled the night, and he felt a slug hit the heel of his boot, numbing the foot. He fired again into the shadows from which he had received some fire and saw that Curly was firing, too. No more shots were fired at them and Jim called to Curly to cease firing.

Silence descended over Hogtown as even the piano players in the saloons paused in response to the gunfire. Ten seconds elapsed, then there was a second volley of shots, this time from pistols, fired from someplace further into the town. That was the end of the shooting.

Jim tried to stand and found that a rifle bullet had removed a sizable portion of his right boot heel without damaging his foot. His left side was starting to burn, too, but he chose not to investigate that just then. He really didn't want to know what he might find.

He hobbled over to Curly, who had managed to roll over onto his back but could not sit up. Jim tore open the sheet to get at Curly's coat, unbuttoned it, and examined the wound high up in Curly's chest. Curly looked up at him, asked him how bad it was, then passed out before Jim could answer. There was little blood in evidence and none at all foaming from Curly's mouth, so Jim decided that Curly's lung had not been touched. He felt Curly's back and could not find an exit wound.

Just then Marcus hollered from the shadows behind the closest of the building to announce that he and the sheriff were approaching. Jim watched as the two men walked across the snow and knelt beside Curly.

"Bad?" the sheriff asked.

"Bad enough, Sam. What did you find over there?"

"You an' Curly got two of the jaspers, an' I got a third in the next alley over. Seems that he'd had enough an' was headed out. Marcus got a fourth down by the creek," the sheriff answered.

"Any able to talk?"

"'Nary a one, I'm afraid," Sam said as he shook his head. "What's worse, I don't recognize any of the three up here. I'll look at the one that Marcus fetched, but I'll bet that he's new in town, too."

"After what Cleary said, do you really doubt who's behind this?" Jim asked.

"I know as well as you," the sheriff responded, "but provin' it's somethin' else. I sure wish I could, but I just can't do it."

Jim grunted in disgust. "Can you get Curly back over the creek an' to the doctor's? I think Marcus an' me ought to finish the rounds."

Sam nodded and motioned over a pair of men from the group of gawkers that had begun to collect. The men picked Curly up carefully and followed the sheriff back to Ruxford.

"What's on your mind, brother?" Marcus inquired softly as the two men started walking down the street.

Jim finished reloading his carbine before he answered. "I think that we ought to pay Simpson a visit. The fact is, we owe it to him. To my way of thinkin', it ought to be a painful experience for him. Cover me while I have my chat, will you?"

Marcus nodded in agreement, then took up station to the rear and slightly to the left of his younger brother. The two men went directly to the Golden Palace, kicked in the front door, and walked to the center of the room.

Del Jackson shouldered his way through the crowd and blocked the lawmen's way. "Hold it right there, Deputy. What do you want in here?" he asked belligerently, his hand easing under his coat to where he carried a pistol.

"Is Simpson upstairs?" Jim asked angrily.

"Yeah, but he's busy right now. Come back tomorrow, same time," he smirked.

Marcus had been standing to one side, his left hand on the forearm of the carbine and his right grasping the stock at the wrist, much in the way a soldier would hold a rifle at port arms. Marcus pivoted to the left and straightened his right arm violently, driving the butt of the carbine into Jackson's face. The blow broke Jackson's jaw and showered bystanders with shards of broken teeth and pieces of shattered bridgework.

"Go ahead, Jim. I'll bet that Simpson can work you into his schedule now," Marcus said.

As if by magic, a path opened before him in the crowd and Jim stepped over the unconscious Jackson as he made his way slowly to the stairs leading up to Simpson's office. Marcus, walking behind him, noticed that a fresh drop or two of blood appeared on the steps as Jim climbed the stairs. It took him a moment to realize that Jim had been hit in the ambush at the edge of town.

Jim paused beside Simpson's door, turned the knob, and stepped quickly through the doorway. Simpson looked up from his desk and started to reach for the pistol he had laying on top of some paper.

"Go ahead, Simpson, pick it up," Jim said almost pleadingly. "Just give me an excuse."

Simpson's hand snapped back to his side, and he stood up to face Jim. "No need for me to do that, Deputy. I do not want any trouble with the law. You startled me, that's all," he said as he tried unsuccessfully to smile.

"We had a little trouble tonight, Simpson. Do you know anything about it?"

"Not me. Like I said, I don't want any trouble with the law," Simpson fawned. "I see that you handled it, whatever it was."

"Yeah, we took care of it, but the sheriff told you that he was holdin' you accountable over here. He spoke for me, too," Horton said as he moved within a step of Simpson. "When we get trouble, you get it, too." With that, Jim unleashed a powerful looping right that caught the surprised Simpson flush on the nose and knocked him backwards over the desk chair and onto the floor.

Simpson rolled over and got to his hands and knees, where he paused for a moment to shake his head in an attempt to clear it. Blood ran freely from his shattered nose.

"Whaa ...," he started to say, but the sound changed into a grunt as Jim delivered a kick to his side that snapped at least one rib. Simpson rolled onto his side as he fought to catch his breath. Horton reached down, grabbed him by the shirtfront, and hauled the barely conscious man to his feet.

"Hear me good, little man," Jim snarled menacingly. "Against my better judgment, you're still alive. Curly got shot up tonight, an' I think that you're behind it. If anything else happens to any lawman in Ruxford, we'll be back to introduce you to some serious pain before we hang you. If Curly dies, I'll kill you myself. I want you to take that as a promise. You understand me?"

Simpson nodded mutely. He did not trust his voice.

Jim let go of Simpson's shirt, turned and walked out of the office. Marcus trailed along close behind. The saloon was absolutely still. The two lawmen walked slowly through the crowd and back out onto the street. Once outside, Marcus turned to Jim and said, "You seem to be leakin' some blood, boy. You hurt bad?"

"I don't know yet. My left side's on fire. Since I'm still on my feet, I reckon that I'll live." In spite of that reassurance, the two men walked as rapidly as they could directly to the doctor's office.

Sheriff Peabody met the pair in the outer office. "Doc's in there with Curly. He got the bullet out an' he thinks that the boy might make it."

"That's good news," Marcus said, "but we got us another patient. Jim picked up a little souvenir out there, too."

The two men helped Jim strip off his pancho, coat, and shirt. The wound was below the ribs and above the hip, in the meaty part of the side, about three inches lower than the scar left by the Utes a few weeks before. While the wound had bled freely and was obviously painful, it was not serious, at least not to Jim's experienced eye.

The doctor chose that moment to come out of his surgery. "Curly'll be fine if nothing else happens to him, like a fever or pneumonia." He spied Jim's bloody side and said, "What's this, another customer? Let's have a look at that." The doctor poked and prodded around while Jim winced.

"Sorry about that," the doctor said. "It looks clean enough. I'll clean it up a little more and bandage it. You need to spend a couple of days off your feet, preferably in bed."

"Oh, he'll just love that!" Marcus exclaimed as he leered at his brother.

Jim shot Marcus an angry look, then followed the doctor into the surgery. Maybe a couple of days in bed wouldn't be so bad after all, he mused.

Chapter 14

The Great Shootout, as it came to be known, was the last attempt to rebel against Sam Peabody's ordinances, at least for that winter. The Christmas season was quiet, and 1879 found more than a dozen fewer saloons and brothels in Hogtown. Will Simpson, his boyish good looks forever marred by a nose that looked like it belonged on a very old prize-fighter, kept Hogtown in line with his crew of thugs. He compensated for his dwindling revenues by increasing his percentage of the take from the other saloon keepers, madams, pimps, and assorted gougers. This increase was in large part responsible for the number of businessmen who locked their doors and quietly took the train for friendlier and more profitable towns.

Del Jackson spent nearly two months with his head strapped in a contraption designed to immobilize his jaw so that it could heal properly. When he emerged from that ordeal, the madness in his eyes never again quite left him. Even Simpson was a little afraid of him and took pains not to antagonize the gunman.

Jackson took great interest in everything Jim Horton said or did and on two or three occasions, the gunman made stealthy trips to Ruxford to spy on him. On one of those trips, he saw Horton in the company of Myrna. Jackson recognized Myrna from years before, and he decided that his revenge on Horton should somehow include Myrna Meloy.

Frog Mayeaux had taken over as the segundo for Simpson while Jackson was healing. It was said that he was reluctant to hand the reins of power back to Del Jackson. One morning in mid-January, Frog Mayeaux did not show up for work and, in fact, was never seen in town again. No one seemed to mourn his passing.

Curly survived his wound, but his recovery was not quick. About six weeks after the gunfight, he showed up one morning at the jail and turned in his badge. It was not that Curly had lost his courage. It was more that he had discovered that he did not need the badge to be a man. He offered to help the sheriff out if Sam ever needed him, and Sam took him up on the offer. Curly had grown up at last.

Jim Horton spent two days in bed after the shootout, Myrna Meloy never left his side, although the need for round-the-clock nursing was never firmly established. A tired and depleted Jim Horton showed up for work on the third day, seemingly none the worse for his experience. He took it upon himself to solve the now-infamous bank robbery mystery. The progress was not particularly fast.

Al Cleary moved across Crystal Creek three days after the shootout. He claimed that he'd had enough of Simpson and his crew and that he'd rather starve in Ruxford than get fat in Hogtown. Sam Peabody remembered the favor that Cleary had done the lawman and offered him Curly's job on a temporary basis until the wounded lawman was able to come back to work. Cleary accepted the offer after some deliberation, and the job became permanent when Curly resigned. Although Cleary was not a fast thinker, he proved to be an honest and dependable deputy who was quite content with his lot.

Jim and Marcus spent a lot of their spare time planning for the spring. Jim thought at first that he would only try to recover the cached gold, but after discussing the matter with Marcus, the two of them devised a plan to return to the mine and work the vein until August. Then they would shut down the operation for good, even if the vein proved to be rich and still productive. They also decided that Marcus would go back to Benton towards the end of March and then meet back up with Jim at the Olsen's place during the first week of April. He was to bring a crew recruited from the main ranch in Texas. Marcus and the crew were to get off the train at Pine City, fifty miles south of Ruxford and avoid Ruxford entirely. Jim hoped that the plan would afford them some sort of secrecy. If it became known that a large crew was going into the hills to mine a strike, it wouldn't take very long before hundreds of others would be following close on their heels.

One thing the men did not want was a boom town surrounding their claim in the heart of the country.

Myrna Meloy was a party to the planning. Jim had finally told her that Marcus was his brother, and both men trusted her implicitly. She made many useful suggestions but made no mention of making more permanent the relationship that she so enthusiastically enjoyed with Jim. For his part, Jim enjoyed each day as it came and gave little thought to the fact that his departure in the spring also meant a departure from Myrna. He had not reconciled his affair with her and his feelings for Sonja, still far away in the mountains.

On the last day of February, Jim got to the jail early. He was in a miserable mood. He had not been able to make any headway with the bank robbery, and he was beginning to take the failure personally. That morning, he tacked some butcher paper to the back door of the jail and waited for the other deputies to come in. When the sheriff and the other two deputies finally got there, he called them over to the back door.

"I want to try somethin' with this bank robbery," he explained. "I'm going to write down everythin' I know about the robbery an' the people involved. I need you to add whatever you know. Maybe then some pattern will come out. I don't mind tellin' you that I'm gettin' desperate."

The lawman started out with theories about the robbery. Sam Peabody stated flatly that he'd wager his reputation that it was an inside job, and he supported that theory with the fact that the safe had been dialed open, not blasted apart as a safe cracker would have done. Jim wrote it all down with his pencil, then listed the names of the people who worked in the bank.

"There!" Jim exclaimed when he had finished. "Now, what do we know about these men? Jack Kirby's been at the bank for a long time an' Morton vouches for him. The bookkeeper is an old man an' couldn't have hauled off the gold. Morton Witherspoon is strong enough to have done it, an' there was a rumor that the bank was in trouble before the robbery."

"Steal from his own bank? Ain't that just a might far-fetched? Most of the money was his to begin with," Marcus stated.

"Actually, most of the gold belonged to Wells Fargo, not to Witherspoon or the bank," Jim said, correcting his brother.

"There's one more name that you ain't got up there yet, an' maybe you should," Al Cleary offered. "Will Simpson was at the bank for some time before he quit. He probably knew as much about the place as anybody workin' there now."

"But Witherspoon changed the combination on the safe every year. How could Simpson know what the new one was?" the sheriff asked. "I gotta admit that the idea of pinnin' the thing on Simpson appeals to me, though," he added hopefully.

"You're a lot smarter than me, Sheriff, but if I was Witherspoon, I'd write the new combination down an' put it where I knew where it was, just in case I forgot the numbers. Maybe Simpson knew the place where Witherspoon kept the paper. That is, if there was a paper, of course."

"That's an awful lot of 'ifs,' Cleary," the sheriff replied skeptically.

"But it makes sense an' it's a lot more than we had yesterday," Jim said. "Is there anythin' else that could tie Simpson to this or to Witherspoon?"

"You ever seen Simpson's hands?" the sheriff asked. "Do they look to you like they know what pick an' shovel work is?"

"His hands are softer'n a gambler's," Cleary offered. "If he's worked at prospectin', it ain't been no time lately."

"I'd better wire Denver an' check with the authorities," Marcus said. "Maybe they know somethin' about Simpson that we ain't learned, like when he struck it so all-fired rich."

"An' I need to check with Witherspoon to see about the chance that he wrote down the combination somewheres," Sam Peabody said. "Hot damn! Maybe we're beginnin' to get somewhere! Anybody got somethin' else to say?"

"Just one thing, an' I don't know if it's important or not," Cleary said hesitantly. "Simpson an' the banker was both sleepin' with the same woman over to Miss Ellie's. We all thought it was a good joke on ol' Mort. The woman's name was Lilly, an' she got herself killed about the time that Simpson left town. Maybe it's just one of them co ... what do you call 'em?"

"Coincidences," Marcus prompted the former bartender. "I don't believe in 'em much, myself. You may have somethin' there."

"I'd love to hang this job on Simpson, but I wonder if all this is makin' sense just because I dislike the man so much. Such things have been known to happen," Jim said as he smiled at Sam Peabody.

"You ain't never goin' to let me live that one down, are you?" the sheriff snorted.

"It makes my point, though, Sam. We'd better be damn sure before we try to put Simpson away for this. Let's see what else we can find out today an' we'll try this again tomorrow," Jim suggested.

The others agreed. Jim put on his hat and coat as he went out the door behind the sheriff. Both men headed for the bank.

Morton Witherspoon was pleasant enough at first, but he got a little huffy when Sam Peabody started asking questions about how things were done around the bank. "It's none of your business whether I wrote that combination down or not," Witherspoon said emphatically. "Are you suggesting that I'd be so stupid as to leave the combination to the bank's safe lying around where anyone could find it?"

"Now, Morton, don't get your balls in an uproar," the sheriff advised. "All we're tryin' to do is find some reason why the door's still on your safe. If we know for sure that the combination was wrote down somewheres, then maybe we won't have to believe that one of the bank's employees done the job."

The banker was somewhat mollified by the explanation. "Well," he said grudgingly, "I do have a little code system for the combination. It's over here on the calendar."

Witherspoon led the sheriff over to the wall calendar and flipped through the months until he came to December. Three dates were circled.

"These are the combination numbers. Someone would have to know the system, because I've got numbers circled on most of the months for birthdays, appointments, holidays, and that sort of thing."

"You been doin' this for long?" Jim asked.

"Twenty years or more. It's foolproof, I tell you," the banker insisted. "I'm the only person in the bank who knows about this besides you two, and when you leave I'll change the combination again."

"I suggest that you don't write it down on the wall this time," the sheriff said. "The only thing that still puzzles me is how the thief got into the building. You an' the head cashier got the only keys, you said."

"That's right. There's a spare in my desk at home, but the one here on my key chain and the one Mister Kirby keeps on his are the only ones that get used. I've never lost one and they are never out of my sight. I guarantee it."

The sheriff rubbed his chin and thought for a minute, then turned to Jim. "You got anythin' else you want to ask?" he asked the deputy.

"I guess not, Sam. I want to thank you for your time, Mister Witherspoon. You've been a big help. I hope that we won't have to bother you again."

The men shook hands. The two lawmen left the bank and walked back up the street towards the jail.

"I guess it's possible that Simpson somehow found out about Witherspoon's system for recordin' the combination," the sheriff said, "but how in blazes did he get into the buildin' without bustin' a window or a lock or somethin'?"

"The woman!" Jim exclaimed. "Damn it, it was right there in front of us all the time an' we never saw it!"

"What are you talkin' about, boy?" the sheriff asked.

"The connection between Witherspoon, Simpson, and the woman at Miss Ellie's. Everybody thought it was a big joke that those two were pokin' the same woman. What if Simpson talked her into makin' a wax impression of the key some night when Witherspoon's gettin' his ashes hauled, then Simpson makes another key an' kills his partner just to tie up loose ends?"

Sam thought about the theory as the two men walked along. After a while he spoke. "It could of happened just like you say. Everythin' fits, not too clean, but clean enough. But it bein' possible an' bein' able to prove it really happened that way are two different things. How are we goin' to do that? The woman's dead, an' it ain't likely that Simpson's goin' to volunteer any information that might hang him."

"You're right of course," Jim agreed. "Right now, maybe all we can do is wait an' see what the Denver sheriff says. It might pay us to check with Wells Fargo, too, while we're at it. Just maybe they've turned up somethin'."

The two men detoured to the Wells Fargo office, where they confirmed that all of the raw gold and almost all of the gold coin taken in the robbery had indeed belonged to Wells Fargo. The insurance company had hired the Pinkerton Agency to look into the matter, but the claim had been paid, however reluctantly. The lawmen learned nothing else of importance.

"Just like the damn Pinkertons," the sheriff snorted when they left the office. "Investigatin' the robbery an' never even checkin' with me. Those folks act like they're some kinda separate law to themselves. Why, I wouldn't ...."

"Like you said, Sam, don't get yourself in an uproar. They couldn't have found out any more than we have if the insurance company paid the claim."

"Yeah, I know, but it's the principle of the thing. We ought to be workin' together on this, not tryin' to outdo each other."

Jim nodded in agreement and the two men went back to the office, where they found Marcus and Cleary pondering the paper tacked to the back door. The sheriff told the pair what he and Jim had learned, then sat down behind his desk and put his feet up on the edge. In a few minutes his breathing slowed, and he started to snore gently.

"So, you think that Simpson did it," Marcus said softly.

"It's possible, maybe even probable. Everythin' fits so far, unless he's got an alibi in Denver. It still strikes me funny that rumors of the bank bein' in trouble stopped after it got robbed. It seems to me that the robbery should have started the rumors, not stopped 'em. Banks have even been known to close after a robbery of that size, but this one seems healthier than ever. It just don't make sense to me, brother," Jim explained.

"Maybe Witherspoon used his own money to make good the loss," Marcus suggested.

"But where would he store the money besides the safest place in town, his own bank safe? An' if he did store it somewhere else, why did he? Did he know that the bank was goin' to be robbed? Was he in it with Simpson?" Jim asked.

"If he was, then why'd someone have to kill Lilly?" Cleary interjected.

"Al's right," Marcus said. "'Pears to me that the case against Simpson gets weaker if you try to make it out that him an' the banker was in it together."

"All we've really got are a couple of theories," Jim lamented. "We'll see what the sheriff in Denver had to say. One thing's certain. Whoever did it was no fool. It was planned down to the last detail an' executed perfectly. I'm not so sure that Witherspoon's up to that kind of thing. He seems to be a little short of guts an' horse sense to me. I'm afraid that if somethin' else doesn't turn up, whoever pulled the robbery is goin' to get away with it."

The other two deputies discussed that for a while, then left to catch some sleep and get something to eat before the night patrol in Hogtown. Jim spent a long time talking to Myrna about the case, but she could add nothing more to what was already known. She and Jim ate an early supper, then went upstairs together. It was not surprising that all thoughts of the case evaporated from Jim's mind.

It took three days, but the sheriff in Denver finally responded to the wire Marcus had sent, and then the information turned out to be virtually useless. The sheriff had heard of Simpson only a few days before he left town with four gunmen, pimps, and assorted ne'er-do-wells. He was not sorry to see them go. The Denver lawman did not know when or how Simpson came into possession of his money, only that he had enough to hire the men he wanted. Simpson had not hired anyone, however, until the week after the robbery took place. The information fit the theory that Simpson was responsible for the robbery, but it was not conclusive enough for Sam Peabody to make an arrest.

Spring came early that year. By the end of the second week in March, patches of ground were showing through the snow, and the main street of Ruxford had been transformed into a sea of mud. The population of the town swelled as prospectors, miners, and the usual riffraff that always followed them stocked up in preparation for another try at stalking the elusive yellow metal. Marcus turned in his badge and headed for Texas to bring back a crew. He would also bring back sufficient pack animals to carry Jim's cache and whatever else they might be able to extract from the ground.

Sam Peabody hired another deputy to replace Marcus and Jim. Abner Bonesteel was from Sacramento and was trying to build up a stake before trying his luck in the mountains the following year. From what Jim could see, Ab appeared to be a pretty good man. He had worked as a deputy in other towns, so he quickly caught on to the routine.

As the March days passed quickly, Jim began to feel the excitement of his impending return to the mountains. In mid-March Jim went to Melethin's General Store and sought out Curly, who had taken a job there clerking. Jim offered him a job, and the younger man jumped at the chance. Curly had had enough of working behind a counter.

While Jim and Myrna continued their relationship on a day-by-day basis, as the day of his departure drew closer, he became increasingly aware of how strong his attachment to her had become.

On the morning that he was to leave, Jim sat on the edge of the bed and pulled on his boots. Myrna walked over to him, her dressing gown tied loosely at the waist. Jim pulled her to him.

"Part of me wants to leave an' part of me wants to stay," Jim said somewhat thickly. "That's never happened to me before."

"Let me guess which part of you wants to stay," Myrna said impishly as she disengaged herself from his arms and backed away from him. It took her a moment or two to pull her robe together and retie it.

Jim recognized her light-heartedness for what it was, an attempt to deal with what promised to be a difficult situation. He played along with her mood.

"You really are a lecherous old lady. I've been treatin' you way too good. An' unless I'm mistaken, all this high livin' this winter had caused you to put on a few pounds," he said appraisingly as he reached for her again.

"Sir! You take liberties!" she exclaimed in mock indignation as she cuffed his hands away. "You are a cruel man, Jim Horton! How could you say such a thing? I'll be glad when you're gone." She sobered quickly and said, "No, I don't really mean that. I'll be counting the days you're gone, and I promise that I'll lose the weight I've gained by the time you return in the fall," she said, the mischief showing again in her eyes.

"I'll be back by the end of August or the first part of September at the latest," Jim promised. "You can be sure that I'll not take a chance on being caught by the snow again. And I was just kidding you about the weight. I like you just the way you are."

They fell silent after that, and Jim finished dressing quickly. They embraced awkwardly, neither of them knowing what to say or how to say it. They finally broke apart and Jim walked out, Myrna went back to the bed and sat on the edge. A wave of apprehension struck her, and she struggled for a moment to subdue it, then recognized the futility of the attempt. She had a terrible premonition that Jim Horton was headed into mortal danger, and she was afraid that she would never see him alive again. "I'll be glad when this is over," she said to herself as yet another wave of despair swept over her. She started praying for Jim's safe return.

Simpson, Jackson, and the rest of the gang had not been idle. Business had picked up with the influx of prospectors preparing for the spring move to the mountains. There seemed to be some unwritten rule that a miner or prospector could not leave town with a dime in his pockets, and Simpson and his fellow businessmen were doing their best to enforce it.

Simpson had directed that Jackson keep a pair of men watching Horton to report back the moment that the lawman left town. Simpson was convinced by now that Horton had made a big strike, and he was gambling that Jim would lead him to the gold. Simpson then planned to keep the site under close watch and attack at the most opportune moment. He was determined to steal the gold and take over Horton's claim.

For Jim he had some special plans, which included being roasted over a slow fire if the opportunity ever presented itself. Whenever Simpson looked at his nose in the mirror, he vowed again that he would make that opportunity happen.

Chapter 15

Jim picked up Curly at the livery stable, and the pair rode along the muddy street past the train depot and on towards the Olsens' cabin. Jim was anxious to join up with the rest of the crew, but he was a little uneasy about seeing Sonja again. He wished that he could avoid the meeting, but the only way he could be sure of finding the cache of gold was by starting out from Ole's place.

The horse Jim was riding was an Appaloosa just young enough to be feeling his oats on that brisk spring morning but old enough to know when to stop the foolishness and get down to the business of covering ground. The dancing and snorting antics of the horse kept Jim's thoughts occupied for the first half-hour or so. After that he became intent on watching the terrain. He rode apart from Curly, yet still close enough to talk without shouting if the need arose. He studied the edge of the woods and the crests of the hills for signs of movement, always on the alert for some tell-tale sign of an ambush. His three years as a cavalryman for the Confederacy and the time he spent as a Texas Ranger had drilled the hard lessons of vigilance into him until it had become nearly automatic.

About ten miles from town, just as the two men were topping the ridge, an elk broke from a stand of trees and made off across the clearing, then disappeared into the wood line in front of them. The elk had not taken five steps before Jim had his carbine out of its scabbard and aimed at the running animal. As the elk disappeared, Jim eased the hammer back to half-cock, but thereafter he rode with the weapon across the pommel of his saddle. He needed no meat, but one never knew what or who else might be lurking in the trees.

When darkness approached, the two men found themselves still several hours away from the Olsens' place. Jim selected a campsite in a copse of trees about thirty yards from a fast-flowing stream. The men hobbled their horses and the three large pack mules that Curly had been leading. Jim built a small fire under a large pine, counting on the heavy branches to break up any smoke that the fire might produce. Curly cut some bacon and produced some biscuits that he had picked up at the cafe that morning, and the men made a meal of that. After they finished their coffee, Curly took the utensils off to the creek to wash them while Jim scattered the fire.

When Curly came back, he deposited the frying pan next to his saddle and poured himself some more coffee before the pot could get too cold. He looked over at

Jim a time or two, then went back to studying his cup without saying a word.

"Somethin' botherin' you, Curly?" Jim asked softly.

"No. Well, yeah, there is," he admitted. "Are you mad at me or somethin'? You ain't said five words since we left town."

Jim's smile was nearly lost in the darkness. "No, I ain't mad at you, Curly. I know I'm poor company on a ride, but I can't jabber away an' pay attention to what's goin' on around me, too. The last time I was out here, a bunch of Utes damn near lifted my hair, an' I still got a scar to show just how close they came." Jim paused for a moment and then continued. "Then there's Simpson. A pair of his boys have been followin' me for the last ten days, an' I thought that I saw movement on our backtrail a couple of times today. Maybe they want to even the score for their boss. Anyway, that's why I ain't been talkin'."

"Thanks for the explanation," Curly said. "I sure am glad you ain't mad at me for somethin'. I ain't been in the mountains much, an' I know I'm a tenderfoot next to you, but I'd like to learn. Want me to take the first watch?"

Jim was about to tell him to turn in, then thought the better of it. "That's fine with me. Wake me at midnight or whenever you start noddin' off, whichever comes first." Curly was getting his first lesson in survival.

The youth picked up his carbine and moved deeper into the shadows. As Jim was rolling up in his blankets, he heard Curly settle down on a fallen tree. Silence fell over the camp. Somewhere an owl hooted and one of the horses snorted. Jim slipped into a light sleep.

Curly woke Jim at midnight and by five o'clock both men were up, saddled, and riding toward the Olsens' cabin. They ate cold biscuits and washed them down with water from their canteens as they rode. Several times Jim took them through streams and across rocky ground in attempts to slow down anyone following them. He knew that a good tracker could follow them, but he had no intention of making the task easier for anyone following behind them.

The men approached the Olsen cabin at mid-morning. Jim was relieved to see a number of mules and horses picketed in open areas and several tents pitched about two hundred yards from the cabin. The crew from Texas had arrived. As the men rode up to the nearest tent, the flaps parted and Marcus stepped out. Right behind him came the familiar sight of Joe Penbrook, the long-time foreman of the brothers' Circle H ranch. Joe was well past his seventieth year but acted twenty years younger when it suited his purpose.

"Joe! You old fossil! What are you doin' here? Who's runnin' the ranch?" Jim exclaimed.

"I'll have you show a little more respect, you young pup. Matthew is watchin' over things, an' I hired me an assistant who may make a decent foreman in another fifty years or so. Marcus said that he weren't up to makin' you toe the line, so I come along to give 'er a try. From what Marcus told me an' what I saw waitin' for you in the cabin, you're goin' to need all the help you can get."

By the time Joe had finished, Jim was off his horse and had enveloped him in a bear hug. "It's good to see you, mean an' nasty as you are. I'm surprised that Marta let you out of her sight. Or did you bring her along?"

Joe grinned from ear to ear. "You might say that I sorta escaped. Caught her at a weak moment. She said she had a ear ache an' would I get outta the house for a while so she could give it a rest, so here I am." Joe paused to scratch his chin, then continued. "Wonder what she said when I didn't come back in from the barn?"

Jim laughed and introduced Curly to Joe and the rest of the men who had heard the commotion and had come to investigate. Marcus had brought several men with him in addition to Joe. They now had a sizable crew, all of whom were used to hard work and could more than hold their own in a fight.

About that time the cabin door flew open, and Sonja came running through the trees and across the clearing. Ole came walking along behind like a giant shadow.

"Jim! I knew that you would come back!" Sonja exclaimed breathlessly as she stopped in front of him. She started to shake his hand, then stopped and self-consciously hugged him and kissed his cheek. Jim hugged her, then took her by the shoulders and held her at arms' length.

"You're as pretty as ever, Sonja. Has that old grizzly bear of a father been treatin' you well?" he asked as Ole came lumbering up to them. Ole laughed and slapped him on the back hard enough to drive the air from his lungs.

"Ha! 'Bout time you came back. None of these old women will try Ole's whiskey. What do you think of that, eh?" the big man said as he crushed Jim's hand in his massive paw.

"I think that they are far wiser than they know, Ole," Jim answered as he tried to restore feeling in his right hand. "I don't know how you find a jug strong enough to hold it," he added.

Ole laughed and tried to slap Jim on the back again, but he dodged just in time. Jim chatted a little longer with Ole, then excused himself and walked off a little way with Sonja.

"Sorry to wish the bunch on you," he said to her, "but I'm not sure that I could find my way back to the cache unless I started from here. I hope that you an' Ole don't mind."

"Oh, no!" she assured him. "They are very pleasant visitors. Especially your big brother Marcus. He is such a fine man! And he knows so many funny stories!"

"He's a smooth-talkin' devil, alright," Jim agreed. "It sounds like you two hit it off just fine,"

"Oh, sometimes I'm so confused, Jim. I thought that you were the man for me because God sent you to me in the storm, but then I meet your brother and I feel things for him, too. Tell me what to do, Jim. I think that I must be a bad woman."

"Don't be silly," Jim said. "There's nothing wrong with you that I can see. Just don't look to me for good advice. You must live your life, Sonja, just as I must live mine. I must tell you that I have met another fine woman and I care for her very much. I care for you, too," he added quickly, "but in a different way, somehow. Does that make sense to you?"

"I don't know, Jim. I love you and I love your brother, too, I think, although I have not spent the night with him," she said, blushing furiously. "Oh, it's so unfair! Why can I not have you both?"

Jim laughed gently at her discomfort and took her in his arms. "Nothin' in this life is fair, my dear, but perhaps I can help you make up your mind. As much as I care for you, I would rather have you for a friend than as a wife. I can't speak for Marcus. You're on your own with him."

Sonja looked at him with wide eyes. "And do friends share the same bed?" she asked innocently.

"No, mostly they don't. Somehow that seems to spoil things. But they do care about each other, and they look out for each other, too. Maybe we should try that for now."

"If you think it is a good idea, we can try. But I have been so lonesome," she said as she put her arms around him and began to move her body against his.

Jim took her by the shoulders and stepped back. "We'd better get back to the others. Think about what I said and then ask yourself whether you really love Marcus an' me or are just very lonely and have confused love with not being lonely anymore."

"Oh, you are so wise!" she exclaimed as she bounded away towards the cabin.

"Oh, you are so wise?" he mocked himself. "If I'm so damn wise, how'd I get in this fix in the first place?" he asked an owl looking at him from a tree. The owl wisely said nothing. Jim kicked an old pinecone and walked back to the tent to see Marcus.

The next morning Jim's crew started out for his claim at first light. There was no sign of the men who had been trailing Jim and Curly, but Jim split the crew and left Curly, two of the Texans, and Marcus behind with orders to follow on later with the pack animals. The reason for that was two-fold: first, Jim wanted a rear guard in case that the group following him from town was a large one; and second, Jim wanted to fool the trailers about the size of his crew if he could. Good trackers could, of course, tell how many men had ridden along a trail, but the pack animals would confuse the issue for all but the most experienced tracker. Jim traded horses and coats with Marcus to further the deception. He did not believe that there was any possibility of ambushing whoever it was that followed them.

Jim halted the lead group several times as they progressed deeper into the mountains. He scheduled one of these halts to rest the animals near the spot where he had cached the gold the winter before. While the others were stretching and taking care of the horses, Jim put on a pair of moccasins and walked several hundred yards to locate his gold. He found it undisturbed. Very carefully Jim returned to the group, erasing all signs of his passage as he went. It was his intention to retrieve his cache on the way back in the fall.

The men were now traveling along the timber line, where the wind was icy and snow still blocked the trail in a number of places. Progress slowed as the men cleared a path through the drifts, and Jim called an early halt to set up camp. It was cold enough that Jim had some concern for the Texans' ability to stay warm, but there was little he could do about it now. The tentage was all with Marcus and Curly. He did make the men change socks and rub their feet, an action which produced more than a few grumbles and snide comments. After a quick meal, all but those on watch rolled up in their blankets and went to sleep without benefit of fires. Light at that altitude could be seen for miles, and there was little in the way of fuel to burn, anyway.

Several miles behind them, Marcus set up camp with the second group deep within the timber.

Randy Talbott and Buck Blackwell were the two men who Simpson had sent to keep an eye on Horton. They had lost a lot of time on the second day trying to find the trail after Jim and Curly lost them again and again by following streams and keeping to rocky ground. The two men sighted the Olsen cabin just as Curly, Marcus, and the others were leaving with the pack animals. Just as Jim had hoped, they mistook Marcus for the younger Horton. Talbott and Blackwell waited until the procession was well out of sight, then skirted around the cabin and followed the well-defined trail leading deeper into the mountains. Simpson's men were cautious. With a clear trail to follow, they had no intention of allowing themselves to be surprised or even seen by the group in front of them.

When night came, the two men were about a mile behind Marcus. Knowing that only a fool would move about in the mountains after dark if he did not absolutely have to, the pair set up camp for the night. Ahead of them, Marcus smiled as he saw the glow of their fire below him. His own fire was small and well-shielded, even though secrecy was no longer a requirement. It wouldn't seem natural if their camp was too clearly marked.

Marcus delayed starting out again until nearly an hour after daylight. Talbott and Blackwell had to backtrack hurriedly when they nearly rode into camp. It was past mid-morning when Marcus rode through the site of Jim's night camp, and it was five hours later when he came across Jim and Joe Penbrook hidden in the rocks overlooking the trail.

"'Bout time you got here, boy," Joe observed. "Jim an' me thought that maybe you couldn't find the trail."

"A blind man could find this one, you old coot," Marcus shot back. "There's a pair of vultures followin' along about a mile behind. You want us to turn around an' take care of 'em?"

"No," Jim answered. "Joe here will take you and the boys into the camp a mile or two up the trail. I'd like for Curly to stay here with me so we can give those jaspers followin' you a proper reception," Jim said.

Curly readily agreed, and Jim and Marcus traded coats again. While Joe led the procession into the camp, Jim gave Curly his instructions. The men picked out good positions in the rocks and settled back to wait for Simpson's men.

Before long, Jim heard the sound of horses' hooves on the rocky trail below him. He eased the hammer of his Winchester to full-cock, then looked over to Curly. He saw that the youngster had heard the sound, too, and was ready.

Talbott was uneasy and had been ever since he and Blackwell had left the timber that morning. He couldn't understand why Horton and his bunch had gone to so much trouble to hide their trail for the first half of the trip, then had made absolutely no attempt to hide their trail after that. Now, out of the protective cover of the timber, he felt naked and exposed. They were deep in the mountains, totally cut off from any support. His partner was of little help. A city tough, Blackwell was lost outside of a town. Talbott cursed Jackson for teaming him up with such an inept man. To make matters worse, Blackwell never stopped bitching about the ride, the food, or the company. When they got back to Ruxford, he'd ....

"Hold it right there!" a voice demanded from the rocks on their right. Talbott jerked his horse to a halt, raising his right hand while controlling his mount with his left.

Blackwell panicked. He jerked his horse around and made a grab for the pistol on his hip. He had barely cleared leather when a shot rang out, and he was knocked backwards off his horse to land like a loose bundle of rags on the trail. His horse, spooked by the shot, bolted off the way he had come. Blackwell's body twitched a time or two and then lay still.

In the rocks, Curly levered another round into the chamber of his carbine and grinned at Horton. It was plain that he thought he had paid Simpson back in some small way for the slug that he had taken in the chest several months before.

Jim looked down at the rider below him. "Before you do anythin' else stupid, drop your gun belt an' your Winchester. After that, pick up your partner an' get out of here," he ordered.

Talbott did as he was told. He knew that it was time to fold his hand and leave the game. The men in the rocks held all the high cards. It took him a while to get Blackwell's body onto the horse. The animal was skittish from the shot and the smell of blood. Blackwell, a large and difficult man to hand in life, was even more difficult to handle in death.

"Go back an' tell Simpson what'll happen if he sends any more of his scum sniffin' around here," Jim said as he emerged from the rocks, his carbine at the ready.

"I don't know what you're talkin' about," Talbott replied testily. "We was just up here mindin' our own business when you an' kills my partner."

"You travel mighty light for anyone plannin' to mind his own business, an' your partner thought he was a bad man with a gun. You do what I told you an' then, if you want my advice, you'll move out of the territory. You got a break today an' lived to walk away. You'll not get another," Jim promised.

Talbott swallowed hard, then nodded and got up on his horse behind Blackwell's body. He turned the horse around and headed back down the trail over which he had ridden just a few minutes before. He hoped that he could catch Blackwell's horse. He wanted the carbine in the scabbard and the food out of the saddlebags. He walked his horse for the better part of a mile before he came to the drop-off he had noticed earlier. He stopped long enough to push Blackwell's body over the edge before continuing on down the mountain. He caught Blackwell's horse an hour later. As he rode on, he pondered Horton's advice and thought that this might be a good time to see what Oregon looked like.

Jim and Curly picked up the firearms lying about and then walked up the trail to the camp. A lot of activity was going on when they arrived. Tents were already lined up, and the animals were picketed and eating from the small amount of forage that the men had brought with them. Vegetation was sparse at this altitude, and Jim knew that tomorrow or the next day at the latest the animals would have to be taken down the mountain to graze.

Nothing in his previous camp had been left standing. The rampaging Utes, angry over Jim's escape, had burned or broken everything he had left behind. The entrance through the rocks leading to the thick seam of quartz laden with gold had not been disturbed, and Jim took the rest of the crew through the opening and into the tiny depression to look at the strike. Several of the crew had never seen gold that had not already been refined and made into coins, watches, or teeth. Everyone was impressed with the richness of the vein. Jim let the men inspect the seam of gold, so rich that the quartz could be broken apart and the gold extracted with a man's fingers.

"Men, let's decide on how we're goin' to split this up," Jim suggested. "Marcus hired you all to come here for a flat wage. If you have no objection, I'd like to change that to shares." A loud chorus of cheers interrupted him, and he waited for the noise to die down before continuing. "I'll take a fourth of whatever we take out, since I'm the man who found it in the first place. You all split the rest, even shares. We leave on the last of August, whether we've cleaned out the seam or not. When we leave, your share in whatever's left behind ends, an' the claim's all mine again. What do you say to that?"

Jim was not surprised when none of the men objected. For the most part, these men were cowmen who had worked most of their lives for forty dollars a month, happy to be working for the highest-paying outfit in central Texas. They had just been given the opportunity to earn more money in a few months than they had expected to see in a lifetime, and it took them a little time for the realization of it to sink in. Once it did, there was another unanimous and thunderous roar of approval.

Jim let the crew caper around for a little while, then brought them back to the business at hand.

"We were followed here today, an' the man who's behind it will be comin' back. I don't know when, but my guess is that it'll be just about the time we get ready to leave. There's eleven of us, an' we'll all take turns guardin' the remuda, the camp, an' workin' the gold. Which one of you wants to be the belly robber?"

Nobody volunteered, so Jim pointed to Joe Penbrook and named him the new cook. Joe stood up like he'd been shot and argued vehemently against the idea. It took Jim a while, but he finally got the old man calmed down.

"You got to understand, Joe, that if we're goin' to get this gold out of here, the crew has to keep up its strength. You're the only one I know whose cookin' won't poison the whole camp. Besides, you're goin' to have to do the huntin', too," Jim said with a sudden flash of inspiration.

Joe grumbled a little longer to show that he hadn't given in too quickly, then finally agreed. Jim set up the guard detail for the day and sent the rest of the men after their tools. Soon the sound of hammers ringing on the rock filled the air. Jim went back to the camp with Joe and helped him set up the kitchen. Very soon wood would become a problem, and Jim made a note to have the herd guards bring enough back for the cook fire when they brought in the animals at night.

"You sure caught me flat-footed with this cookin' business," Joe groused. "I'm as good a hand with a pick as any of them pups. Why, I remember the time when ...."

"Joe, you're so damned ornery an' contrary, if you was a salmon, you'd swim downstream to spawn," Jim observed. "Besides, you're the only man that I can trust to hunt alone an' not get himself hurt. With you doin' the job, I don't have to take another man off the diggin' to go along as a wet nurse."

Joe looked hard at Jim for a moment to see if the younger man was putting him on, then smiled when he saw that Jim was serious. "Maybe you're right, boy. Maybe you're right," he grudgingly agreed. As far as Joe was concerned, the matter was now settled.

Chapter 16

J oe Penbrook stepped over a dry branch and turned to warn Curly before he could step on it. Curly was a good man in many ways, Joe knew, but lately the boy had been given to daydreaming when he should have been paying attention to what was going on around him. The trouble had started when the crew had stayed with the Olsens. One look at Sonja and Curly could no longer be counted on to stay alert. He decided that the boy would probably outgrow the mooning in time, but Joe wasn't all that sure that Curly would live that long if he didn't change his ways pretty soon. That was why Curly was out here with him today. Joe was going to try to talk some sense into the boy.

Joe usually went hunting alone while the rest of the men worked in the mine or stood guard. In the beginning, Joe had taken the mules and the horses down to grass every day and had returned with them at night. It soon became plain to him that he was blazing a trail that a blind man would follow, and after Jim's trouble with the Utes the year before, Joe didn't believe any of the braves had developed eye trouble. He convinced Jim to take the herd down to the lower meadows to graze for the summer. Two of the crew stayed with the animals, freeing Joe to spend his time hunting for camp meat. Today he had decided to take Curly along to see if he could get the boy's attention back where it belonged.

The two men had been following the tracks of a large elk for nearly an hour. They were very close now, Joe judged. There was a clearing just ahead, and he signaled for Curly to stop. Joe slowly eased his way to the wood line and crawled the last few yards to the edge on his belly. He eased his head around the base of a large tree and scanned the clearing. The elk was grazing about a hundred and fifty yards to his front, oblivious to the hunters stalking him.

Joe motioned Curly forward, and for once Joe was gratified that Curly moved noiselessly into position to the older man's right. Curly smiled and eased his rifle up into firing position. Joe did the same, thumbing the hammer of his Winchester to full-cock as he brought the rifle to his shoulder. He started to take the slack out of the trigger when Curly reached over and slowly pushed down on the barrel of Joe's rifle.

Joe turned to Curly and started to make an angry comment when the younger man put his finger to his lips in a sign for silence, then pointed toward the far side of the clearing. At first Joe could see nothing, then he spotted a slight movement. Moments later Joe spied a young Ute stand up slowly, level his bow, and loose an arrow at the elk. The arrow struck the big animal just behind the front leg. He took a mighty leap, but it was to be his last. The aim of the young Ute had been true, and the elk's front legs collapsed as it died from an arrow through the heart and lungs.

The two men watched silently as the youth ran up to his kill and slit its throat. A moment or two later he was joined by five older men who helped carry the elk back into the wood line. There had been no wasted time or motion. One minute the elk had been alive and grazing peacefully, the next he was dead and carried from the field with nothing more than a pool of blood to mark his passing. Although the Utes were gone, neither of the men moved for nearly half an hour. When they finally did, it was slowly and as noiselessly as possible.

When they had reached the relative safety of the deep forest, the men stopped to consider their position. The Utes had not been a war party, that much was clear, but both men knew that that could change in an instant. What was important now was to put as much distance as possible between themselves and the Utes. They gave up any thought of a hunt for that day. With luck the hunting party would be miles away by the morning and the two men could try again. Joe made a mental note to scout for signs before he even thought of firing a shot at anything.

"Boy," Joe said in a low voice, "I wouldn't say this to just anybody, an' I'll deny it if'n you was to repeat it, but you sure saved our bacon today. I never even seen that buck 'tll way after you stopped my shot. They'd of had our hair for sure if you hadn't of seen 'em. An' to think that I was goin' to lecture you on payin' attention!"

"I was just lucky, Joe," Curly said modestly. "That young fellow wasn't payin' attention to nothin' but that elk, an' I saw him about ten seconds before he let go with that arrow. If he don't pay better attention than that, he won't live to get much older, I'm guessin'."

"Those was goin' to be my words, exactly," Joe said. "I'm glad that you've got good eyes an' that you finally decided to use 'em. You've been moonin' around so much lately that I'd about given up on you."

Curly blushed. "I'll deny this if you was to tell anybody else, Joe, but I can't stop thinkin' about Miss Olsen. She's about the prettiest girl I ever did see, an' she doesn't know that I'm alive," he said miserably. "She can't see any farther than Jim. What do you reckon he's got that I haven't? An' he don't even act like he wants her around!" he added in exasperation.

"What he's got that you don't is two females makin' fools of themselves over him. Sooner or later, he'll make a choice or they will, an' then he'll be no different than you. 'Til then you'd be well-served to keep your eyes open, your mouth closed, an' your fly buttoned. You makin' a fool of yourself won't put you in good with Sonja, an' if some Ute finds you daydreamin', you're the one who won't get to be no older. Lookin' like a love-sick sheep never helped a man out with a woman like Sonja. Just relax an' be yourself. If you wasn't good enough to take along, you wouldn't be here. Jim's mighty particular about who he trusts his hide to. Just don't let him down. If you was to, I'd take it real personal. An' if you think it's bad to have trouble with Jim, you ain't seen trouble 'til you've had it with me!" Joe's smile kept the warning from stinging too much.

Curly was silent for a while, then sat down on a fallen tree. "I guess you're right, Joe. I've been actin' like a kid. I'll do better. Just do me a favor, will you? Don't tell anybody that you had this talk with me."

Joe cackled softly and patted the younger man on the back. "Far as I'm concerned, we never said nothin'. Now let's get our butts back to the camp. Jim'll want to know about them Utes."

The two men made their way cautiously back to their horses. That night Jim doubled the guard on the horse herd and the camp, but nothing more was seen of the Utes. No one objected.

Chapter 17

Spring and summer passed quickly in Ruxford. Business in Hogtown was brisk, but not in comparison with that it had been before Sam Peabody laid down the law the winter before. Will Simpson bided his time, content to wait before making his move against first Horton and then the law. Randy Talbott had reported back to Simpson with the location of the Horton strike. He also reported that there were only four men working the claim. After he made his report, he drew his time and left town, never to return to Colorado.

Del Jackson was given to longer periods of brooding. Several times he crossed the creek into Ruxford, each time to watch Myrna Meloy at the Golden Nugget. As the summer passed, Myrna spent less and less time with her business, and by the end of May she rarely left her rooms at the Excelsior. The town doctor made several calls on her, and the rumor that she was not well started to make the rounds.

Sam Peabody, Al Cleary, and Abner Bonesteel continued to enforce the law on both sides of the creek. The sheriff had not given up looking for something else that he could use to tie Simpson in with the bank robbery, but he had not had much success. He was beginning to wonder if he would ever bring anyone to justice for the crime.

Morton Witherspoon still managed to prosper. He took over the shack in Hogtown previously occupied by Cyclops Mary, rebuilt it, and moved in his current favorite from Miss Ellie's old establishment. The woman's name was Abigale Carpenter, and she was a lovely thing by anybody's standards. She was also a greedy wench with a natural instinct to love for money. She had grand designs for luring Morton away from his wife on a permanent basis.

Bertha Witherspoon knew practically from the start of their marriage that her husband was unfaithful, but as long as he was somewhat discreet, she could pretend total ignorance and raise their four children as she thought best. In many ways she was grateful to Abigale when Morton started to spend two and then three nights a week "working late at the office." The banker's habit of infrequent bathing, the smell of his cheap cigars, and his obvious lack of concern for his wife made him a less than desirable bed partner as far as Bertha was concerned. She was also determined that she would not bear him any more children. She believed that she had quite enough to do already.

Towards the middle of August, Simpson called Jackson into his office to put in motion his plan for taking over the Horton claim. Jackson was more than ready.

"Next week I want you to take the boys up to the hills and settle this thing with Horton once and for all. If we are to believe Talbott, Horton has only got three other men up there with him. You and a dozen or so of the boys should have no trouble taking care of the whole bunch. Just leave me three or four men to keep things going here."

Jackson got out of his chair, walked over to Simpson's desk, and poured himself a drink from the private stock that the saloon owner kept in the bottom drawer. He extracted a cigar from the box that Simpson kept on top of his desk, bit off the end, and lit it. He walked back slowly to his chair and sat down.

"This is one expedition I wouldn't miss for nothin'," Jackson announced. "I got some unfinished business here in town that I gotta attend to before I go, but that won't take me long. You want to go along on this one, too?" Jackson asked insolently.

"It would be better if I stayed here, just in case the sheriff ever wants to look into this thing. You handle it any way you want. Just remember that there must be no survivors. I recommend that you set up an ambush on the trail and catch them on their way back down the mountain. You had better take along plenty of supplies. You may be up there quite a while."

"You let me worry about the details," Jackson spat. "Today's Wednesday. We'll ride out of here on Saturday. That should put us where we want to be sometime on Monday. A week from tomorrow or the day after should put me in control of the claim."

"It will put *me* in control of the claim, Jackson, not you. Don't ever forget who runs the show around here," Simpson said angrily.

"Slip of the tongue, boss," Jackson said as he tossed off his drink and stood up. "Don't worry about a thing. As soon as the boys an' I get back, you'll never have to worry about money again." Jackson smiled wickedly as he stuck the cigar in his mouth and walked out of Simpson's office.

In spite of himself, Simpson shivered. Jackson was getting to be more uncontrollable with each passing day. Simpson resolved to send a telegram to a friend in Denver. It was time for Jackson to be eliminated.

The same thought went through Jackson's tortured mind as he started to alert the crew for the impending expedition. He promised himself that when he returned from the mountains, he would kill Simpson and take over his whole operation. He meant to establish in this town the eminence he had enjoyed in Benton before the Hortons had come home from the war and had driven him out of Texas, one step in front of the law. He was determined to have everything back the way it had been, and that included Myrna Meloy.

That Friday night a shadow moved through the darkened alley behind the Excelsior Hotel, then inched along the rear wall of the building before it came to a flight of stairs leading to the second floor. The figure silently ascended the stairs and tried the door at the top. Finding it locked, he took a Bowie knife from his belt and quickly forced the lock. He slipped through the opening and closed the door gently behind him. A lamp burned dimly halfway down the corridor. He blew it out as he crept softly towards the door that he knew led to Myrna Meloy's suite.

The man paused to listen at the door for a moment and, when he heard nothing, tried the knob. It turned easily under his hand and the door opened with hardly a sound. The man waited for an instant before he stepped through the doorway and into the room. The room was dark except for a light that showed faintly beneath the door along the left-hand wall. As the man walked across the floor towards the light, a board creaked loudly under his foot.

"Who's there? Jim, is that you?" Myrna asked from the other room. She repeated the question when she heard no reply.

The man opened the door and walked boldly into the room. He found Myrna Meloy dressed in a simple dressing gown, leaning against the near side of the bed. Her long, red hair spilled across her shoulders and down to her waist. In the dim light she was the loveliest sight that the man had ever seen, and he felt his throat thicken as his desire for her mounted.

"No, Myrna, it ain't Jim," the man said as he drew nearer.

"Who are you and what do you want here?" Myrna demanded.

"Why, Myrna! I'm surprised at you. After all that we've meant to each other. Don't you remember the man who took you out of that whorehouse in Texas?" he asked, grinning evilly. "Now, don't you go puttin' on airs, sweetheart. Once a whore, always a whore, as they say."

Recognition came flooding over Myrna. She turned very pale and staggered back a bit. She might have fallen if she had not grabbed hold of the post at the foot of the bed.

"Jack? Jackson Delacourte, is that you?" she asked incredulously.

"It sure is, Myrna baby. Only my name ain't Delacourte no more. It's Del Jackson now, an' I've come back to get what's rightfully mine."

"You won't find it here, Jackson. Now get out of here before I call for help," she said firmly.

"You call an' I'll kill you where you stand. You make me sick, actin' so high an' mighty," he sneered. "You wouldn't be actin' like the Queen of Sheba if folks around here knew that you used to work at Fat Ethyl's for a dollar a poke."

That statement was not exactly true, Myrna knew, but it was close. In the closing days of the War Between the States, the Union Army had overrun her parents' farm in Alabama. One night some drunken troopers raped her, her mother, and her older sister. Her sister had died as the result of the attack. Myrna had been just fifteen at the time. A few weeks later her father had come home to find his women abused or dead and the farm burned to ashes. He had gathered his family and set off for Texas to build a new life. Luck had not been with them. Cholera took Myrna's parents somewhere north of Austin, near Round Rock. Myrna made it to Benton more dead than alive. Fat Ethyl nursed her back to health and gave her room and board in exchange for Myrna's cleaning up around the bordello that Ethyl operated. Jackson Delacourte had seen her there and had taken her home.

Myrna had wanted desperately to love the man, but that first night she had learned just how deep his depravity ran. He was far more cruel and sadistic than the drunken Union troopers had been. Yet she had lived with him for more than a year, believing at first that he would marry her, and then gradually understanding that at best he would only use her to satiate his own warped appetites. Seth Horton, one of Jim's older brothers, had set her free from that slow death and had run Delacourte out of the state. Myrna thought that she had been finished with that nightmare, yet there he was again, threatening to pull her back into that old, terrifying life. She felt as though she was on the edge of insanity.

"What's the matter, Myrna? Can't you say anything? How about a little welcome home kiss?" Jackson asked as he walked up to her and grabbed her by the arm.

Myrna spat in his face.

"Bitch!" he hissed and he wiped the spittle from his eyes. Suddenly he struck her a vicious blow to the mouth, splitting her lip and spilling blood into her mouth. Still holding onto her arm, he grabbed the bodice of her gown and tore it down past her waist, then released her and stepped back to observe his handiwork.

"Why, ...," he started to say in astonishment.

"Yes, Jackson, that's right," Myrna interrupted, "but that shouldn't make any difference to you. You've never let common decency get in your way before. I expect that you would insist on having your way with me even if I were on my deathbed." Myrna paused, then continued, her voice turning harsh. "Yes, you'd try even then, if you thought that your manhood would let you."

Jackson stepped forward and struck her again, knocking her onto the bed.

"You always needed the sight of blood to get that thing of yours to work, didn't you, Jackson?" Myrna taunted.

Jackson flung himself at her with a roar, striking her again and again as he finished tearing off her gown. He took off his gun belt and threw it aside, then loosened his trousers. He had lost all reason.

"I'll show you who needs what," he spat as he began to lower himself onto her prostate form.

Suddenly an excruciating pain tore through his body. It seemed to be centered on his left side. He couldn't catch his breath, and he forced himself to rock back to a kneeling position, sitting on his heels.

"Whaa ...," he gasped as he looked down below his left armpit and gazed stupidly at the knife handle that protruded from his ribs.

"You'll have to try harder, Jackson," Myrna said as she slid off the bed, taking her dressing robe with her as she went. When she had slipped into the robe and belted it, she picked up Jackson's gun belt and drew the pistol. She cocked the Colt as she aimed at Jackson.

Jackson made a feeble attempt to pluck the blade from his side, then gave up. He looked slowly around, then tried to focus his eyes on Myrna.

"You've killed me," he managed to whisper in awe. "You've murdered me!"

"Like I would a cockroach," she told him as he fell from the bed and crashed to the floor. He groaned once and then lay still.

Myrna waited a few minutes to be sure that he was dead, then staggered past the body to the bed. There was very little blood. Myrna tugged several times on the bell cord near the head of the bed.

Moments later she heard the sound of a man running down the hall toward her rooms. Suddenly Amos Stewart, the desk clerk, appeared in the doorway of her bedroom. His gaze went from Myrna to the body on the floor and then back to Myrna's bloody face.

"Are you alright, Miss Meloy?" the clerk asked anxiously.

"I don't know yet, Amos," Myrna said through bloody lips. "That man broke in here somehow and attacked me. When he knocked me to the bed, I was able to get to a knife from under the edge of the mattress. Do you think you can get the body out of here without anyone seeing you?"

"You can count on me, ma'am. I'll take it out the back way," he said.

"I want you to hide the body, Amos. Hide it where no one will ever find it. This will be our secret, ours and no one else's. Do you understand?"

"Whatever you want, ma'am," the clerk said as he hoisted the body onto his shoulders. "Do you know who it was?" he asked.

"No, I have no idea," Myrna said, grimacing as a pain shot through her body. "And send someone for the doctor. Tell him to hurry," she said as she lowered herself back onto the bed. "Please tell him to hurry."

Chapter 18

It was nearly noon on Saturday and Will Simpson was absolutely furious. Eleven riders had gathered behind the Palace at dawn and then stood around waiting for Del Jackson to show up. They had rations for three days and two hundred rounds of ammunition per man, but they still had no leader. In the six hours they had gathered, they had not progressed a single foot beyond the boundary of Hogtown.

Every inch of Hogtown had been searched at least once. There was no trace of Jackson. Simpson considered sending some men into Ruxford to look for him there, then decided against it. Sheriff Peabody would have been sure to notice the activity and become suspicious.

Simpson considered placing one of the other men in charge of the expedition, and he would have if Frog Mayeaux had been there. Unfortunately, Mayeaux had been missing for several months and no one else in the group had shown any talent for leading men. It was not surprising, considering the fact that Jackson had systematically and ruthlessly discouraged any leadership other than his own.

Simpson took another look at his watch and stuffed it back into his pocket in disgust. He could wait for Jackson no longer. He sent one of the men to the stable to fetch his horse while he went back inside to get his gun belt. When the man returned with his horse, Simpson swung awkwardly into the saddle and headed west, out of town. The other men fell in behind him.

Simpson pushed the men and the animals hard, and it was nearly dark when he called for a halt for the night. The horses were tired and offered no protest to being hobbled. One or two cook fires appeared, but most of the men were content with eating their food cold. Simpson was so exhausted that he skipped the meal altogether and rolled up in his blanket as soon as he had taken care of his horse. At that point he wanted nothing more than a good night's sleep. Minutes later he felt someone shaking him by the shoulder. He sat up quickly and rubbed the sleep out of his eyes.

"What do you want?" he snarled.

"It's Purvis, Boss. Me an' the boys, we want to know if you was plannin' on settin' a guard tonight. We was also wonderin' what time you was thinkin' of movin' out in the mornin'."

Simpson groaned and gave the matter some thought. He had little experience in these matters and had relied upon Jackson to take care of such things. He felt foolish because he had not thought to give the needed orders and had needed to be coached by his subordinates. He felt a need to reestablish his authority.

"Yes, go ahead and set a guard," he said. "We'll leave at first light. Have the guard wake the men an hour before."

The rider stood up and started to walk away. Simpson called him back. "Purvis," he said, "I need a new second-in-command. You're it. From now on, you take care of these details. I want you to tell me if anything seems strange to you or if you think that we need to do something different. Do you know what I mean?"

"I think so, boss," Purvis answered after taking a moment to think about it. "You want me to take over Mister Jackson's job. Ain't that right?"

"Exactly. Do you think that you can do it?" Simpson asked.

"Yeah, I can handle it, but what happens when Jackson shows up again? Who's in charge then?"

"You let me worry about Jackson," Simpson said. "As of right now, you've got his old job permanently. I'll take care of Jackson if he ever comes back."

Purvis nodded and walked off to tell the other men of the plan for the next day. Simpson laid back down and wished that he felt as confident about dealing with Jackson as he had just sounded.

Morning came, but departure was delayed again. The men in the crew, long used to town work, were slow to stretch their sore muscles and get about their business. Simpson was impatient, but the truth of the matter was that he wasn't moving any faster than the rest of the men. There were other problems as well. There had been a heavy dew during the night, and no one had thought to throw a blanket over the kindling to keep it dry. The damp wood was hard to get burning and produced a vast amount of smoke when it did finally catch, so breakfast was delayed. Two of the horses had wandered off when the guard fell asleep, and it took the better part of an hour to find them and bring them back to the camp. Everything considered, Simpson was surprised that they were only two hours late getting back on the trail.

The men rode slower now, aware of the need to save their horses as they went higher into the mountains. By late afternoon they passed wide of the Olsen cabin and made camp about three miles beyond. Purvis had detailed one man to cook, and before long a fire had been started and the horses picketed for the night. One of the men had gone off into the timber and returned shortly with a haunch of venison. The men ate well that night. Purvis doubled the guard to make sure that someone stayed awake. Simpson watched the activity in camp and decided that with a little more time the crew just might turn out pretty well. That night wolves came to investigate the horses, but the man-smell kept them at a distance. None of the crew knew why the horses were nervous.

Ole Olsen raised his head slowly and looked around the side of the tree that he was using to conceal himself from the riders. He counted twelve men as they rode past. He waited a few minutes to see if there was a rear guard and, when he was satisfied that there was none, he trailed the men at a distance. He watched as they made camp, then set off for his cabin.

Sonja met him at the door. "Why do you hurry so, father?" she asked. "Supper will not be ready for another hour."

"I have no time for supper tonight, daughter. Twelve men just rode past, headed for the mountains. They have no pack animals, but they carry many guns. They are evil men, I think. I must warn Jim that they are coming. Fix me some food for the trail while I saddle the horse," he said, a troubled expression fixed on his face.

"Oh, father! I must go, too. I cannot bear to stay behind while you, Jim, and Marcus are in danger!" she exclaimed.

"You stay here, close to the house, while I'm gone," Ole said firmly. "If there's to be any trouble, I want to know where you are. If you set foot out of the cabin, take a rifle with you."

Sonja knew better than to argue with her father. It would not do her any good, she knew. She turned away from him and sullenly prepared the food as she had been told. She had just finished when Ole came back, took up the bundle of food, and kissed her on the cheek.

"Don't worry," he said. "Nothing will happen to Ole or the Horton boys. You be a good girl and do what your father tells you." With that admonition, Ole left the cabin, mounted his horse, and rode off into the night.

Sonja waited an hour, then took a second parcel of food and an ancient Spencer and went to the corral. She caught and saddled her horse, then set off up the trail after her father. Before long she saw the fires of Simpson's crew through the trees. She dismounted and led her horse in a wide arc around the camp. Once her horse nickered softly and she put her hand over his muzzle to silence him. She listened to see if he had been heard, and when nobody challenged her, she continued on her way.

She kept going for another two hours, then stopped for the night in a concealed spot about two hundred yards from the trail she knew the men behind her must follow. If she was alert, she was sure that she would be able to find some way to help her father and the Hortons.

Ole rode all night, feeling the trail more than he actually saw it. Jim had been a little vague about describing the location of his camp, so Ole had tracked the crew when they left his place last spring. His action was not motivated by greed. The big Swede was simply curious, so he had followed along behind. He was glad now that he had, for it enabled him to ride directly to Horton's camp.

It was late in the afternoon when Ole heard a challenge from high up in the rocks overlooking the trail. Ole identified himself and the guard, who recognized the huge man immediately, sent him on into the camp. There he found Jim and Joe Penbrook slicing up venison for the evening meal.

Jim looked up from what he was doing. "Why, Ole," he said in surprise, "what are you don' here?" Then, remembering his manners, he invited the big man to dismount and share in the meal.

Ole swung off the horse with obvious relief. He usually traveled wherever he went by foot, and both he and the horse were vastly relieved that this trip was over, at least for the moment.

"I have some news that I thought you might need to know," Ole said as he inspected the stew pot and sniffed approvingly. "I think that you got big trouble coming. Last night twelve men passed my cabin headed this way. They are not mountain people, and they know where they want to go. Do you expect any company?"

"We do, Ole," Jim replied. "A pair of men trailed us from Ruxford last spring. One of them got back home again. I reckon who you saw was Simpson's gang, on their way here to hijack the gold we dug out this year."

"I saw that pair," Ole said, "and I buried the dead one after his friend threw his body over the cliff. May heaven spare me from friends like that!" he exclaimed as he turned his eyes to the sky.

"You saw what happened?" Jim asked the grinning giant.

"Sure, I saw. How do you think that I found this place so quick? You find much gold here, Jim?" he asked casually. Without waiting for an answer, he continued. "I been here three, maybe four times and always thought it was a pretty good spot. But gold always brings trouble, I think. Now, with furs it's different. It takes too much work to take pelts, so bad men like those behind me don't bother to try. They try to steal money after the furs are sold. That is why I drink my own whiskey. I make sure that I get home with all my money."

"Well, Ole, I guess we did find a little color," Jim admitted. "In fact, we found a lot of gold. The seam ran out last week an' we're tryin' to see if we can find it again before we quit for the winter. Centuries ago, this land experienced a tremendous upheaval and parts of it were pushed hundreds of feet into the air. It's worn down now, an' just because there's a seam of gold on one side of a crevice don't mean that the rest of the gold is on the other side."

"Maybe this is a good time to stop for the winter," Ole suggested. "That way there is nothing for anyone to find."

"We just about figured the same thing," Joe Penbrook offered. "It's for dang sure I ain't fixin' to stay much longer. It's gettin' plumb chilly at night, an' my blood's gettin' a might thin."

"Ho, ho, ho!" Ole boomed. "What you need is some of my good whiskey. Too bad I got none with me."

"That's not whiskey, sir," Jim corrected. "That's embalming fluid, an' Joe don't need any. He only smells like he's dead."

Joe sniffed disdainfully, then turned to Ole. "I don't smell so bad that he don't eat my cookin', I notice. Drag up a rock, Ole. This here venison stew'll be ready in a few minutes."

The sound of shod horses on rocks reverberated through the camp, followed closely by a pair of riders leading the crew's horses and mules back from the graze. The riders dismounted and put the animals into a stone and rail corral. When they were done, they came over to check on the stew. They exchanged howdies with Ole and Jim before Joe ran them off with a large wooden spoon.

"Worse'n damn kids," the old man grumbled as he stirred the pot vigorously. He tasted the contents, screwed up his face and spit into the fire. He walked to his tent and emerged a minute later with a handful of chili peppers, which he dumped unceremoniously into the pot.

"If'n you got the guts to eat this stuff, don't break wind too close to the fire," he warned. "The flame could melt the rock you're sittin' on."

Ole bellowed another of his laughs, then sobered abruptly. "Jim, those men will be close sometime tomorrow. What are you going to do?"

"We'll double the guard an' see what happens. If they don't do somethin' right away, I figure them to be settin' up an ambush somewheres. Then maybe Marcus an' I'll sneak down to their camp an' run off their horses. That'd slow 'em up plenty. It'll take a whole lot more men than what you saw to overrun this camp. I think they'll try the ambush, myself."

"If they knew how many you are, I agree with you," Ole said, "but if they don't, I think they will attack the camp. These men were riding light. They are not prepared to wait very long. After I eat, maybe I will take a little walk, like a big bear. I can look at their horses' teeth and they would never know. Tomorrow they can start walking home. What do you think?"

Jim smiled and slapped the big man on the back. "It's not your fight, Ole. You've done enough already, an' we're grateful. After you eat, why don't you kind of slip off an' go home? We've got plenty of men an' Sonja will be worried."

"You think that Ole is afraid?" the big man asked, insulted by such a suggestion.

"I think you'd charge hell with a pan of water, my friend," Jim answered. "I just don't want to see you get hurt in a fight that's not yours."

"I been in plenty of fights. I never get hurt. Do not worry about me," Ole said, grinning. "I have a good time breaking heads."

Jim gave up. It was plain that Ole would do whatever he wanted to do, and no argument was going to change his mind. One by one the crew drifted in and helped themselves to the stew. Ole tried a bowl and his eyes started to water, and his nose began to run.
"Damn! That's good stuff!" he exclaimed as he helped himself to another bowl. When he finished his fourth, he wiped his mouth on his sleeve, belched loudly, and got up.

"I think that I will take a little ride now, and maybe a little walk, too. Perhaps the men behind me will be a little longer getting here than they think. I will be back after the sun comes up, so do not wait up for me," Ole advised.

For such a large man, Ole was incredibly light on his feet. He made it to his horse and was riding out of the camp before Jim could muster an argument against it. The sun was setting behind the mountains, so Jim set the guard and went back to the fire to talk with Joe and Marcus. He had few illusions. Simpson would come whether or not Ole ran off his horses, and Jim intended to be ready for him.

As darkness fell, Sonja put out the small fire that she had started to make coffee and repacked her gear. She had trailed Simpson's crew all day, and now she intended to move as silently as possible along their trail until she could see their camp. She knew from what her father had told her that Jim's camp was only a few hours away. Her heart raced at the thought of seeing him again. Or was it because she would also be seeing Marcus, she wondered. It made no real difference, she reminded herself. She would see them both. She mounted her horse and started up the trail.

It took her little more than an hour before she saw the glow of Simpson's fire, but during that time it had turned pitch black. The moon was not up yet, so movement was slow. She dismounted and tied her horse to a tree, then took her Spencer and crept towards the fire. Her moccasins made no noise as she moved from tree to tree, stalking the camp as if it were a wild animal. It took her nearly an hour to get close enough to the camp to distinguish the figures huddled around the fire. It took another hour to get close enough to hear what the men were saying.

"I tell you, it's plumb loco to ride all this way an' just sit in them rocks waitin' for 'em to come off of that damn mountain. There's only four of 'em. I say we ought to just ride over 'em, get the gold, an' ride home. I didn't hire on to live on a rock like some damn lizard!"

a large, bearded man with a big piece missing from his left ear exclaimed.

"Shut up, Smitty," the man to his right said. "You ain't runnin' the outfit. Mister Simpson, he's got his reasons for givin' those orders. You can run your mouth off all you want, but you know that you're goin' to do what he says, same as me."

"Watch who you're tellin' what to do, Purvis," the man called Smitty warned. "You ain't near the man that you think you are. Why, for two cents I'd carve you up an' leave you for the bears!" He spat as he drew a thin-bladed knife from his belt. The long blade glittered in the light from the fire.

Sonja started to back away from the fire as a plan started to form in her mind. If she could only make it to their horses, she thought ....

She heard a twig break behind her and she swung to face the sound. A dark shape loomed over her and made a grab for her carbine. Sonja fired as the Spencer came to bear. The sound of the shot and the man's scream of agony blended together as the camp behind her came suddenly alive.

Sonja was blinded momentarily by the flame from her carbine's muzzle. As she made her dash to escape, she tripped and fell headlong into a tree, stunning her. As she fought to regain her wits, she felt her carbine being ripped from her grasp and strong hands hauled her to her feet.

"Now looky what we got here!" Smitty exclaimed. "I ain't never seen no woman built like this one here! We ought to pass her around before we finish her off."

"Nobody's doin' nothin' 'til the boss has his say," Purvis said calmly. "Let's take her back to the fire an' find out what she's doin' here."

"What about Pete?" another man asked. "He's layin' back there with a hole in his gut big enough to drive a freight wagon through."

"I'll send a couple of the boys back to get him. Maybe it ain't as bad as it looks," Purvis said hopefully.

"Don't count on it," the other man said. "I seen a lot of belly wounds durin' the war, an' I ain't never seen any worse than this."

The three men walked back to the fire, half dragging, half carrying Sonja. Her head was clear now, and she vowed to herself not to say a word to these men.

Simpson joined them near the fire. "Where did you find her?" he asked.

"About fifty yards into the trees," Purvis said. "She gut-shot Pete when he come across her, I guess. I'll send a couple of the boys to fetch him in."

"Do that," Simpson directed. "Smith, you tie up the girl. I want to find out what she's doing here."

"Can I have her when you're done?" Smith pleaded.

"Nobody's getting anyone," Simpson said. "A woman like her is bound to have somebody out looking for her. We don't need any outside trouble before we finish what we came here to do."

The rest of the men were drifting back to the fire. "Say," one of them said, "I know her. She was at that cabin back down the trail. I seen her when we went past."

Simpson turned to the man. "Are you sure?" he snapped.

"Well," the man considered, "I'm pretty sure. There can't be two of 'em like that out here."

That brought a roar of rough laughter from the rest of the men. Simpson considered the situation for a while. Talbott had told him that Horton's crew had spent time at the cabin, so Horton had to know her. Given Horton's reputation with the ladies, it was possible that this tall blond meant something to him.

"We'll keep her with us," he decided. "Maybe she'll prove to be handy later on," he explained.

"Yeah, real handy," Smitty smirked.

"That's enough, Smith," Simpson snapped. "Nobody lays a hand on her unless I say so. Purvis, get a guard back on watch while I talk to this woman."

Purvis nodded and the group broke up. Simpson walked over to where Sonja was crouched next to a fallen tree. "What's your name, lady?" he asked.

Sonja remained silent but shot him a hate-filled look.

"Silence won't help you any. Talk to me or I'll have to let the boys have you. If you can't be of use to me, you certainly could be of use to them," he warned.

Sonja let go with a torrent of Swedish.

"Well, at least we know that you can talk. Now let's try it in English. What is your name?" he asked slowly.

Just then one of the horses started to scream and men began to shout. Several horses broke loose and ran through the camp, headed for the valley below. Simpson saw Sonja struggle with her bonds. He drew his pistol and struck her on the head with the barrel. Sonja slumped back, unconscious. Simpson rolled her into the shadow of the fallen tree and set off with the rest of the men in pursuit of the horses.

Ole Olsen crouched in the shadows and laughed silently at the antics of the men in the camp. He could not believe his good luck. Just as he was preparing to attack the guard and set the horses loose, a shot and some sort of commotion on the far side of the camp had drawn off the guard and diverted the group's attention. He had been able to free the animals without being seen and it looked as though he would have no trouble getting away.

When the last of the men had disappeared into the night, Ole stood up and walked past the camp on his way to his horse. He passed within twenty feet of Sonja's inert form without seeing her.

Chapter 19

With the dawn came a light, drizzling rain that soaked nearly everyone in Simpson's camp within a matter of minutes. Practically none of the men had brought slickers with them, and the grumbling and complaints that had already begun on the trail now assumed major proportions. The most popular topic of conversation seemed to be the stupidity of trying to ambush the Horton crew. Simpson's men were cold, wet, and unused to life in the mountains. Few of them expressed any interest in staying there a minute longer than absolutely necessary. Purvis finally detached himself from the group and went over to talk with Simpson.

"Boss, we got trouble," he began.

"Tell me something I don't already know," Simpson responded. "You can hear those thugs three states away."

"Yeah, I know," Purvis said. "I think they want you to hear. If you're goin' to stay with your ambush plan, I don't think you're goin' to have a crew at all. Fact is, if it keeps rainin' like this, they may be lightin' out by the end of the day. There's somethin' else that's botherin' 'em, too. Smith an' a couple of his pards think that you're hoggin' that woman for yourself. If we stay in camp any time at all, we're goin' to have trouble over her."

"The same thought has occurred to me," Simpson admitted. "From what I overheard, they just want to overrun Horton's camp now and take their chances. Is that right?"

"Yeah, that's about it. They figure the odds at three to one, or they was until last night when Pete cashed in his chips. They think that them odds make it a pretty sure thing if we rush the camp right now. There's tents an' food up there, so we could hole up for a while before we start back down."

"I can just see us holed up with the gold and the woman," Simpson said in a sarcastic tone. "That bunch of rabble would kill themselves off before the day was out. How did Jackson keep them in line?"

"They was all scared of him, Mister Simpson. Jackson wasn't all right in the head, an' they knew it. They ain't scared of me or of you, either, if the truth was known, probably because we ain't crazy. If you have any hopes of gettin' the gold back to Hogtown, you better hope that Smith gets himself killed in the attack. I can see that it happens that way if you want, boss."

Simpson considered the proposal for a while. There were sure to be casualties of his crew if they tried to rush Horton's camp, and Smith might as well be one of them. He had more than enough men to make the plan work. Simpson had no more loyalty to his crew than they had for him. He was concerned only with getting the gold. On the other hand, if he insisted on an ambush to minimize casualties to his crew, the men would slip away one or two at a time until he would not be able to rush the camp or set up an effective ambush. He realized that he really had no choice at all.

"Alright, Purvis," he said finally, "tell the boys that we go in today. You take care of Smith. How many of the horses did we get back?"

"We got seven, Boss, countin' the one the woman here had tied to a tree over yonder. One of the boys is still out, so maybe we'll get one or two more, but a lot of them will have to ride double."

"Put the woman on her horse and I'll take another. Work out the rest the best way you can. Some of them may have to walk. We'll leave here in an hour," Simpson commanded.

Purvis nodded in understanding and set off to get the crew ready to move out. Simpson walked over to Sonja and sat down on the fallen tree trunk next to her.

"We're moving out in an hour," he said. "You'll go with us, just in case we need you. I still want to know what you were doing here in our camp."

"I was on my way home from hunting. I saw the fire and came to see who it was. Your man surprised me and when he grabbed my carbine, it went off. I am sorry that he died, but it was not my fault. It was an accident," Sonja said in a small voice as she tried to brush the wet hair out of her face with her bound hands. "When my father finds out what you have done to me, he will kill you," she added.

Simpson nodded his head in agreement. "He may try, if he ever finds you. If you want us to untie you and let you go, you'd better tell me all you know about those men up ahead."

"All I know is that they stayed the night at our cabin last spring, then they rode away. I know nothing more," she lied.

"They didn't even say who they were?" Simpson asked incredulously.

"If they used their names, I do not remember," she replied. "They just wanted a place to spend the night."

Simpson grabbed her by the shirtfront and jerked her to him. "Lady, I don't believe you, and my men won't, either. I've been able to keep them away from you up until now, but I won't be able to stop them from taking you if they really want you. Do you understand that?"

"I understand that you are an evil man to do this to a helpless woman," she said passionately.

"Pete didn't find you so helpless, and the men are plenty sore about what you did to him. If you cooperate with me, I'll see to it that you get away before the men do anything to you," Simpson promised as he stroked her cheek. Sonja twisted away.

"No. I know nothing more," she insisted.

"Very well," Simpson said. "You asked for it."

Ole had ridden off after stampeding Simpson's horses, intending to put some distance between himself and the camp before finding a likely spot to spend the rest of the night. He started to circle the camp and head back to the cabin, then changed his mind and reversed his course and headed back to Horton's camp. He traveled for an hour or more before he came across a deadfall that he considered to be adequate for his purposes. He hobbled his horse and made a crude shelter from his groundsheet and slicker. He did not risk a fire but just wrapped himself up in his blankets and went to sleep. He had no fear of four-legged mountain animals, but he did have respect for the two-legged kind that might be drawn to anything that looked like a fire.

Ole slept soundly, and he was on the trail again as light began to filter through the trees and the rain began to fall. He put on his slicker as he passed the timberline. Shortly after that a guard waved to him and he rode into Horton's camp.

The smell of food was the first thing that assaulted his senses as he dismounted and walked over to the cook fire. The second thing that assaulted him was Joe Penbrook's wooden spoon as the big Swede tried to scoop stew out of the pot with an empty bowl.

"It's too late for breakfast an' too early for dinner, you hairy critter," the old man informed him. "If you can't wait, then you'd better go an' cook somethin' your own self. Now get out of here before I pin your ears back for you real good," Joe threatened.

Ole laughed good-naturedly. "Little man, that would be a good trick that I would like to see you try. But I will wait, all the same. Will you put in chili peppers again?" he asked hopefully.

"You liked them there peppers, now did you? Well, seein's how it's you, I guess I can add a few." And with that, Joe tossed in a handful before he stirred the pot again. "Any man who likes chili peppers can't be all bad, I guess."

Ole took one last sniff of the stew and then set off in search of Jim. He found him under a rock overhang, mending a pack saddle.

"Jim, I got big news for you," Ole said as he eased his big frame onto a rock. "I run off all of Simpson's horses last night. I bet that slows him up plenty."

"Maybe it did, Ole, but not by much, I reckon," Jim said. "I figure him to at least scout us out sometime to-day. You probably saw the boys in the rocks when you came in."

"I seen them, alright. But it is a long way for a man to walk," Ole observed.

"They're probably mounted again by now, and they may think that their surprise is gone if they believe that something besides a bear ran off their horses last night. Were you seen by anybody?"

"Naw, nobody saw me. There was a shot on the other side of the camp, and then a lot of shouting. I did it then, when everybody was busy."

Jim thought for a minute. "Unless someone shot himself in the foot, they'll think that we know where they are. I may mosey down the trail a little an' give 'em a little surprise."

"Sounds like a good idea. When do we go?" the big man asked anxiously.

"Not we, Ole. Me. I keep tellin' you that this ain't your fight."

"You said that last night. It will be better if two men go. One can cover the other," Ole argued.

The two men discussed the plan for nearly an hour. Finally, Jim gave up and sent for Curly to join them. The three men came up with a plan that Jim thought might have a good chance of working. It was really quite simple. Ole and Curly would find a place in the rocks about four hundred yards from the spot where the other men were guarding the camp. Ole and Curly would let Simpson and his men pass, then cut off their only route of escape, trapping them in a murderous crossfire. In the unlikely event that Simpson succeeded in breaking through the camp's defenses, Ole and Curly could fire at the attackers' rear, which would cause them to split their forces in order to deal with two threats instead of one. To Jim's way of thinking, the major advantage of the plan was that it would get Ole and the least experienced member of the crew away from the major part of the battle. Ole was a big target, too big to be missed by anyone but a blind man.

Once the details were settled, Curly and Ole were allowed to eat and move down the trail to take up their positions. Shortly after that the other members of the crew came drifting in to eat quickly and then go back on guard or finish last-minute preparations for leaving the mountains.

Simpson's men had recovered a total of nine horses by the time they moved out. Simpson detailed Purvis to stay to the rear of the formation with Sonja, where she would be handy if she was needed. Three of the men had to double up riding with others, so Simpson stopped from time to time to allow the extra riders to shift to mounts that had not yet been subjected to the heavier loads.

In spite of the stops, progress was swift. The men, well-soaked by then, were spurred on by the thought of dry tents, hot food, and an end to life in the mountains. The thought of a share of the gold did not slow them down any, either. As the morning wore on, the men riding double began to dream of horses of their own. It was one more reason for taking Horton's camp quickly.

Ole and Curly heard the horses coming long before they saw them. The trail was narrow and the men rode in columns, hunched over in a vain attempt to dodge the rain. The two men watched as the riders passed below them. Suddenly Ole jumped up and pointed.

"The bastards got Sonja!" he exclaimed as he gestured toward the blond woman, who was then more than fifty yards past them.

"Be quiet and get down!" Curly demanded.

"But the bastards got Sonja!" the big man bellowed as he turned to look at Curly. "We got to do something!"

At that moment a volley of shots sounded from up the trail. Ole turned back to look for Sonja and Curly swung his carbine, catching the giant behind the knees and knocking him to the ground. As he fell, a bullet from Purvis's rifle knocked Ole's hat from his head and laid open a gash along his crown. Ole rolled over and sat up against a rock, fingering the cut in his scalp.

"That man almost killed me!" he exclaimed in wonder.

"He damn sure did, Ole, an' if you don't keep down, he may do it yet," Curly advised.

"But the bastards got Sonja!"

"I heard you the first two times," the younger man said. "You ain't goin' to help her none if you get your head blowed off. Get down behind those rocks an' get ready to stop 'em when they try to get away."

Ole didn't like it very much, but he did as he was told. By now a full-fledged battle was developing up the trail. The sounds of rifles, ricochets, shouting men, and panic-stricken horses were very clear in the thin mountain air. The big man fidgeted anxiously as he strained for another glimpse of his daughter.

Jim Horton levered another cartridge into the chamber of his carbine and sighted in on another of Simpson's riders. He squeezed the trigger and felt the weapon recoil against his shoulder. A hundred yards away, the rider threw up his hands and fell from his horse, mortally wounded.

The battle was less than a minute old, but already four of the raiders lay still on the wet ground. Two horses were thrashing in agony as they tried without success to regain their feet and escape from the carnage. Smoke from the rifles hung thickly over the scene of the battle, threatening to obscure the vision of both opponents in this desperate struggle. Most of the raiders who had not yet been hit had dismounted and were seeking whatever cover they could find in the rocks near the trail. A rifle fired to Jim's left, and a man crouched behind a rock screamed in pain and stood up, only to be struck by a fusillade fired by the defenders.

The volume of fire on both sides began to diminish as casualties began to mount and targets became fewer.

Jim saw two of his men go down, but he could see at least seven of Simpson's gang sprawled in grotesque positions along the trail or among the rocks. It was then that he caught sight of Sonja trying to control her plunging mount. A tall, thin man was attempting to grab its bridle. Just as Jim was about to shout a warning to his men, he saw Simpson spring from the rocks and vault up behind Sonja on her horse. He grabbed the reins from her hands and urged the animal back down the trail, away from the murderous fire. The last two of his mounted riders wheeled their horses and followed him, A rifle thundered and the rear-most rider was plucked from the saddle as if by an invisible hand.

Ole crouched in the rocks and waited as the fleeing riders approached. When they were no more than fifty yards away, he stood up, took careful aim, and fired. Sonja's horse crumpled silently, shot through the heart. Curly fired a second later, the slug from his carbine tearing out the throat of the remaining rider, the tall man known as Purvis. The gunman toppled from the saddle, clutching his neck as he strangled on his own blood.

Simpson felt the horse begin to fall and grabbed Sonja around the waist and flung himself from the animal, dragging her with him as he went. When they hit the ground, he slipped his left arm around her throat and drew his pistol.

"You in the rocks!" he shouted.

"What do you want?" Curly answered.

"I want your guns out here on the trail and a fresh horse or I kill the girl!" he replied quickly.

Ole bellowed in rage and charged out from behind the rocks, intent on breaking Simpson's neck. Curly made a dive for the big Swede, but his fingertips only grazed the back of Ole's slicker. Simpson kept his chokehold on Sonja as he calmly sighted his Colt and shot the charging giant twice in the chest. Ole bellowed again, this time in pain, and he staggered a few more steps before he collapsed.

Sonja went crazy.

"Papa! Papa!" she cried as she struggled to break free.

Simpson momentarily lost his grip on the fighting girl and Curly took that opportunity to fire. The bullet caught the raider leader under the right armpit and passed through both lungs before exiting through his left side. Sonja, free from restraint, rushed to the side of her fallen father and gently rolled him onto his back. She cradled his head in her lap and tried to wipe the mud and the rain from his face, but Ole was past caring. The big man was dead.

Curly walked slowly from the rocks and knelt beside Sonja. He spoke softly as he attempted to comfort the grief-stricken girl. Sonja rocked back and forth, trying to will her father back to life. Curly caught a movement out of the corner of his eye and turned just in time to see Simpson level his pistol at Sonja.

"Look out!" he shouted and flung himself on top of the startled girl just as Simpson squeezed the trigger. Curly felt a tremendous blow strike him in the leg. His vision dimmed and a roaring filled his ears. He struggled to disengage himself from Sonja and reached for Simpson, but the effort was too much for him. He passed out.

Jim came running down the trail and arrived just in time to kick the pistol out of Simpson's hand before he could fire another shot. He hurried over to the others. It took him only a glance to tell him that Ole was dead. Curly was bleeding badly from a wound in his thigh. Jim quickly stripped off his own shirt and used it to staunch the flow of blood. A few moments later Joe Penbrook and the rest of the crew got there, dragging a lightly wounded raider with them,

Joe watched Jim work on Curly, then knelt down and elbowed Jim out of the way.

"Let somebody who knows what he's doin' work on the boy. Another minute or two an' the kid'll either be dead or crippled for life," Joe said cantankerously, but his eyes showed concern for the youth. "You better go look at Simpson. I don't think that he's got much longer afore he crosses over."

Jim nodded and moved over to Simpson, whose breathing had become very labored. Blood frothed at his mouth and flowed freely from the holes in his sides. Jim wiped the dying man's mouth clean and raised his head. Simpson's eyes flickered open and focused on Jim's face.

"Am I killed?" he asked weakly.

"I'm afraid so, Simpson. You didn't give anyone much choice."

"Maybe. Such a sweet deal. Got too greedy."

"Tell me about the bank robbery," Jim urged.

A light glowed in Simpson's eyes and a smile played at the corners of his mouth before a spasm of pain changed it into a grimace. "That one was a beauty, huh?"

"That it was. We had no proof at all," Jim admitted. "Tell me, how'd you get into the bank?"

"The woman, Lilly. Hid in the closet when Witherspoon came. Took the key from his pocket while she entertained him. Wax cast. Simple," he said, his voice becoming fainter.

"And you killed her later," Jim stated.

"Yeah. Couldn't have ... witness."

Jim asked him about the getaway and Simpson told him in a halting voice. Then Jim asked him about the money.

"Put the bills in … saddlebags. Used it to bankroll me in town. Some … still in … safe," he gasped.

"What about the gold?"

A puzzled look came over Simpson's face. "Gold? What gold?" he asked. "I only … took … paper. Couldn't … carry gold." Simpson breathed raggedly and Jim changed subject.

"And Eff King?" he asked.

"Dead."

"Jackson?"

"Don't know. Couldn't find."

"What do you know about Witherspoon?"

But Simpson could say no more. He had joined King, Purvis, and most of the rest of his gang somewhere in hell.

Jim stood up and walked over to Joe Penbrook who, along with Sonja, was busy supervising the movement of Curly back up the trail to the camp. Two other men were struggling to carry Ole's body while the remainder of the crew disposed of the other bodies. It would take several hours to finish the job and to round up the horses and other fear scattered about,

Jim saw that Sonja was back in control of herself and fully engaged with helping Curly, so he walked over to the only surviving raider. The man, only lightly wounded, was surly and uncooperatjve. Jim had the man tied and taken back to camp, then went to find Marcus.

The elder Horton was back in camp, burying the two dead members of the Horton crew. Sonja had decided that her father should be buried with them, so Jim picked up a shovel and helped him scoop out shallow graves. The exercise helped to relieve some of the grief that he felt for the loss of Ole and his two men. When the graves were filled, the rest of the crew gathered around and Marcus said a few words, then everybody went back to work.

Marcus and Jim decided to wait a day before starting back for Ruxford in order to give Curly a chance to gain a little strength. They called over a member of the crew and prepared him to take a message to the sheriff in the morning.

"Charlie, I want you to take the prisoner in an' tell the sheriff that Simpson told me all about the bank job. We'll be a day behind you, maybe less if you don't make good time," Jim guessed. "Have him send the doctor out to the Olsen cabin an' tell him to keep banker Witherspoon close by. I think that I've got all the answers to the robbery."

Charlie repeated his instructions, then left to get ready for his trip in the morning. It was a subdued group that spent the night in camp. Their losses more than offset any joy they might have felt as a result of winning the battle.

Chapter 20

The sun was well up into the sky the next morning when Charlie Bartlett left camp with the prisoner and Jim's message for the sheriff. The rest of the crew checked packs for what seemed like the hundredth time and sat around waiting to start back down the mountain. A guard was still posted, but there was little likelihood of another attack on the camp unless the Utes came back to finish what they had started the year before.

Over at Joe Penbrook's tent, Jim stepped inside to check on Curly. Sonja looked up as he entered and smiled a little. Dark circles showed under her eyes and she looked very tired. Someone had given her a fresh shirt, and she had fixed her hair into one long, golden braid that extended to her waist. Jim had to admit that she did a lot more for the shirt than the previous owner had.

"He's much better today," Sonja said. "Mister Penbrook said that the bone is not broken and that the wound is clean." She stroked Curly's head and said, "He's such a brave man. He saved my life when that evil man Simpson would have killed me like he did my father. I don't know how I'll ever be able to thank this man."

"It's likely that he'll be able to think of something' once he's mended some," Joe opinioned, "though it's sure that you've saved his life, too."

Sonja looked questioningly at Joe. "How have I done such a thing?" she asked.

"Why, back there at your cabin, ever' time he saw you he couldn't pull his eyes off of you. Kept fallin' over things an' crashin' into trees an' such. If you hadn't of sat here an' talked with him, he'd of broke his damned fool neck by now."

Curly's face flamed. "Now Mister Penbrook, that ain't exactly true!" he protested. "I never crashed into no trees an' that horse that kicked me caught me off guard."

"Yeah, an' we know why, too, don't we?" Joe said, jerking his head in Sonja's direction.

"Jim, I hope you're not stayin' here just for me," Curly said, changing the subject quickly. "If I can't ride, I can sure stay put on a travois. I'm feelin' pretty good."

"Do you really mean that or are you puttin' on a good front?" Jim asked him seriously.

"Honest, Jim, I'm ready to go. If I get worse, we can always stop. Let's travel while we can."

The more Jim thought about it, the more Curly's suggestion made sense. The boy's wound was clean and the bleeding had stopped. Infection was not very likely in the high mountain air, but if it came, Jim would rather that it happened as close to the Olsen place as possible. Jim knew that if were in Curly's place, he would want to move, too.

"You've convinced me, Curly. I'll tell the boys we'll start just as soon as we get you loaded up an' we can eat. Noon ought to see us on the trail."

Jim left the tent and scouted around until he found Marcus and told him of the plan. Then he called the rest of the crew together and made the announcement. Cheers filled the air and a couple of the more exuberant Texans fired a shot or two into the air, The gloom that had hung over the camp was suddenly lifted, and a flurry of activity broke out everywhere. Tents came down in a matter of minutes, mules were loaded, and horses saddled. No one wanted to stay to eat the noon meal, not even the three men who had received minor wounds in the fight the day before. They all wanted to get to town where they could begin to live the lives of wealthy miners. Jim was sure that half of them would be dead broke in a month, but they'd have enough memories to last them a lifetime.

By mid-afternoon the crew entered the timberline, where Jim stopped the crew for a rest. Joe Penbrook built a travois for Curly, who was showing the strain of trying to sit in a saddle with a hole the size of a silver dollar in his thigh. Jim took Marcus and several of the other men with him to recover the gold that he had cached nearly a year before. When they had it loaded on the extra mules, Jim stopped to take a last look around. The bones from the mules that had died in the blizzard were strewn over a wide area, the result of hungry predators that had come across an unexpected meal. Of his horse he could find no sign. Jim was glad. He hoped that the big animal had managed somehow to survive.

"How much gold do you reckon that we got here?" Marcus asked Jim casually as they led the mules back to the rest of the crew.

"I figure that we've got close to a million here, countin' what we just picked up. I don't think that there ever was a richer seam than the one we've been workin'. Too bad it's all played out."

"It'll make a pretty good payday for the boys when we get back to town. Should come to more than fifty thousand dollars a man, even with the shares goin' to the kin of the men we lost. That's a hell of a bankroll, little brother."

"Sure is. My share of what we dug, put alongside this cache we just picked up, will run to more than a quarter million, if gold prices stay put an' this gold is as pure as we think it is."

"What are you goin' to do with it?" Marcus asked.

Jim thought for a minute before answering. "Morton Witherspoon is not goin' to be in business much longer, if my hunch is right. I think I'll try to buy out the bank an' maybe start up a ranchin' business on a few of the high meadows around here. I'll try to talk

Curly into managin' that part of the business. I've got a feelin' that he's goin' to want to stay in the hills."

"I don't think that Sonja is goin' to offer him no choice in the matter," Marcus said, grinning. "She told me that him savin' her life made everythin' clear to her. She's plannin' on devotin' the rest of her life to him. Speakin' of which, part of your woman problem seems to be solved. What are you gon' to do about the other part of it?"

"I've been thinkin' about just that for six months. Part of the reason that the bank looks so good to me is that I want to marry Myrna if she'll have me. I'm pretty sure that she won't want to go back to Texas. Too many unpleasant memories are there for her. This place is fresh an' growin'. It's a good place to start a new life."

"It's a good enough place, I guess," Marcus agreed, "but make sure that Myrna really wants to stay before you sink down roots. Hell, half of the women in Benton have a past, an' the others are too danged ugly to have been anythin' but virtuous. Myrna's a lady, sure enough, an' there ain't anyone in town worth anythin' at all who wouldn't be proud just to shake her hand."

Jim laughed. "I may be gettin' ahead of myself. She hasn't agreed to have me yet. I'd better not be makin' too many plans 'til I ask."

"Fat chance you got of escapin' the preacher. I bet that the first thing we hear when we hit town is the organ tunin' up."

"You're on, brother. Ten bucks an' a hot bath says that you're wrong. An' I hope I get to pay off," Jim said as they rejoined the rest of the crew. A few minutes later they were on their way back through the timber, headed for Sonja's cabin.

Charlie Bartlett took a full three days to reach Ruxford. It was mid-morning when he tied up in front of the jail and walked into the office. Al Cleary was on duty, and it did not take him long to lock up the prisoner and take off at a run to find the sheriff. Twenty minutes later Sam Peabody came through the doorway, breathing heavily from his exertion. Charlie delivered the message as he had been instructed, then set off in search of the doctor right after the sheriff finished pumping him for details of the fight.

"Hot damn!" the sheriff exclaimed to Cleary after Charlie finally made good his escape. "I knew that Jim would figure out what happened in that robbery. I'd better go down an' tell Morton the good news. We might even get to recover some of the money."

As he started to leave, two of the local ranchers came into his office. Both men were agitated. It took them a little time before they settled down enough to be able to present a clear story to the sheriff. Sam finally learned that the two men had been losing a few horses and cows on a regular basis, not many at any one time, but a constant loss over the course of the summer. The men had written the loss off to Indians, weather, predators, and other natural causes, but the night before they had caught a group of four men helping themselves to more stock. There had been a fight, or more accurately, a pitched battle. The results were that two of the outlaws were now enriching the Colorado soil and the other two had been trailed to a box canyon, where some of the ranchers' men were keeping them bottled up.

The sheriff took a Winchester from the gun rack and motioned for Cleary to do the same. Then the four of them went to the livery to get the lawmen's horses. It was full dark by the time the sheriff and his prisoners made it back to the jail. Sam sent Cleary to the livery with the horses while he put the rustlers into a cell. Suddenly he remembered Jim's message and realized that he had not stopped to tell Morton Witherspoon the good news. He toyed with the idea of stopping at the banker's house, since the bank had long-since closed, but he decided against it. He would talk to the banker in the morning. After all, there was no real hurry. The banker wasn't going anywhere. Sam put on his hat and headed for the Excelsior Hotel. He was sure that Myrna Meloy would like to know that Jim Horton was on his way back in.

Jim Horton and his crew caught sight of the Olsen cabin just as the sun was beginning to set on their second day on the trail. Curly seemed to be no worse for having made the trip, although the wound still looked angry. Jim and Marcus carried him into the cabin under Sonja's close supervision. They put him in the bed that Jim had used during his stay the previous winter. Since it was late, Sonja insisted that the entire crew use the cabin as a bunkhouse. After the animals had been cared for, floor space in the cabin began to diminish as bedrolls were rolled out. Joe and Sonja fixed a quick meal, and shortly after that the crew went to sleep.

Daylight was still an hour or so away when Jim rolled up his blankets and started waking the crew. He lit a candle and took Joe with him to look at Curly's wound. They pushed aside the curtain that divided the bedroom from the rest of the cabin and found Sonja sitting there in a chair, just looking at the sleeping man.

Just then Curly opened his eyes and saw Sonja. He smiled gently and said, "You know, the most wonderful thing in the world is to wake up in the mornin' and look at a beautiful woman."

"Maybe so at your age, young feller," Joe said, "but when you get to be my age, the wonderful thing in the world is to wake up an' find out that your bowels ain't all stopped up. Now quit tryin' to be a smooth-talkin' devil an' let me have a look at that there leg of yours."

Curly did as he was told while Joe removed the bandage and poultice that he had made from tree moss, tobacco, and several other ingredients whose identity he did not volunteer, and Curly didn't want to know about. The wound did not look as angry as it had the day before. Joe bent low and sniffed. There was no smell of rot.

"Boy, I think that you just might keep that there leg," Joe said as he applied a fresh poultice and bandage. "When that doctor gets here, let him look at it an' poke around. If he gives you any pills, take 'em. When he leaves, put this here poultice back on. Them doctors can kill you if you take 'em real serious. An' speakin' of killin' you, make sure that he washes his hands before he goes pokin' around in that wound. Sonja, you might have the doc rinse them paws of his in some of Ole's firewater."

Sonja and Curly agreed to follow Joe's directions, so the old man left them and began to fix breakfast for the crew. Jim, Marcus, and a pair of the other Texans went outside and began to chop wood to replenish the supply near the cabin. From time to time, other members of the crew relieved them, and before long everyone had eaten while a vast quantity of wood had been cut. After a while Sonja came out and took Jim aside.

"Jim, I have decided that I really love Curly," she said shyly. "He risked his life to save mine. I hope you do not mind if I stay with him. I know he loves me, too."

"Of course I don't mind, Jim said gently. "I only want what's best for you. I hope that you'll both be very happy."

Sonja threw her arms around him and kissed him soundly. "Thank you, Jim," she whispered. Then she was gone.

It was closer to noon than to breakfast when the rest of the men said their goodbyes and rode off towards Ruxford. They had started out from the mountain about three hours after Charlie Bartlett and had by now fallen at least half a day behind. The heavily laden pack mules could not travel as swiftly as saddle horses could, so the crew was camped seven or eight miles west of Ruxford when Sheriff Peabody locked up the rustlers and told Myrna Meloy that Jim would be riding in the following day.

In the camp that night, Jim and Marcus advised the men to go directly to the Wells Fargo office when they reached town and to ship all but a little of the money back home to Texas so that they would have something besides a massive hangover to show for the work they had done. It was Jim's intention that Wells Fargo weigh the gold and make the split so that there would be no argument over who got the larger pouches. Although the men were all friends and had worked together for months or, in some cases, for years, gold had a way of bringing out the worst in a man. Horton had seen gunplay over far smaller sums of gold than this, and he was relieved when the men agreed to his plan. Marcus posted the guards and the camp settled down for its last night in the field.

Morning came and the crew rode directly into town and stopped at the Wells Fargo office. Jim separated the cache gold from his expedition the year before, then gave the division instructions for the rest to the Wells Fargo agents, who became visibly nervous when they realized just how much gold had been placed in their care.

Before Jim was able to leave the office, Sam Peabody walked in. "Glad to see you, son," the big man said as he pumped Jim's hand. "Heard that you got the lowdown on the bank robbery an' settled Simpson's hash at the same time. Tell me about it."

"I will, Sam, but not right now. I need a bath an' a change of clothes before I go see somebody. How about me meetin' you an' Witherspoon at the jail right after lunch?"

"Well, I guess I can wait that long, but you sure got my curiosity aroused. Oh, by the way, that 'somebody' you was talkin' about knows you're comin' in today," the sheriff said with a grin that went from ear to ear.

Jim made a rude comment to the effect that the sheriff ought to mind his own business, then left the Wells Fargo office and rode to the livery stable. He dropped off his horse and took his bedroll and Winchester with him to the Excelsior. He had no sooner walked into the hotel than he saw Myrna, more beautiful than ever, standing at the desk, talking with the clerk, Amos. The man's eyes widened when he saw Jim and he started to speak until Jim gestured for him to be silent. The clerk nodded slightly and turned his attention back to Myrna.

"Can a tired old man get a room around here?" Jim asked as he stopped next to Myrna.

"Jim!" she exclaimed as she threw herself into his arms. "I'm so glad you're back safe and sound." Further discussion was postponed while she kissed him full and hard on the mouth.

"Lady, do you greet all of your guests like this?" Jim asked as he slowly disengaged himself from her embrace and held her at arms' length. "And just look at you. Slender as a young girl and twice as beautiful as I remembered."

"Thank you, sir. And may I say the same about you?" she inquired impishly.

Jim laughed. "Maybe so, but I must smell like a billy goat an' I passed needin' a shave a week ago. Suppose I get a room an' clean up, then we can talk a little."

"My thoughts exactly, sir. Just come this way. Your room is waiting for you," she said as she turned and led the way upstairs. She stopped in front of her rooms and opened the door. Jim entered and Myrna followed him in, closing the door behind them. In moments they were embracing again.

"Myrna, I want you to marry me," he said thickly as soon as he was able to break away.

"Are you sure?" she asked. "You weren't when you left."

"I'm sure now. I was just a little slow figurin' out what's really important to me."

Myrna smiled and stepped back into his arms. "Then I'll marry you if you still want me. But you need to know that while you were gone, another man came into my life."

Jim eased back from her a little and looked at her questioningly for a moment. Myrna just stood there and smiled at him. "I guess that's my fault," he said. "I should have spoken sooner. It makes no difference to me as long as he's gone now."

"You're absolutely right, Jim Horton," she scolded. "You were responsible. I was, too. And he's not gone. In fact, he's right through that door, in my bedroom. I think it's high time that you two meet. Come with me," she said as she took him by the hand and dragged him into the bedroom.

"Alright, Myrna, I give up. What's goin' on?" he said as he looked around the room. "Where is he?"

"This way, dear," she said as she led him around to the other side of the bed. "Jim, I want you to meet James, junior, the new man in the house," she announced as she picked up the baby from his crib. "James, meet your father."

For the first time in his life, Jim was absolutely speechless. His son looked at him and cooed as he wiggled his fat little fists. Jim took him gently from Myrna.

"How ... When ... What ...?" he stammered.

"You know very well 'how,' Jim Horton!" she said indignantly. "As far as 'when,' he was born nearly two weeks ago."

Jim looked up from his son. "Myrna, why didn't you tell me before I left? Surely you knew. I could have married you then," he said, still somewhat in a state of shock.

"Because I can think of a lot of reasons why we should get married, but this child isn't one of them. I wanted you to want me, not just a name for the baby. We can get married in a month or so, now that you know what you want, too."

"Why so long?" he asked.

"Sometimes, Jim Horton, you really are pretty dense. Someday I'll explain it all to you," she said as she kissed him lightly on the lips.

Jim handed his son back to Myrna, then hugged them both. Myrna and Jim both suddenly began to talk excitedly, and, what with one thing and another, Jim barely made his appointment with the sheriff.

Chapter 21

Sam Peabody was pacing the floor when Jim arrived just after noon. "There you are!" he exclaimed. "I've been waitin' all mornin' to find out about that bank job. Now spill it before I have to shake it out of you!"

Jim laughed at the older man's impatience and pulled up a chair next to the lawman's desk. "Sit down, Sam, an' I'll tell you all about it. Where's Witherspoon? He ought to hear this, too."

"I told him to be here right after I saw you this mornin'. No matter. I'll tell him later. Now get busy an' tell me what happened!"

"It's pretty important that Witherspoon be here, Sam." And then Jim told him what Simpson had said as he lay on the trail, dying.

"If Simpson didn't take the gold, then who did?" the sheriff wanted to know after he had heard the story.

"I think that it was Witherspoon. When he found the safe empty an' so much money missin', he saw a way to get the bank out of trouble by stealin' the Wells Fargo gold an' blamin' it on the robber. Wells Fargo got paid off by the insurance company, who raised its rates to cover the loss. I guess that Witherspoon figured that nobody'd end up gettin' hurt when he took the gold."

"Why, that dirty thief!" Sam exploded, following that statement with a string of choice cuss words. "Grab your hat, we're goin' after that jasper!"

The two men left the office and set off at a brisk pace for the bank. When they walked in, Jack Kirby was the only man there. Jim and the sheriff walked over to the cashier's cage.

"Jack, where's Witherspoon?" Sam Peabody asked.

"I don't know, Sheriff. After you left this morning, he went back into his office and stayed there until the agent from the Wells Fargo office came in about an hour ago to make arrangements for storing some of the gold that Mister Horton here brought in this morning. As soon as the agent left, Mister Witherspoon left here with a carpet bag. He acted like his coattails were on fire and the nearest water was ten miles away."

"Do you have any idea where he went?" Jim asked.

"I thought that he went to Wells Fargo, but I guess he didn't. He didn't say anything at all to me when he left."

Jim turned to the sheriff. "Sam, we'd better check his house. I've got a feelin' that he's tryin' to fly the coop, an' if we ever want to see him again, we'd better find him real quick."

"What's this all about, anyway?" Jack Kirby asked, shaking his head in confusion. "Why would Mister

Witherspoon want to run away? I just don't understand what's going on."

"We haven't the time to tell you the whole story right now, Jack, but we will when we come back," Jim promised. "If Witherspoon comes back, keep him here and send for us. Use a gun if you have to."

Kirby nodded, but it was plain that he had no idea about what was going on. The lawmen left with Jack still shaking his head in confusion. They met Marcus on the boardwalk and the three men set off down the street.

When Morton Witherspoon left the bank, he did not go home. The sheriff's visit that morning had alerted him to the fact that Simpson had been the man who had stolen the money from the safe last November. He also knew that the man had talked before he died. Witherspoon had spent the majority of the morning trying to come up with a plausible explanation for the disappearance of the Wells Fargo gold from the safe. He had little success. The last event that shattered what was left of his composure was the visit from the Wells Fargo agent, who announced that Jim Horton was in town. Panic seized the banker. He took a carpet bag from his desk, stuffed it with bills from the safe, and went directly to the livery stable. It took him ten minutes to make the trip over to Hogtown. He pulled to a stop in front of the cabin occupied by Abigale Carpenter and ran inside.

"Abby, get your things together. We're leaving town now!" he announced as he started gathering her clothes and throwing them on the bed.

"Morton, calm down!" Abby advised. "It will take me a while to pack, so you might as well sit down and stop messing up my clothes."

"Don't you understand? There's no time!" he exclaimed. "I have a hundred thousand dollars in the buggy and at the house, and we've got to leave now!"

"I can get new clothes later," she said as she put on her bonnet, picked up her purse, and walked swiftly to the door. She paused to look back over her shoulder at the banker. "Are you coming, Morton?"

Witherspoon helped her into the buggy, then got in and drove like a madman to the house that he shared with his wife, Bertha. He parked the rig in the shade in front of the house and ran inside. In his bedroom he threw some clothes into a valise.

"Morton, what's wrong?" his wife asked as she came into the room.

"I've got to leave town for a while," he said without looking up from his packing. "I'll explain later."

"Explain to me now, dear," she said as she grabbed him by the arm. "Explain to me who that woman is in your buggy out front."

The banker shook her off his arm and stuffed more clothes into a second bag. "I'll explain, all right. I'm leaving town, Bertha. Permanently. That woman out front is going with me. Now are you satisfied?" he asked as he turned and started down the stairs to the first floor of the house.

Taken aback by her husband's brusqueness, Bertha hesitated for a moment before running after him. She caught up with him as he came back into the house after throwing his bags into the buggy. She grabbed ahold of his arm again.

"Morton, what about me? What about our children? Surely you won't just abandon us!" she cried.

The banker wheeled around and struck her viciously across the mouth, splitting her lips and loosening a tooth. The blow knocked her back into the room, and she grabbed for a chair to steady herself. Both she and the chair tumbled to the floor.

"Get this straight, Bertha," he said as he stood over her weeping figure. "I don't care what happens to you or to your brats. Look at yourself. You've let yourself go. You're too fat, your hair is getting gray, you nag all the time, and you don't share my bed. Why should I be concerned for you?"

Bertha got unsteadily to her knees and threw her arms around her husband's legs. "Don't leave us, Morton. I beg you to think of the children if you don't care about me. What will become of them if you leave?"

Witherspoon struck his wife until she let go and crumpled to the floor at his feet, weeping hysterically. The banker looked at her with disgust.

"You and your brats can go to hell as far as I'm concerned. Now you stay out of my way, or I'll break your damned neck!" he exclaimed.

The banker stalked into the room that he used as a study, pulled back the rug that covered the center of the floor, and opened a small trap door. He reached through the opening and grunted with exertion as he pulled a small but very heavy box out of the recess and onto the floor. Without bothering to close the trap door or replace the rug, Witherspoon started backing out of the room, dragging the box with him as he went.

"Morton!" his wife cried.

"Shut up!" he demanded as he backed through the front door and out towards the buggy.

"Goin' somewheres, Morton?" a voice behind the banker asked. Witherspoon froze in his tracks. He looked around and found Sheriff Peabody standing there with his hands on his hips, looking him in the eye.

"I asked you a question, Morton. Are you goin' somewheres?" the sheriff repeated.

The banker had a trapped look in his eyes as he dropped the box and turned to challenge the sheriff. Then he saw Jim as he walked out from behind the buggy.

"I'd like to hear the answer to that one myself, Morton," Jim said. "I'd also like to look in the carpet bag and that box, if you don't mind."

"Yeah, me too," Marcus said as he came around the corner of the house.

"That makes it unanimous, Morton. You'd better open 'em up," Sam advised.

The banker was visibly deflated, and he hung his head in defeat. "You got me, Sheriff. I did it. I took the gold from the safe after I discovered the other robbery."

"How'd you get it home?" the sheriff asked.

"I put it in my desk and brought it here a little at a time," he answered.

"You mean that it was in the bank all the while I was investigatin'?" Sam asked in amazement. "Mister, you got a pair of brass cajones!"

"I had no choice, believe me," the banker pleaded. "I was over-extended at the bank and would have had to close the doors if this opportunity had not come along. Anyway, nobody got hurt. Most of the gold I fed right back into the bank."

Witherspoon raised his head slowly and wiped tears from his eyes. "I guess you're going to arrest me," he said weakly.

"Right you are, Morton," the sheriff said as he watched the battered figure of Bertha Witherspoon approach the group. "I figure that you ought to be makin' little rocks out of big ones at the state pen for ten years or so."

"May I speak to my husband for a moment before you take him in, Sheriff?" Bertha asked through swollen lips.

"Good heaven, ma'am! Did he do that to you?" the sheriff asked, unable to believe his eyes.

"It doesn't matter, Sam. May I talk with him? Please?" she pleaded.

"Of course, ma'am. But please don't take too long," the lawman said as he motioned Jim and Marcus back so that the woman could have more privacy.

Bertha thanked the sheriff, then turned to face her husband, her hands hidden in the folds of her skirt. Tears flowed freely down her bruised cheeks.

"Morton," she said in a cold, angry voice, "you have whored around for years, disgracing yourself and your family name. I could live with that because you went through the motions of keeping it from me. But that wasn't enough for you. You have stolen from the bank, lied to me, and, on occasion, even struck me. I could stand that, too, and perhaps even forgive you. But to-day you did something for which I can never forgive you. Today you shamed me by bringing your whore to my house, for all of the town to see."

"Just who are you calling names, you old sow?" Abigale demanded from the seat of the buggy.

Bertha ignored the woman. "Morton, I'm saying goodbye. The next time I'll see you will be in hell!" she exclaimed as she drew a pistol from the folds of her skirt and shot her husband through the heart.

Morton Witherspoon lived just long enough to clutch his chest as he fell back against the front wheel of the buggy and then slid into the dust of the street, a look of surprise still on his face. Bertha stepped around his body and brought up the big Colt as Abigale screamed and the horse, startled by the gunshot, reared and plunged. Bertha's next shot removed the right side of Abigale's jaw and the third caught the woman in the left breast, knocking her from the seat and into the dust on the opposite side of the buggy from her lover. She was dead before the dust settled. The horse snorted and danced nervously between the bodies.

Bertha walked slowly over to Sam Peabody and handed the pistol over to the thunderstruck lawman, then held out her hands.

"Put on the handcuffs, Sam. I'm glad that I killed him," she said between sobs.

The lawman got his wits about him as Jim and Marcus walked over to the pair. "I'm sorry, Bertha, but I got to take you in," he said regretfully.

"Why, Sheriff?" Jim asked as he looked at the battered, tear-streaked face of the woman. "I saw the whole thing, an' it looked like a clear case of suicide to me."

"Yeah, Marcus agreed. "It was a double suicide, sure enough. No reason to arrest the poor widow."

Sheriff Sam Peabody, upholder of the law in Ruxford, thought for a minute and then said, "Damned if you two ain't right. Damned if you ain't right," he repeated as if to convince himself further. "Help me get the bodies into the buggy an' down to the undertaker's. We got better things to do than hang around here."

Jim and Marcus loaded the bodies and the gold into the buggy while Sam Peabody soothed the widow. A dog barked down the street, and the sky began to cloud over. With a little luck, Jim thought, it just might rain before the day was out.

~ The End ~

Colonel R.C. Hartjen joined the Army at age 17 and was commissioned six years later. He has commanded an Armored Cavalry troop in Germany, an Airborne Cavalry troop in Viet Nam, and a tank battalion in the United States.

He holds an earned doctorate in counseling psychology and is a graduate of the US Army War College. *The Gold Stalkers* is his third novel in his Horton Family Historical Western series.

Colonel Hartjen is retired and makes his home in Leavenworth, Kansas along with his wife, Helen, and their devoted yellow Labrador, Annie.

Other books by Col. R.C. Hartjen

Cowhouse Creek Showdown

The Last Stage From Cedar Station